BANG UP

KAREN WOODS

EMPIRE
PUBLICATIONS

First published in 2016

EMPIRE PUBLICATIONS
1 Newton Street, Manchester M1 1HW
© Karen Woods 2016

ISBN: 978-1-909360-43-3

Printed in Malta.

ACKNOWLEDGEMENTS

As always, thank you so much to the people who support me and read my work. Thanks to my children Ashley, Blake, Declan and Darcy. A big thanks as always to my mother Margaret for all her hard work, also a big massive thanks to Rebecca Ryder for her expertise.

Bang-Up is my 15th novel and I hope you all enjoy the insight into a life we never really see behind bars. Since I've started writing its opened so many doors for me and I've enjoyed meeting many creative people. The 'Ard Knox Theatre Company has now been set up in North Manchester and this year at the Lowry theatre I will be putting on my fifth sell out show called "My Big Fat Jobseekers Wedding". I hope some of you will attend it.

Big Thanks to Ashley and John from Empire and to all my followers on Facebook and Twitter. Check out my website www.karenwoods.net for more information on the play and forthcoming titles.

My last thanks goes to my son Dale in heaven, always in my thoughts.

Love

Karen

Life doesn't give, you have to take.

CHAPTER ONE

Mikey Milne stood in the dock at Manchester Crown Court with his hands tucked neatly behind his back. His shoulders forced forward, his chest expanding with every breath he took. He was a cocky fucker and he didn't give a shit who was watching him, he was here to impress. The young offender looked into the public gallery and showed little remorse for the crimes he'd committed. His nostrils flared as he jerked his head forward slowly. "I'm ready, you cunts!" he mumbled under his breath.

Mikey shot a look at his co-accused and smirked. What a smacked arse his mate was! This was just a bit of jail, nothing to lose any sleep over. He'd do the time on his head. The guy was a pussy. Mikey stuck his hand down the front of his tracksuit bottoms and flicked his fingers across his cock rapidly. His solicitor had advised him to dress smartly for court but he had told him straight to get a grip. There was no way he was dressing up for a court appearance, not now not ever. They could get to fuck. The prosecution could take him as they found him; rough and ready. He didn't really care anymore. Brendan was shitting himself; fidgeting, gasping for breath, panic had clearly set in. The corners of Mikey's mouth began to rise. He sniggered through his fingers and leaned in to the side of his mate's ear. "Fuck it mate, do or die isn't it. We'll have to soldier it. Don't let these twats get to you."

Brendan Mellor dipped his head, he didn't reply. His

heart was in his mouth and he wasn't as confident as Mikey. Brendan was just a lad who had been in the wrong place at the wrong time. A follower, his dad had always called him. A daft fat prick who would do anything to gain a bit of street cred. This sentence was going to break him in two, his arse was twitching already, his heart pumping inside his rib cage. Mikey nodded as he studied the judge in his large black leather chair. He was like an Indian chief talking to his tribe. Mikey weighed him up. How did he sleep at night playing about with the destiny of people's lives? He looked a right grumpy old fart too; grey hair, rotund figure and a bright red nose.

They were all seated at the Crown Court today for the sentencing of these two criminals and the wig brigade were out in full force; a gang of them in grey curly hair and black gowns. The police officers wanted the pair of them off the streets and they had made that clear in their statements to court earlier in the case. Mikey knew that, regardless of the verdict, this judge was getting a mouthful from him today. Who was this tosser anyway? How could *he* judge *him* and tell him what was right and what was wrong? He was just another do-gooder telling him what he already knew. Fuck it! He was ready to kick off, he had nothing to lose. Mikey Milne was a law unto himself and lived every day by his own code of conduct. Nobody could tell him what to do or say. The courts had tried in the past to put him in his place but to date no one had ever controlled this young tearaway. He would spit in their eye and tell them he'd do this sentence on his head. Jail meant fuck all to him, it was his second home. A place he was familiar with, living with lads just like he was - fucked in the head. They didn't know how easy they had it. Three meals a day and no worries about paying bills – it was a piece of piss compared to some people living on the outside.

Mikey stretched his hands above his head and yawned, mouth wide open, eyes fully closed. He ragged his hands through his thick dark hair and looked at the uniformed security guard just to the right of him. The youth licked his lips slowly and studied him for a bit longer than necessary. Was it worth it? Could he take him down and jump the dock, he wasn't sure. Smirking at the guard, Mikey ground his teeth tightly together. A slight nod of the head towards him was all it took to unsettle the man. The prisoner stood cracking his knuckles as he sneered at him. The way he was feeling right now he could have broken him in two; snapped his jaw, ended his worthless life.

Mikey's girlfriend Sarah sat in the public gallery looking over at him. She was tearful and knew her boyfriend was going down today no matter what. Mikey had already been found guilty of supplying Class A drugs along with a few other charges. She thought he was just unlucky. The dibble had caught him bang to rights and no matter how much he tried to worm his way out of this one he had to admit to himself that he was getting a long stretch no matter what. Mikey had done a deal with the prosecution earlier and held up his hands to a lesser charge. He'd probably saved himself a few years already, so in a way he'd got off lightly. It could have been a lot worse.

Mikey's mother was at court today. She nodded towards her son, feeling guilty that she'd let him down all his life and never been there when he needed her most. Rachel was as hard as nails – her face betrayed no emotion. Life had made her like this. She'd had such a hard miserable existence and it wasn't all her own doing for sure but still she struggled, she'd had to fight all her life. Nothing had ever been simple. Rachel kept her chin up and listened to everything that was being said about her son. Her head dipped as she listened to the prosecution talk about his criminal record. There was whispering from others sat near her. Already her son was being judged. Mikey's mother had done a bit of bird too. In her day she was always getting a few months here and there. She had been a top shoplifter - a professional one in her day and she knew how the justice system worked more than most but to watch her boy go down hit her hard. Rachel sucked hard on her gums, praying for a good result.

Sarah, Mikey's girlfriend, was a pretty little thing; long blonde hair and such lovely baby blue eyes, she looked angelic. She wasn't like Mikey at all; she came from a good home and knew right from wrong. Her family thought her relationship with this dead-leg had ended long ago but it had never really stopped. If they ever found out he was still in the picture he would have been in a body bag. They had connections; big men who would take anybody down for the right price. Money talked and her family had more than enough of it to make sure this scrote disappeared off the face of the earth if need be. Mikey had been warned off already. He kept that on the low though, he didn't like admitting that he was vulnerable. There was no way anyone could know that he had backed down to these hard nuts and admitted defeat. One night he was cornered and had a gun held to his head, one thug had rammed the cold silver barrel to the back of his throat until he gagged. But, still, even though he should have kept away from Sarah he carried on seeing her. It didn't deter him, he loved a challenge. And, if these pricks came for him again he would be ready for them next time. Sarah loved her bad boy with all her heart and couldn't imagine life without him. She was smitten, besotted. He was her world. Mikey loved her in his own way too but she was so needy, always wanting more from him, always wanting him to spend more time with her. She made him do things that made him feel weak. He was never really a romantic guy and he found it hard to display any kind of emotion. Holding hands and kissing in public was for wimps, it just wasn't his style. She thought she was better than him sometimes and it really pissed him off.

The court room was silent as Judge Mayor started to speak. He cleared his throat, sipping on a glass of water. It was time to hear their fate. Everybody was hanging on his every word. Journalists, their pens held tightly in their hands, were ready to let the world know Mikey Milne was no longer at large on the streets of Manchester. They would word his story in the usual way, making him sound like a thug, a lowlife, a danger to the public. Rachel swallowed hard and shook her head slowly knowing it wasn't good news. She had a gut feeling and by the looks of things this was going to be a nightmare. This judge had a moody look about him, his expression was sour. He looked like he'd smelt a fart and he was looking around the courtroom for the culprit. Mikey whispered to Brendan and nudged him in the waist with a single finger. "This is showtime mate. Here we go. Don't let these fuckers break us. Keep it real." Rachel Milne hung her pale wrinkled hands over the brass rail and gripped at it tightly, her knuckles turning white. Her eyes squeezed together, her mouth was moving but no words were coming out. Perhaps, she was praying, the poor cow. She needed a miracle.

The criminals stood patiently in the dock and knew after a few minutes that their fate would be announced. Brendan Mellor had bright ginger hair and a plump waistline, he loved food, he loved eating. Ever since being a small child he had loved sugary snacks, he was a carb-junkie. He was shady too, very deep and you just couldn't get to the bottom of him. This youth had never been to prison before and the colour drained from his cheeks as he stood waiting to be sentenced. His father was in court today and he was eager to hear his son's fate. He hated Mikey Milne with a passion and from the minute he'd set eyes on him he knew he was nothing but trouble. A gob-shite he was, always the first there when anything was going on. He'd corrupted his son, led him astray. Mr Mellor snarled over at Mikey and wished him dead. Brendan was doing fine until he had got mixed up with this scumbag. He could have had a job and a career. His family were ready to support him in anything he wanted to do. He'd fucked it all up now, and for what, to gain his mate's respect. What a complete arsehole Brendan was. He never thought this through, he'd dropped a bollock.

Mikey had done a couple of stretches in jail over the years. An eighteen month and a six month. A shit and a shave he called it, it never broke him. It just made him stronger, more streetwise perhaps. At the age of twenty-two it was something he was proud of. He liked to think he'd earned his stripes amongst the lads on the estate, put his name on the map. Mikey's nostrils flared as he stood cracking his knuckles, his chest rising with speed and the large vein at the side of his neck pumping rapidly. He was ready now.

The judge leant forward in his seat and held some

paperwork in his right hand. The guards behind the prisoners stood up and moved closer to the offenders. They were preparing for it to kick off. When men got sent down anything could happen, this could get messy. Mikey was like a ticking bomb. The judge began in a firm tone, eyes looking directly at the convicts. "Michael Milne, I have read over your case and you have to realise that no matter what has been said here today, a custodial sentence is the only option I have left for you. You're a dangerous young man who needs to learn that your life style is not a healthy one. You have had chance after chance from the courts and not once have you mended your ways. "

Mikey jerked his head forward and tickled the end of his chin with a single finger. "Get on with it you old cunt," he whispered under his breath. This was pissing him off now, he just needed to know his sentence so he could crack on with life. He shot a look over at his mother and bit hard onto his bottom lip. Any second now he was going to blow. His ears were pinned back and his cheeks were beetroot. Mikey closed his eyes as he continued to listen to the judge rambling on about the way he'd lived his life in the past.

Brendan was fidgeting about at the side of him, he was breathing heavily and sucking hard on the edge of his thumb. He couldn't keep still. Judge Mayor lifted up a white sheet of paper from the case file and he was now ready to pass sentence. Rachel gripped Sarah close to her and held her tightly in her arms. She rested her head on top of hers, inhaling the apple fragrance from her thick blonde hair. The journalist nearby rolled the blue biro in her fingers rapidly and she was seconds away from getting the story she wanted for the local press. Mikey pushed his nose against the glass panel and slid it slowly against it. Here it was, he didn't have to wait any longer. You could have heard a pin drop. "I sentence you Mikey Milne to five years' imprisonment." Mikey sniffed hard and lifted his eyes to the ceiling and stood in deep thought. It was taking time for him to digest what had just been said. He listened eagerly as the case continued. "Brendan Mellor, I have taken into consideration your previous criminal record and that you have not been in prison before. Therefore, I sentence you to two years in prison. I hope you two young men use this time to become better people and learn that crime doesn't pay."

Mikey was bubbling with rage, nostrils flaring. Rachel sprang up from her seat and punched her rounded fist into the air. She was going sick and ready for punching somebody's lights out. Her voice was loud and the people in the public gallery were on edge as she booted the wall near her. "What a fucking liberty this is! He's a kid for crying out loud! You could have given him a probation order you old cunt! He's not been in trouble for over a year now, surely that should count for something," she pointed her finger around the courtroom. "You're all the same you lot, useless wankers who know fuck all about the real world. Silver spoon bastards the lot of you!"

The distraught usher ran to her side and gripped her by the arm. "You need to leave. This kind of behaviour is not tolerated inside the courtroom. Come on, leave."

Judge Mayor's back was up as he peered over his gold-rimmed glasses and pulled a sour expression. He was in no mood for this woman and he was ready to have her detained for contempt of court. Rachel was escorted kicking and screaming from the courtroom with the help of the two security guards. What a foul mouth she had!

Mikey Milne was up in arms and there was no way he was taking this lying down. His clenched fist pounded against the glass panel that separated him from the rest of the courtroom. He shrieked at the top of his voice. "Jail won't break me you wankers. I'll do this sentence on my head. Mam, don't you worry about me. I'll show these bastards, just you watch." Judge Mayor sprang to his feet. He watched as the Group Four guards tried their best to deal with the convict. Mikey was throwing punches, kicking his legs out, there was no way they were taking him without a fight. "Pricks, come on, is that all you've got, you shower of bastards. Let's have it."

Sarah bit hard on her fingernails and wiped the cuff of her jumper across her eyes. She was sobbing her heart out, unable to breathe properly. Standing to her feet she screamed. "Mikey, you're just making it worse. Please stop, please, for me, just calm down." Her words fell on deaf ears though, there was no way he was listening to her. He was in the zone now and trying his best to break free.

Brendan Mellor stood in shock. There was no way he was making any trouble for himself. He shot a look over to his father and his eyes clouded over. He was ready for breaking down, his lips trembling. He mouthed the words "Sorry" over to his dad and his head dropped. Loud banging noises and screaming could be heard as more security guards came into the dock. Mikey Milne was twisted up in seconds. It took six of them to restrain him. Even now, when he couldn't move a muscle, he was still shouting the odds out with his face pressed firmly to the floor. "Come on you cunts, you'll never break me." The journalist had her story now; a ruthless, psychotic criminal is sentenced.

Rachel paced up and down outside the courtroom, her hands ragging through her hair. She was fuming and speaking on her mobile phone. "The bastards have slammed him. Gary, I swear he's kicking off. They're going to hammer him once they get him into a cell. Just you watch, if they put one mark on my boy's body I'll sue them." Rachel held the phone to the side of her ear and bit down hard on her lip. People were coming out of the courtroom now and there was no way she wanted them to see her like this. She took a deep breath and tried to hold back the tears. People were pointing and whispering. The phone call ended suddenly and Rachel stood waiting for Sarah. Each person that walked out from the room looked her up and down, judging her, knowing now why her son was the way he was. Rachel stood tall. If they wanted trouble she'd give them trouble alright. She'd dealt with these sorts of people all her life and, like her son, she was scared of nobody. Tilting her head to the side she placed her hand on the side of her hip and held a cocky expression. A woman was eyeballing her from the opposite side of the corridor. "Have you seen enough or do you want me to spin around for you to get a better look, you nosey cow?" She was ready for her, she was ready for them all. They were no better than her, she'd scratch their eyes out if she needed to. They were just regular people thinking they knew her story.

The courtroom door flew open and crashed against the wall. Sarah appeared, her eyes were red raw and her voice was low. "They've took him Rachel, they've took my Mikey." Sarah's legs buckled from underneath her as she fell to the floor. She was hyperventilating and finding it difficult to breathe. People just walked past her as if she was a big dollop of dog muck on the bottom of their shoes. Not one person stopped to see if she was alright; inconsiderate bastards the lot of them. She could have been dying for all they knew and not one of them gave her a second thought. Rachel sprinted to her side and held her tight in her arms. She didn't need this, she had her own grief to cope with without nursing somebody else. She'd told Sarah not to come to court but she just couldn't stay away; she was in love, totally head over heels in love with her boy.

Rachel composed herself and put her own troubles to the back of her head. "He's going to be alright. Our Mikey will deal with them. You know he won't take any shit from anyone. Come on, sort yourself out and let's get home. Everybody's looking at you. For fucks sake I don't really need this!"

Sarah snivelled as she lifted her head up slowly, tears rolling down the side of her cheek. "What am I going to do without him? He's my world. Nobody knows me like he does. I just want to die. Leave me here on my own, just leave me be." Rachel shrugged her shoulders and remembered when she had been in this situation. Her own heartache had destroyed her, ripped her heart out and if she was being truthful she'd never really truly loved anyone again after it. John Pollock had been her world back in the day and when he got slammed for ten years it broke her in two; shattered her heart into a million pieces. At the time she declared she would wait for him and be faithful to the end of his sentence but in her heart she knew that was always going to be a big ask. Things change, time moves on and even with the best intentions she had to admit to herself that she was lonely and needed a man beside her. Rachel had received death threats from Johnny from behind the prison walls. Once he heard she had moved on he pledged to end her life, make her suffer. And he would too, he was a sick bastard who liked to make his victims suffer. Any time soon John Pollock would be walking the streets of Manchester again, the police had said they would inform her of his release date. Rachel pretended she was over it all but she was scared, very scared. This man was a head the ball and he would never forget what she had done to him. The sleepless nights she'd caused him, the humiliation. She was living on borrowed time.

Mikey was flung into a holding cell by the scruff of his neck. He was bleeding from the side of his head and thick red blood trickled down his cheek. Once the door was slammed shut he swung his leg back and booted the steel door rapidly. He made sure they all heard what he had to say too; his words echoing throughout the corridor. "Wankers, it takes six of you to put me in here. Just you wait until it's time to get me out you clowns. You just watch, one of you is getting your jaw snapped." Mikey let out a menacing laugh as he stumbled over to the wooden bench at the back of the room. He was wounded. His heart was racing and he was pumping sweat. He had nothing to lose anymore, he was a ticking bomb. "Argghh," he screamed as he punched his fist into the concrete wall. Mikey had to calm down, he was going to have a heart attack if he didn't. His face was white and his eye balls were bulging out of their sockets, he was on the edge. It was such a shame for this lad. He was a car crash waiting to happen. Life had let him down and he was a victim of circumstances, lost in the system. Just like a lot of other youths really. Nobody had ever showed him love and he was calling out for help. Mikey crashed down onto the bench and looped his arms above his head, his body still trembling. Closing his eyes, he tried to hold back the emotion he was feeling deep in his heart. This was a mess, a fucked up dirty big mess. His mother needed him on the out. What was she going to do now with him locked away for years? They would come for her as she was his only family. They would make her pay his debt. Rachel wasn't strong enough to deal with them on her own. They were ruthless. Mikey stroked a single finger down the cold wall. Up and down it went, up and up and then back down again. He was thinking.

Brendan Mellor sat in his cell with his knees pulled up towards his chest. His eyes scanned around the room and he was blubbering like a big baby. He wasn't a criminal, he had just got mixed up in something he knew nothing about, trying to impress the other gang members. Brendan had few friends and Mikey had helped him out when he was at an all-time low. He felt part of something when he was with Mikey and the boys, they had his back and nobody would ever hurt him again. Not even his father. But prison life scared the shit out of him and he wasn't afraid to admit it. How was he ever going to survive on his own in the prison system? Mikey couldn't protect him every hour of every day could he? He sat rubbing at his arms as goose bumps appeared all over his skin. "Mam, I want my mam," he sobbed.

CHAPTER TWO

Rachel stormed out of the courts. She was fuming and cursing as she left the building. Sarah was behind her and she was embarrassed at the way she was acting. "Fuck them, fuck them all," Rachel shrieked. The clouds overhead were grey and the rain pounded the pavements lashed by strong winds. Dipping her head, Rachel dodged a large puddle. "For fucks sake, every day it's pissing down here. Come on, let's peg it to the bus stop." She grabbed hold of Sarah by the arm and dragged her across the road. This woman had to keep a low profile and she didn't want to be spotted in the town centre. Her bail conditions said she could never set foot in Manchester City Centre again. The judge told her straight, she was on her last warning – either Rachel kept to her bail conditions or she went back to jail. But this woman was always a risk-taker and just like her son, she thought she was untouchable. "Have you got any money for the bus," Rachel asked as she wiped the drops of rain dangling from her nose. "I spent the last bit of money I had on cigs before. Brassic I am, potless."

Sarah gasped, she knew she was lying, she was always on the scrounge and would do anything to earn an extra few quid. Sarah dug her hand in her back pocket and pulled out a crisp ten pound note. Rachel snapped it out of her grip and rubbed her palms together rapidly. "Lovely jubbly, we can get home now then. I thought we would have to jib on the bus. It's shit being skint all the time, it does my head in."

Sarah looked her up and down and couldn't believe she was serious regarding sneaking on the bus. Was this woman for real? She acted like she was still a teenager; she had no respect, few morals. Manchester city centre was busy today and the shoppers were out in full force. As Rachel walked past the shop windows she stopped and licked her lips slowly. She was edgy and taking one step forward and one step back, hesitating. "Just hang on here for me, chick. I won't be long. I've just got to do something. Stand at the bus stop over there and wait for me. Get under the shelter and stay out of the rain. You'll get piss wet through otherwise." Sarah was just about to say something but it was too late, Rachel had gone.

As she walked into the store, Rachel clocked the security guard to the left of her, she had an eye for detail when she was grafting. A big guy he was, a porker. Just there for show really. He would never have caught her if it came to a chase. She would have dusted him if it came on top. Pulling her coat up over her long thin neck, she headed up the escalator to the women's department. This was going to be a hard graft. She had no bags with her, no other way of concealing anything she stole. Yes, she could shove it in her coat but that was so on top and not the way she worked. It was back to basics. Rachel liked working alone, she was straight in and out of any store she shoplifted. She was fast and very rarely got spotted. It was all about being confident and in her day Rachel had more of that than anyone, she was a barefaced criminal. Walking over to a pile of jeans, she quickly picked up five pairs and casually walked around the store holding them in her hand. There wasn't a second to spare, she had to be quick. Wasting time would bring attention on her, raise doubts that she was up to no good. Rachel entered a changing room with haste.

The assistant stood smiling at her and looked her up and down. She wasn't the usual type of customer she was used to and she approached her with caution. "How many items are you trying on Miss?"

Rachel kept her cool and made sure there was no way the young girl could see how many garments she was carrying. "Just two chick, which changing room is free?" Rachel wasn't hanging about, she headed straight into the changing room before the woman got a chance to check what she was holding. Rachel sat inside the changing rooms and pulled the alarms from three pair of jeans. She always had the tool to get the alarm off on her, she never went anywhere without it. The alarms were yanked off in seconds. Rachel quickly grabbed a price tag and smirked at it. She could get twenty pound a pair for these jeans all day long. Half price was what she charged for most of the goods, it was the going rate and very few people ever moaned about the price. People loved a bargain and even the rich were always willing to get stuff on the cheap. She had a few buyers already who bought in bulk and she rarely struggled to sell her knocked off gear.

Lifting her head up, Rachel clocked her reflection in the long mirror in front of her. Slowly she stroked underneath her eye with the tip of her finger and pulled at the baggy skin. She'd aged so much over the last few years and any good looks she once had were long gone. She was haggard. Her once pearly white teeth had crumbled away and all that was left were brown stumps, decayed teeth and stale breath. Rachel scooped her thin greasy hair back from her face and tucked it behind her ears trying to smarten herself up. Staring at her reflection, her heart sank. What on earth had happened to her? She'd let herself go big time. Rachel gnawed at the end of her thumb. This was no time to be having regrets about how her life had panned out, she had a job to do. Rolling the garments up tightly, she shoved them down the front of her pants, tucking them neatly beneath her knickers. Standing in the mirror she turned from side to side making sure nobody could see them. Rachel yanked her coat down over the top of her sparrow legs and picked up the remaining garments. She gave herself one last look in the mirror. Taking a deep breath, she was ready to leave. Her hands were shaking as she unlocked the door. Calm down girl, calm down, she told herself. A few steps forward and she met the eyes of the assistant. "No good these love. I've piled a bit of weight on recently and I don't think my body is ready yet for skinny jeans. Maybe next time, ay. I'll just stick to my fat arse jeans for now?" The young girl smiled. She was used to customers hating their body image and today Rachel was just another one in a long line of body haters. Rachel searched the store as she planned her escape route. Once she had the goods concealed she rarely waited around for long, she was in and out like a ninja. Her chest tightened as she shot a look over at the security guard. Did he know she was up to no good or was she being paranoid? Her heart was pumping and her palms were sweaty. "Keep it real girl, come on, you can do this," she muttered under her breath. Rachel spotted a group of middle-aged women getting ready to leave the store and quickly hurried to stand behind them. They were chatting and never really noticed how close she was to them. Rachel tried to mingle in with them but stuck out like a sore thumb. These women were all well styled and there she was dressed like a scally, stinking of stale tobacco. It's a wonder they never clocked her. Here it was, the moment of truth, she was nearly at the exit.

Sarah stretched her neck out as she stood at the bus stop. Rachel was so selfish and she had no thought for the way she was feeling in her time of need. She could have done with a cuddle, a few wise words of advice to help her from sinking into a deep dark depression. Sarah was like that, she let things get on top of her and she was known to be dark and moody when something was on her mind. She controlled her emotions by talking about it, even though it might have only been to herself, she liked to analyse things until she came up with an answer for the way she was feeling. Loyalty was all she asked in life and if someone let her down, there were no second chances, nothing, she was gone. Sarah could see Rachel motoring towards her. She was checking over her shoulder as she crossed the busy road, the cars honking their horns at her. She rammed two fingers up at them and sneered over at the drivers. "Piss off and watch the road, you stupid bastards." Rachel sniggered as she sat down inside the bus shelter. Her breathing was short as she quickly swiped the sweat from her forehead with the side of her hand. "I just can't help myself can I? I'm on my arse so I needed a quick graft to put a bit of money in my pocket. I can get some gas and electric now."

Sarah's eyes were wide open, she was mortified. "What if you had got caught, don't you ever think about going back to prison? You're off your head you are! You're just asking for trouble!"

Rachel licked the edge of her front teeth and replied. "Life's life isn't it. I have to keep my head above water. Money doesn't grow on trees you know. We're not all handed it on a plate like you are Miss Fancy Pants." Sarah watched as she pulled out the jeans. Rachel checked nobody was watching and kept her voice low. "Here, stick them in your bag until we get home. I'll get Gary to get on the estate to sell them. He'll easily get a score each for them."

Sarah was alert, her eyes were twitching. Was she now a criminal? She was handling stolen goods and if the police were to search her she would have been arrested for her part in the crime. No way was she being involved in this. Rachel could do her own dirty work. "Here, you can carry the bag then. I'm having nothing to do with it. My family would go ape if they knew I was even speaking to you, never mind being involved in any crime."

Rachel growled at her and rolled her eyes. Sarah was a right smacked arse and if she'd have had her own way she would have got Mikey to cart her months ago. She was so prim and proper and she never really knew what it was like to struggle for anything in her life. She was a brat, fed with a silver spoon. Rachel bagged the stolen goods up and rested it on her lap. This daft bitch was doing her head in already and she would rather sit in silence than try and make conversation with her, she was winding her up, pressing her buttons.

★

Mikey watched the cell door like a hawk. He was aware the guards kept lifting the hatch up and looking at him through it. He could hear the sneaky bastards. They were wary of him and he knew it. Cupping his hands around the side of his mouth he shouted in a loud voice. "Brendan, can you hear me mate, which cell are you in?" Mikey held his ear to the wall and waited for a reply. There was no answer. He looked puzzled and sat back down on the floor. Was Brendan still here or had he been shipped out already? They usually moved inmates out of the holding cells about four o'clock, surely it was that time now. He had no sense of time and he was just hoping he didn't have to stay here much longer, he was bored shitless. Where would they send him? Which jail was he going to? Mikey sat twisting his fingers, he was edgy and wanted to know where he would be spending the next five years. Well, it wasn't really five years exactly, he'd only serve half of it but still it was a long time to be away from the outside world. Would things change that much in his absence? Would Sarah still be waiting for him on his release date or would she move on? His girlfriend was faithful, he knew that, but time changed people and love could be lost in the blink of an eye, a click of a finger. He'd seen it happen one hundred and one times before; guys in the nick threatening to end their lives, inmates smashing their pads up because a loved one was no longer waiting on the out for them. It was selfish of him to think she would wait, he had nothing really to offer her, only what he was standing up in. He couldn't give her the big house and car she wanted, he could give her nothing but his love but was that enough? Only time would tell.

Standing to his feet, he walked over to the door and hammered on it with his fist, booting it for good measure. "Oi boss, what time's tea? I'm starving in here. Any chance of a curry before I go on my travels?" Mikey smirked to himself and chuckled as he carried on yelling from behind his door. His tone changed and he was playing with them now. "Come on lads, give me a break, ay. Sort us some scran out before I go. I'm wasting away here. You know prison food is crap. Just give me a decent meal before I land in the chokey." There was still no reply. Mikey started to sing at the top of his lungs, hoping to get some response. "When you're chewing on life's grizzle, don't worry give a whistle," he took a deep breath and pelted out the chorus. "And, always look on the bright side of life," he was whistling and pacing his cell, dancing, wiggling his arse. Mikey froze as the cell door swung open. The guards stood warily, waiting to see if he was going to give them a hard time. They'd dealt with his sort many times before and they were ready to use as much force as necessary to get this convict out of here. Mikey licked his bottom lip and smirked at them. He stood with his back to the wall. "Evening ladies, any chance of a bite to eat. I have rights you know."

One guard stood with his hand resting on the doorframe. He sneered over at Mikey and he was ready to kick the living daylights out of him if he needed to. His jaw moved rapidly as he chewed on his gum. "You're going to Lancaster Farms, lad. The baby jail."

Mikey nodded slowly and casually flicked the invisible dust from the top of his shoulder. "Standard pal. I've been to worse places. When am I going? Is Brendan allocated there too?"

The security guard was in no mood for chit-chat. This cocky kid was doing his head in and he wanted him gone as soon as possible. It was Friday night and he wanted an early finish. To have a few pints with his mates down the boozer. He locked eyes with Mikey. "It doesn't matter where anyone else is going so don't concern yourself, nosey bollocks. You're going there and that's all you need to know." The man looked over his shoulder at his work colleagues and nodded. He had this under control. The other men were ready to go into the cell. One wrong move and Mikey was getting dealt with. This was how it worked behind closed doors and nobody knew the half of it. Some serious attacks had happened inside these walls but when the reports were filled out the guards stuck together, never once did they snitch on their workmates. It was the circle of trust, nobody grassed.

Mikey flicked his eyes about the room. He was the underdog and knew he would never win when they were team handed. His expression changed and he was co-operating for once. "So, am I going now or what? No point in waiting about is there ladies?" This youth was full of himself and he was getting right under their skin. He knew what he was doing and he loved winding them up. Mikey walked towards the door and stood tall, a bounce in his step. He never flinched. Each officer was alert and aware he could strike at any minute, he couldn't be trusted. He left the cell and didn't look back at them once.

The white Group Four van had eight doors inside it and behind each door was a small window. This vehicle was used to transfer prisoners to jails all around the country. Some of the most notorious criminals in the United Kingdom had sat in these vans; murderers, rapists, kiddy fiddlers. Mikey had been inside one of these before and he knew the crack. As he stepped inside he shouted out in a loud voice. "Brendan, are you on the bus mate?"

Mikey smiled as he heard a reply. "Yeah, I'm going to the farms, where you going?"

"I'm going there too, see you when we land. Don't worry about fuck all I'll look after you. It's going to be a doddle."

Before he could finish his sentence he was pushed

inside a door. Turning his head quickly he met the eyes of another officer who thought he was top dog. "Enjoy the trip mate." Mikey just sat down on the seat and rammed two fingers into the air over at him. "Don't you worry about me you faggot, just you worry about who's stuck up your wife while you're out working." It was game set and match – Mikey had won the argument. The security guard was trying to come back with something but Mikey started to sing and ignored him. The door slammed shut and Mikey was alone with his thoughts.

Mikey imagined some of the landmarks around Manchester disappearing one by one through the small window. It was going to be a long time before he ever set foot on those streets again. Dropping his head into his hands the reality of his life for the next few years kicked in. He was sobbing, tears rolling down his cheeks. No one must hear him though, nobody could see he was weak. Mikey rested his head on the wall to the left of him. The rain hammered against the van and he sat listening to it as if it was calming him down. He loved listening to the rain. Ever since being a small child he remembered how peaceful it made him feel. He loved being tucked up in his warm bed at night watching each droplet of rain run down his window pane.

Most nights he would lie there never knowing if his mother was going to return home. He didn't know if she was safe or if she'd been beaten within an inch of her life again. Rachel had received some bad beatings over the years. She'd been admitted into hospital several times and had stitches, concussion and broken bones. Trouble just followed her. Mikey spent most of his youth being shipped about to different relatives and anyone who would give him a bed for the night. He never really had a place to call home and from an early age he had to fend for himself. His father Dennis had only been in his life until he was five years old. He was a criminal too and he was forever in and out of jail. God only knows what for but Rachel had always said he was a bad penny and deserved to be locked up for good. Mikey would never have a bad word said against his father though. He loved him no matter what and on the night he left after yet another heated argument with his mother, he'd come into his son's bedroom and lay stroking his head with a flat palm. "Son, I can't do it anymore. She's driving me insane. I'll end up killing her if I stay. She's saying bad things about me that aren't true, honest, don't listen to her. Don't end up like me son. I'm fucked in the head. You're so bright and have a great future in front of you. Make me proud son, just do something with your life and don't end up a washed up worthless fucker like me." Mikey would remember those words for the rest of his life, they were all he had left to remind him of his old man. He'd not seen the guy for years and didn't have a clue where he was living. Word was that he was doing another stretch in jail but he didn't know if that was true or just gossip.

Deep down he knew he'd let his dad down, he'd never once made him proud. All of his life so far had been nothing but trouble. He'd been expelled from school when he was thirteen and left school barely able to read or write. It never bothered him, he thought he knew it all. Common sense was all he needed to get by in life, or so he thought. He was a know-it-all, nobody could ever make him see sense when he had a bee in his bonnet. He had a lot to learn and it looked like he was going to learn it the hard way. Somebody needed to give him a shake, a slap around the head, something to make him see that crime didn't pay.

Rachel was the one who'd got him grafting in the first place. It was shocking really, she had no shame. It was her need to score, her greed for the drugs that controlled her body that made her the way she was. Rachel started using heroin when she was first in jail. At the start it was just a few toots to calm her down, to get her through the hard times. She never thought that it would become her master and take over her life like it had. Those were dark days. Well, that's what she called them now whenever she spoke about them. Those were the times when she'd sold her body to feed her habit, times when she'd sucked dirty old men off to stop her rattling for drugs. Rachel had been clean for over three years. She was on a methadone script and her need to go out to commit crime had reduced dramatically. She'd never be fully clean from the drug though, it had a grip on her and wasn't for letting go. Even to this day she still had the occasional urge to feel the buzz from the drug that ruined her inside and out. That feeling would never truly disappear.

Mikey looked after Rachel as soon as he was old enough. He'd seen her on her hands and knees crying for drugs, begging him to help her. This was something no child should ever see. He had to look after her, she had nobody else. All her family had deserted her years earlier. Could you blame them? She'd robbed them and shamed them, what did she expect? There was only so much they could take. Mikey started out in his criminal career just doing a few easy grafts to earn some money, stuff his mother had put him on to. Cars with SAT navigators inside them, vans with boxes and valuables left on the seats. Yes, Rachel was eager for her son to learn the tricks of the trade from an early age. She showed him how to survive. If nothing else, his mother gave him the ways and means to make money and put food on the table any way he could.

CHAPTER THREE

Mark Fulton was at the dining table flicking through the newspaper. He was studying the horses and he was thinking of having a flutter. The names of the horses he fancied were circled in black biro. Tips of the day he liked to tell people, it was a load of shit really, none of them ever won a race, donkeys they were. The radio was on quietly in the background and he was only half-listening to the local news. It was the same old shit, just a different day. The crime rate in the area was soaring and he shook his head slightly as he listened to the news about a vicious attack on a local shopkeeper. Two thirteen year-old kids had kicked the fuck out of a sixty-two year-old man and left him half dead. They took one hundred pounds out of his till and snatched a few packets of cigarettes. Apparently, the youths were high on drugs and could only apologise for their behaviour. They wanted a good kicking, someone should have smacked their arse until it bled. A bit of old-fashioned parenting was what was missing here; a few clouts around their ear hole every now and then to keep them in line was what was missing. Kids were too cheeky these days and they had no respect for anybody, not even their parents. Mark hated crime and detested how the youth of today thought they knew it all. He flicked the pages over and sipped at his coffee.

His wife Tracey came into the front room, stressing. She was a right moaning cow and it always seemed to be somebody else's fault that she was in a mood each morning;

a right hormonal bitch she was. His wife tapped him on the shoulder as she rushed past him. "Mark, have you seen my bleeding car keys. I'm going to be late. I put them on the table last night. Have you shifted them again? You know what you're like for moving things about?" Wow, this woman was a right nagging bitch, nag nag nag, non-stop. This guy was henpecked.

Mark and Tracey had been married for three years and the honeymoon period had ended years ago. Sex was crap and he had to make a date with his missus for a leg-over weeks in advance. He was lucky if he got her to spread her legs once a month, an ice maiden she was. Mark was living like a monk, tiptoeing around her, doing anything to stop her yapping at him all the time. Tracey had been gorgeous in her day and all the men queued up to take her out, she had been a prize catch. But once Mark put a ring on her finger she stopped looking after herself and had let herself go. Her once slimline figure had gone from a comfortable size ten to at least two sizes bigger. She was a cake addict and never stopped eating. Mark had only mentioned that she should curb the bread in future and that had caused World War Three. He would never be straight with her again. He left her to her own devices and just sat back watching her get bigger by the day. He was actually starting to hate his life with her, she was a misery and every day she had some drama going on in her life. There was never enough money coming into the house, everything was such a big effort with her. "Make sure you put the money in the bank Mark, the mortgage is due at the end of the month. Don't forget, we don't want to be charged for a late payment again do we?" She stressed her words and made sure he got the message.

Bang Up

Mark pulled a black jumper over his white shirt. He wanted a peaceful morning but that was never going to happen while she was in the same room. She never let up. Mark kept his calm and snarled over at her. He could have strangled her, ended her life at that second, she made his blood boil. He gasped his breath and raised his eyes. "I'll do it for fucks sake. I told you last time it was a mistake on their part. It's not my fault if the bank fuck things up is it? Just go to work anyway. I'll sort it out, like I always do."

Tracey bent over slightly and kissed the side of his cheek. She knew she'd rattled his cage and tried to make amends but he just pushed her away and wiped the cherry coloured lipstick from his cheek. Heading to the door she shouted back at him. "What time are you home tonight, is it a late shift?"

Mark didn't even look at her as he carried on reading his newspaper. "Yep, I'm on a double shift so I'll see you when I see you."

Tracey casually slung her handbag over her shoulder. "I wish you would find another job with normal working hours. I hate sleeping on my own at night. You need to switch jobs and work sociable hours like I do."

Mark picked his cup of coffee up and sipped the last bit of it. He rammed two fingers in the air behind her and let out a laboured breath. "Don't come back home then! Suits me fine," he growled. The front door slammed shut and he threw the newspaper down on the table. He dropped his head into his fanned fingers and sighed. Something was troubling him. Pulling his wallet out from his trouser pocket he opened it and looked at the cash there. Mark spread the notes out on the table and sat staring at them, his finger touching the notes and slowly gliding across them.

He was short again, one hundred and fifty pounds short. This was all getting out of control. What a prick he was, would he ever learn? Mark liked to gamble. He loved to chase his money, he was addicted to gambling and had been for a few years now. Scratch cards, roulette, anything that he thought could win him the jackpot. Ragging his hands through his hair he sat looking at the notes on the table again. Something had to give, his luck needed to change somehow, someway. Just a few grand would land him back on his feet and clear the debts he'd accrued.

Mark quickly checked the time on his wristwatch and sprang to his feet. He couldn't be late again, he'd already had his collar felt about his time keeping. He just didn't have the get up and go anymore, he had no motivation whatsoever. Mark worked as a prison officer in a jail not too far from where he lived. The role of a screw had made him see life in a different light. There were some bad people living in this world, dangerous sick bastards who were not right in the head. When he first started working at HMP Lancaster Farms he was a bit wet behind the ears. He knew nothing about prison life and how cunning some people really were. He'd learned the hard way. Nobody could ever be trusted in the big house. He was wise to this now. Every day he worked there he was living on borrowed time. Screws were being stabbed, attacked, fighting for their lives in a hospital bed the moment their backs were turned. The job was hardcore and very stressful. Every night he lay in bed thinking about what had gone down on his latest shift. There were lads stringing themselves up, inmates self-harming, bullying, and then, there was the dark side of the jail: the paedophiles. He'd always struggled on the high-risk wings. He could never look the kiddy-fiddlers in the eye without wanting to punch their lights out. They were dirty bastards, lowlifes. And yes, he'd turned a blind eye on a few occasions to let them take a good beating from the other prisoners in the jail. They deserved it; they were the scum of the earth.

So, why did he still work there? Why did he put himself through this rigmarole every single day when he could have had a nice office job, a cushy number with no idiots wanting to end his life every minute of every day? Deep down Mark was a control freak, he liked to rule his wing with a firm hand, he liked the power he held over the inmates. His father was the same and he hated that sometimes when he looked at his reflection in the mirror he could see his old man staring right back at him; a fierce, controlling bully who intimidated everyone he saw a weakness in. When Mark first started the job, he had sympathised with the convicts on his wing and thought he would give them a clean break, never judging them. But, after a sneaky attack that led to a large scar on his left cheek, he never trusted any of them again. His head was always in the game now, he never let any of them get close to him. Once bitten, twice shy. The good Mark had gone and all that was left was a moody, grumpy screw with no time for anyone anymore. Every shift he worked he would never let his guard down, never turn a blind eye. He had to be on the ball twenty-four-seven.

Mark picked his car keys up from the table and shoved the money back in his wallet. There was just enough time to nip to the bookies before his shift began. He'd had a tip from his pal about a horse that was running and he'd already checked the form on the horse, it was easy money. In fact, it was his last hope of getting the money back he'd already lost.

Mark pulled up in the car park outside the prison and dropped his head onto the steering wheel, banging it slowly. Small beads of sweat were forming on his brow and he looked like he was going to burst out crying. His luck had run out and he'd lost every penny. The crumpled betting slip on the seat next to him had been spat at and cursed all the way to work. Why did he listen to his mate, the four-legged donkey came last and didn't even put up a fight for a place! If he'd have had a gun at that moment he would have found the horse and shot the lazy fucker right in the head! He was up shit street now, he had nowhere else to turn. The minute he walked through the door his missus would be on at him and it was only a matter of time before she found out he'd done the mortgage money in again. He was a bad liar and she could always see right through him, his eyes blinked rapidly when he was telling porkies, he fidgeted about and he could never look her in the eye when he was trying to pull a fast one.

Turning his head slightly, he could see the prison gates facing him. It was a modern jail and not like some of the other joints he'd worked in the past but it was still a jail and behind its walls were the rejects of life. The Artful Dodgers of the world, men nobody would ever trust. Smithy banged his palm onto the window and made Mark jump. "Are you ready for the shift lad, come on, the sooner we get in, the sooner we finish!" he chuckled. Mark grabbed his holdall from the passenger seat and opened the car door. There could be no more tears now, it was work time. He had to be the confident, happy-go-lucky man everybody thought he was.

Smithy had been his pal for as long as he could remember and they'd both started working in the prison service at about the same time. Smithy loved his job and he always did his best to work alongside the inmates. He'd gained the respect of the offenders on his wing and it was very rare he ever got any trouble from them. B-wing had always been a black spot inside the jail and each screw dodged it like the plague. It was full of youths who didn't like rules, lads who had chips on their shoulders, cocky fuckers who would bow down to nobody. Men who would stick a blade in you the moment your back was turned. Mark stood back from the path as a white van drove past them both. Smithy smirked over at him and punched him playfully in the arm. "Some new prisoners for the jail, fucking shoot me now! More head the balls to deal with, more pricks who think the world owes them a favour!"

Smithy sniggered and zipped his coat up tightly as they continued to walk to their place of work. Mark shot a look over at the sweat box and snarled at it. He knew each inmate inside was another reason why his job was so hard these days. These prisoners were a new breed of criminal; ruthless and not afraid of anything. Most of them were in for violent crimes and they didn't think twice about taking a man down. Prison didn't scare them, it just made them stronger. The days had long gone when a young offender came through the prison door who had made one silly mistake. These inmates were full of attitude and had respect for nobody. Yes, there was the odd one who wanted to turn their lives around but they were few and far between. For most of the men behind these walls, this was part of their everyday life.

The men stood at the entrance to the jail. Smithy punched his digits into the silver key pad. Once they stepped inside, everywhere they went the process was more or less the same. Everything was under lock and key. Mark followed Smithy into the reception area and they went straight to the lockers to put their personal belongings away. Nothing of any value was ever taken into the main prison.

Jerry, the man in charge, was chewing the end of his blue biro and sat at his desk watching the CCTV with concern. He was around fifty-five years of age and most of his working career had been spent in the jails around the country. Jerry had been in the army before this job and he knew how hard it was to make sure rules were followed. The army had turned him from a boy to a man, he always said, and every chance he got he was telling his co-workers about his days in the forces. They were the best days of his life and he recommended that every man should join the army as soon as they were old enough too. Lifting his head up from the screen, he chuckled as he spoke to Mark and Smithy. "Right lads, I need you both to muck in and help out in reception with these new prisoners. I've got two staff who have phoned in sick and we're short-staffed on that side. We need to pull together and get this lot settled without any hassle."

Smithy rubbed his hands together and sniggered. "Yep boss, no worries. Glad to help in your hour of need. You know me, I don't mind getting my hands dirty."

Jerry smirked over at him and knew he was being sarcastic. This man was always so happy and nothing ever seemed to bother him. He was the life and soul of the party, never negative and always ready to put his neck on the line for others. Mark raised his eyes and sucked hard on his gums. All he wanted to do was to get onto his wing and do a day's work. This was not what he needed on a day like today.

The van doors opened and Smithy stood there with a black clipboard in his hands. He rolled the pencil around in his fingers, looking at the names on his sheet. Here they were, the new recruits. One by one they started to come out of the van. Smithy smiled at the prisoners and tried to make this as easy as possible. He had a big heart really and knew for some of these lads it was going to be hard. Yes, they'd broken the law but he always saw the good in the men, he always gave them a chance, unlike his workmate. Mark opened the doors inside the van and guided each prisoner into position. He was in a mood, slamming doors left, right and centre. There were eight prisoners in total landing at the jail. Brendan Mellor appeared from the doors and he looked like he was going to fold in two. His legs buckled beneath him and he had to hold onto the side of van to steady himself. His head was spinning and he looked like he was going to spew his ring up. Prisoners stood talking to each other and each of them was disclosing why they were in the jail. Most of the sentences were for the same kind of stuff; drug charges, robbery and violence. The last door of the sweat box opened and a young male walked out. This kid was so young, he was thin and small and looked like he was going to break down crying. Surely he wasn't old enough to be inside this jail? Mikey clocked him instantly and nudged one of the other inmates in the waist. "Check fucking Harry Potter out over there. Wow, doesn't he look like him?" They were all looking at the young offender now and his eyes were wide with fear. He was the double of Harry Potter and all he was missing was the black cape and magic wand in his hand.

Mikey knew the crack in the jails and knew the next few hours would involve sitting about in the reception area waiting, filling out forms, picking up uniforms and learning a bit about how the jail ran. Mikey edged closer to the young lad and made eye contact with him. "What you in for Potter?" The offender wiped his round black rimmed glasses on his white shirt and placed them back on the end of his nose trying to focus. Mikey hated waiting for an answer and spat near his feet. This kid was getting a dig if he didn't answer him any second soon. He asked him again and his ears pinned back. "Oi, fucking deaf lugs. I said what are you in for?" All the others were waiting on his answer now. If he was a kiddy-fiddler or a wrong-un he was getting sorted out the moment the screws turned their backs. They would kick the living daylights out of him, mark him for life, brand him. That was the rule of any jail. Any crimes against children were frowned upon and they were sitting ducks every second they walked about the landings.

The male was stuttering and his voice was low. He croaked. "I'm in for fraud."

Mikey twisted his head over his shoulder and laughed out loud. "What, you're a fraudster. Tell me more because I think you're chatting shit. You only look about fifteen, should you even be in this jail?"

The inmate swallowed hard and stood fidgeting. "I was making driving licenses, IDs and passports. I just did it to earn some money for college and that. The guy told me

I would never get caught but once they arrested him he admitted that I was the brains behind it all."

Mikey liked this kid already and now he'd proved that he wasn't a nonce he was allowed to join the group. Mikey placed his hand around his shoulder and ruffled the top of his thick black crop of hair. "Come on Potter, you're sorted. We'll look after you, won't we lads?" A few inmates nodded and he was welcomed into their realm. He was good like that, Mikey. He had a heart of gold and when he was in the right mood he could be a loving, caring person. Brendan edged closer to Mikey. He stuck to him like a fly around shit, wherever he went, Brendan followed. There was no chance he was dealing with this alone. Mikey owed him and he was making sure everyone knew he was his wing-man, his sidekick.

The new prisoners walked into the reception area and were placed into a single cubicle. The prisoners were shouting to each other and trying to make the most out of the situation. Mikey stood at reception and gave his details to the officer in charge. His uniform was now issued; blue pants and a blue and white striped shirt. He ran his fingers over the shirt and pulled a face. This wasn't his usual swagger and a far cry from what he would wear on the outside. He tried to make light of the matter and thought he'd have a bit of banter with the screws. "Can I have Armani jeans and a Hugo Boss shirt? I can't wear this load of shite, it makes my body itch. I'm used to the finer things in life, not rags like these." There was laughter and already Mikey was standing out from the crowd. He was never one to be quiet and his voice was heard throughout the room. Smithy stood watching Mikey from a distance and smiled. This guy had charisma and even though it was his first day in the slammer he was already making them laugh.

When he was finished Smithy shouted over to him. "You need to see the doctor now, mate. Just in there she is. It's only basic stuff she'll want to know so don't worry about anything."

Mikey picked up his clothes and placed them on a chair outside the room, he raised his eyes over at Smithy. "Hope there's a few ladies in here who will appreciate my lean body. I can put a show on for them if they want?"

Smithy sniggered. "Just get your arse inside and stop fucking about. If we ever need the Full Monty, I'll give you a shout but for now you know what the rules are regarding any ladies in the jail. One wrong move and they'll report you. Hormonal they are, you know what women are like."

His voice was low and his eyes were wide open as he chuckled. Mikey walked into the medical room and he was asked to sit down facing the female doctor. She didn't waste any time asking him questions. Time wasn't on her side and she wanted to go home sooner rather than later. Here it was, the tick list. She didn't looked at him once, her eyes were on the medical form. Ignorant she was, up her own arse.

"Do you have any illnesses or do you feel suicidal? Is there any regular medication you take?" she began.

Mikey pulled a face and sat forward in his seat twisting his fingers. "Nope, no illnesses yet and I don't take any regular medication. I do get migraines though but not all the time just when I'm stressed." The doctor was jotting this down on her pad.

Lifting her head slightly she watched him for any reaction. "And, how's your mental health, do you ever have suicidal thoughts?"

Mike gasped, what the hell was she asking that for? He was a normal inmate. His head was fine. "Nar, I'm sound as a pound me, love. I'm a bit gutted about the sentence but nothing that I would want to end my life for."

"Excuse me! Don't ever call me love!" she hissed.

The medical was nearly over and after a few more questions the form was complete. "Can you get undressed while I carry out a few more checks? Just go behind that screen and wait for me." Mikey strolled behind the white curtain. He was whistling and confident of showing his body off to anyone who was interested. Hours at the gym and a healthy protein diet had given him a body most men would die for. His six pack was his baby, the ripped stomach muscles were always tensed and any chance he got he liked to show them off. Peeling his clothes from his body he folded them neatly on the chair next to him. It was cold in this room and goosepimples were appearing all over his body. He stood jumping about on the spot rubbing at his arms with speed. A quick pull of his penis and he was ready to be examined. This man was hung like a donkey! A big girth and a long, solid member that would make any woman's eyes water for sure. Looking down at his semi-hard cock he sniggered to himself. He loved watching the females when they clocked his manhood for the first time. They tried not to look at it but he knew they were happy with what they could see.

He shouted from behind the curtain whilst cupping his nuts in his hands. "I'm ready when you are. Any chance of getting this done as soon as possible? I'm freezing my balls off stood around here. My knob's the size of an acorn," he sniggered.

The doctor stepped behind the curtain to examine him.

"Right, I need you just to relax and I will be as quick as I can." He was watching her closely now and the moment she spotted his semi-hard cock she started to blush. She was gobsmacked and stuttered. "Can you hold your arms out to the side of you and turn around slowly please?" Mikey did as he was asked and even though he was stood there in the nude, bare-arsed, he was still flirting with the doctor. He clenched his arse cheeks together and flexed his biceps. Smithy stood watching Mikey from the side of the room and he was making sure he was doing everything he should be doing. He was amused and the corner of his mouth started to rise. He too spotted his penis and he had to give it a second look to make sure he wasn't seeing things. It was like a baby's arm holding an apple. He'd never seen anything so big before. Grabbing at his own crotch he tweaked his member. It would never be that size but still he was happy with what God had given him.

This part of the induction was always something every inmate hated. Being touched, being probed, it was so undignified. Smithy stood behind Mikey making sure he had nothing concealed on his body. They made him open his mouth, lift his ball-bag up and now they had him squatting down to make sure he had nothing shoved up his arsehole. The anal passage was somewhere most prisoners concealed their contraband; phones, drugs, you would be amazed at would they could fit up their shitters. Some of them were like clown's pockets, they could get anything up there with a bit of Vaseline on it to help it inside.

Mark came into the room and he was alert. Mikey was squatting down and Smithy was bent down looking underneath his undercarriage with a mirror on the end of a long pole. This kid was clean, he wasn't holding anything.

There was a special chair to the back of the room that Mikey was now led towards. The boss chair, as it was called by the inmates. This was used to detect metal objects a prisoner might be concealing inside their bodies, usually mobile phones, or a blade. Once again Mikey was clean, nothing was detected. He smirked over at Smithy and chuckled. "Clean as a whistle I am lads, nothing up my ring-piece," he gave them a cheeky wink.

Smithy nodded slowly and made sure he had his attention. "Just keep it like that son and everything will be fine. Some of the lads think we don't know what goes on inside these walls but we do. So let that be a lesson to you. We're all over it." Smithy giggled and looked at the prisoner for a bit longer than necessary. They both knew what he meant without him going into it.

From nowhere Mark stepped forward and snarled at Mikey. He'd taken an instant dislike to him and hated his cocky attitude. He was in no mood for him today and he was on a short fuse. "Right, get ready and I'll take you back to the waiting area. It's going to be a few hours until you're ready to go onto the wing."

Mikey started to pull his boxers over his legs. He looked up at him. "Yep, no worries pal. It's not like I've got anywhere else to go is it?"

Mark licked his lips slowly. There was no way he was having anyone getting over familiar with him, especially a newcomer. "Oi, smart arse. Keep it shut and go where I've told you to go. You need to get one thing straight. I'm not your pal and never will be."

Mikey sniggered, he just couldn't help himself. He knew exactly what he was doing and carried on winding him up. "Whoa, relax bro. I'm just saying that's all. Where's your sense of humour? Don't tell me you're one of them moaning cunts who takes everything to heart?"

Mark went nose to nose with him. Heads touching, eyes locked. Mikey was game as fuck and he would never back down, there was too much at stake. Mark's stale breath was all over him. "I don't have a sense of humour in this place. So remember that. It's not a holiday camp here either, it's a prison. Carry on with your attitude and you'll end up down the block."

"Like I'm arsed, do what you have to."

The two of them stared each other down and Mikey knew this screw was one to watch out for in the future. There was always a prick like Mark in every jail and he knew his card was already marked. He was a wanker and thought he was untouchable because he was wearing a uniform. Mikey looked the screw up and down and knew he would be wasting his breath if he thought he could have a bit of banter with this guy. He was miserable and up his own arse. Smithy diffused the situation and nodded at Mikey to go back to return to the other prisoners.

Once he left Smithy grabbed hold of Mark's shoulder and stopped him from walking away. "A bit harsh that don't you think? He was only trying to have a bit of fun. You need to chill out and stop being so hard on them."

Mark broke free and scanned around the area to make sure nobody was listening. He was raging inside and he could have easily head-butted his pal, put him on his arse for giving him grief. "I'm not in the mood today mate, just leave me alone." Smithy watched as he stormed off.

Mark was such a hot-head lately and he was always on a downer. He scratched the top of his head and let out a laboured breath. "Please your bleeding self," he whispered under his breath.

Mikey sat down in the cubicle next to the kid who looked like Harry Potter. He shouted from behind his wall so he could hear him. He hated being alone and any chance he got he would always make sure he was in company. Perhaps, it was something from his childhood that made him feel like this; all those times he had sat in his house alone waiting for his mother to come home, the times when all he needed was someone to talk to. "So, what's your real name Potter? I bet it's something posh like Marvin or Nicolas?"

The inmate's voice was low and Mikey was struggling to hear him. He screwed his face up as he tried to make out what he was saying. "Christian Moore," the low voice replied. Mikey digested his reply and tipped his head to the side. What a lovely name that was. A bit posh but still, he liked it. Christian seemed liked a rich person's name, a man of style, a man of knowledge, a spiritual human being. He shouted back to him with a smile on his face. His fingers gliding down the wall slowly.

"Well, I'm going to call you Potter from now on. Are you okay with that?"

Christian smirked from behind his door. He was relieved he had a friend. He'd never met anybody like Mikey before in his life. He was well educated and most of his friends came from money. His own family had money in the past but they had lost it all when the family business went bankrupt two years before. If he was being true to himself, nobody had ever taken the time to get to really know him. He was so quiet and his self-confidence was low. "That's fine by me. I kind of like the name Potter anyway. I've never had a nickname. It's cool. I like it."

Potter rubbed his hands together as he sat waiting. He was a gang member now with one of the top dogs as his friends. He even had a nickname, how cool was that? As soon as he got chance he was going to write home and tell his friends and family all about it. Mikey placed his head next to the wall that separated them both and knocked the side of his napper against it. "So Potter, tell me about you. Whereabouts are you from. Have you got family? You sound like a right posh twat by the way?"

"My family lived in Cheshire. Well, we did up until two months ago. We're living in Ancoats now just near the town centre in Manchester."

Mikey closed his eyes and visualised the place he was talking about. "I've got a few mates who live around there. Is it near the old hospital?"

Christian replied with an eager voice. "Yes, our apartment is just behind it." It was so comforting to know someone knew the area where you were living. It was nice to talk to people who could relate to the area.

Mikey ran his finger slowly along the cold wall above his head and carried on speaking. "It's rough as fuck around them parts, lad. I've done a few grafts with a couple of guys from around there. How are you finding it Potter?"

Christian thought long and hard before he answered. He didn't want to offend anyone. "It was hard at first I suppose. I was only there a week and my mountain bike got nicked from me. Two lads it was. They shoved a knife to the side of my neck and threatened to slice me up if I didn't give it to them. I panicked I can tell you."

Mikey was holding his stomach laughing. He'd done similar things himself and it was all in a day's work to him. "Yep, that sounds about right. You don't look like one of the normal residents, that's why. They must have known you'd just hand it over without a fight. You got off lightly really. I would have chinned you before I left, if it was me."

Potter sniggered as he answered him. "I crapped my pants I can tell you. My father wanted me to phone the police but I told him straight that wasn't going to happen. There was no way I ever wanted to meet those two creatures again, ever."

Mikey nodded slowly. He admired this lad's honesty. "You done the right thing. If you would have snitched on them, your windows would have gone through. Nobody likes a grass you know. You need to remember that, especially inside the jail. Keep what you know to yourself and you'll be fine." Mikey started to hum a tune, he was bored now. His eyes were closing and he started to nod off.

Day turned into night and the new inmates were led to the induction wing. Each of them had their kit folded in a neat bundle in front of them. Potter could barely see over his pile and every now and then he was dropping things. Brendan Mellor had tried to get a double pad with Mikey but the screw told him straight he was going where he put him. What a slap in the mouth that was for him. Brendan was devastated and hated that Mikey had never said a word about it. Mikey stepped inside the pad with Potter not far behind him. His eyes shot about the small room and he sucked in a deep breath of air. So, this was it. This was his home for the next few years. Potter sat down on his bed and folded his arms tightly in front of him. His bottom lip trembled and his eyes clouded over. This was the real deal now. No more waiting, no more not knowing how things would turn out, their sentences had begun. Mikey jumped onto his bed and looped his arms behind his head. He was taking ages to get comfortable and his hand was slamming hard at the mattress trying to get rid of any lumps. That would have to do, he gave up trying. Mikey turned his head and gripped the pillow folding it in half ramming it back behind him. He could see his pad mate was struggling and remembered his very first night being locked up away from the people that he loved. Prison was a daunting place when you didn't know the script. The noises throughout the night; crying, screaming, inmates shouting... Yes, this place was enough to break even the strongest of men.

"For fucks sake Potter, are you going to sit like that all night long, get your head down? Listen, I'll tell you straight, the first few weeks are going to be hard but once you get used to the swing of it you'll be sorted. I've told you already I've got your back, so you've got fuck all to worry about. Just keep your head down and this sentence will be like a walk in the park for you. How long did you get slammed for anyway?"

Potter lifted his legs up onto the bed and lay back slowly. His eyes were wide open and reality was hitting home. "I got twelve months. I'm lucky really I could have got three years my solicitor said."

Mikey dragged the thin grey blanket over his body and tucked it under his chin. "That's a baby sentence, you'll only do half of that anyway so six months you're in for. If you're lucky you might even get out before that date on a tag, you know, an electronic device?"

Christian flexed his fingers on his chest and turned to face Mikey. "Thanks for helping me out. I don't know what I'd have done if they would have put me in a pad with someone else. I'm not very good at mixing with other people. I'm a loner really."

Mikey turned on his side and faced the wall. His eyes were still wide open. He was ready for some shut eye and any second now he would be dead to the world in a deep sleep. "No worries. Now, get your head down and get some sleep, you fucking fairy. Tomorrow is another day. Let's see what these bastards have planned for us."

"Night Mikey," Christian whispered.

"Shut up and get to sleep, "Mikey sniggered back over to him.

Brendan Mellor sat alone in his cell. The cold brick walls seemed like they were closing in on him. Shivering at the small window he sucked in the night air from outside. He wasn't coping well and hated being alone at night. He was weak and full of anxiety. Brendan ran to his cell door and he banged his clenched fist into it desperately. "I can't do this, please, somebody help me. I'm dying here, I can't breathe." He was hysterical, he was having a panic attack. The screws on duty that night could hear the inmate from behind his door. It was something normal that happened on the induction wing. Smithy had seen even the strongest of men fold once the door was locked behind them at night, so he was used to it. He was about to stand up to go and give Brendan a bit of comfort when Mark grabbed his arm to sit back down. "I was just going to see if he was alright. For fucks sake Mark, he's only a young kid. Have a bit of heart will you?"

Mark let go of his arm and sneered. He shouted behind his workmate as he approached the cell door. "This is a prison, not a fucking nursery, remember that. Leave the tosser to it."

Smithy shook his head and started to open the cell door. He couldn't be arsed with the drama anymore. He was telling him straight, he was doing his head in. He shouted back to him. "Stop being an inconsiderate prick. This image you're trying to portray of yourself isn't working anymore. What the hell has got into you? You're like a raging bull."

The cell door was opened now and Brendan fell to his knees gasping for breath. "I want to go home, please let me go home. I want my mam, please just get my mam."

CHAPTER FOUR

Rachel was rolling a cigarette at her kitchen table. The tobacco smelt like camel shit, it was cheap, nasty stuff that she'd picked up cheap down the local market. You could always get a bargain on Conran Street if you were in the know: dodgy CDs, snide trainers - they were all up for grabs if you knew who to ask. Rachel was edgy and had something on her mind, she stood up and then sat back down – she was on pins. She began sucking in large mouthfuls of air and stood biting her fingernails. "Gary, we need to book a visit and get a parcel sorted out for our Mikey as soon as possible. And," she stressed, "I mean quick, he's got fuck all in that place and he needs to get back on his feet."

Gary turned his head slowly and yawned with his hands over his head. All of a sudden this kid of hers was God and she was running around like a headless chicken after him. Usually, she was cursing him and wishing that he never came home. Now Gary had to tread on eggshells. He knew one wrong word against the Holy child and he would have been binned. He'd bad mouthed Mikey in the past and to this day she was still reminding him about how much he hurt her feelings. Rachel never forgot anything, 'you forgive but you don't forget' she always said.

"Sort him out with what? We're skint, love. Fuck all is happening in terms of graft so I don't know what you expect me to do. Money doesn't grow on trees you know?"

"I know we're on our arse but we need to do something.

We can't just leave him to rot in there can we?" Rachel folded her arms tightly across her chest and continued. "He's bunged us enough times in the past and it's down to us to make sure he's sorted while he's in the slammer," she smiled and tried to make light of the matter. "He only needs a few bags of spice to get started. A bit of white and brown and he'll make his money back in weeks. You know what it's like to have fuck all in jail so instead of being negative you need to start coming up with some ideas."

This woman was actually talking about her own flesh and blood dealing in heroin and cocaine, did she have no shame? What kind of mother would ever be involved in anything like this? Gary sat tickling the end of his chin, thinking. He'd been in the big house before and knew more than anybody how it all worked but money was short and like he'd already said, they were both on their arses.

Rachel and Gary lived from hand to mouth every day and they'd already spent their jobseekers allowance. He looked over at Rachel and reached over to touch her hand. He licked his lips slowly and held a cunning look in his eyes. "What about his stash?" before he could finish his sentence Rachel jumped down the back of his throat and rammed a finger into the side of his head.

"Don't you dare mention that money again! That's his nest egg for when he's out and if anyone gets a whiff of it we're all dead meat. Just keep your big trap shut. Nobody must know about it, ever." Rachel stood up and popped a cigarette in the corner of her mouth. Flicking the lighter slowly she held her fag down towards the burning yellow flame. "Gary, I'm scared. It's only a matter of time before they come looking for us. We're his family and we'll be first on the list. Davo is no fucking idiot and he'll put us in a body bag if he ever finds out."

Gary was laid back and it was obvious he wasn't taking this seriously. This wasn't his beef and if the shit hit the fan he would drop Mikey in it at the drop of a hat. He was a coward. "Stop being daft, Rachel. Nobody knows about it except us. If we both keep it shut, it will still be there when Mikey gets out of nick. I'm just saying for now, borrow a few ton out of it and sort him out. We don't have any other option do we?"

He watched her from the corner of his eye and casually sat back down in his seat. Rachel paced the floor and sucked hard on her cigarette, cheeks sinking in at both sides. A thick grey cloud of smoke filled the living room as she looked over at him. She was angry and her defences were up. "I knew I shouldn't have told you about the money. Mikey will go mad if he knows I've told you," she rubbed at her arms and the hairs on the back of her neck stood on end. She was fighting with her thoughts. "I had to tell somebody though, what if they come here, what if they find out I'm his mother?"

Gary stood and cradled her in his arms. He was such a shady character and something about him was just not adding up. "I won't tell a soul. For one, you've not even told me where the money is, have you? How much are we talking anyway, a grand, a few grand, how much?"

Rachel pulled away from him and sat back down in her seat. She tapped her fingers slowly on the wooden table and kept her eyes low. "Ten grand. It's a lot of money and we should never speak about it again. I'll get the cash together for him, somehow, someway. I'll make sure he's alright in jail but there is no way I'm touching his money. No way in this world." Her eyes started to cloud over and she dropped her head low. "I've never been a good mother to our Mikey, have I? And I blame myself for the way things have turned out with him. You know how it was when he was growing up. I let him down big time. If I could turn back time, I would. I'd have been a proper mother and done all the things I should have done for him."

Gary had heard this story over and over again. He was sick to death of hearing it... Rachel had let Mikey down in his life but what did that matter now? He was a grown man and he should have been able to fend for himself. The apron strings needed to be cut and as far as he was concerned, he wouldn't have been arsed if he never saw her son again. Rachel snivelled and wiped the end of her nose on her jumper. "I need to see him. My mind's all over the place at the moment. Do us a favour Gary, nip down to the shop and see if we can get a bottle of vodka on tick until next week. Mr Patel is usually alright with me when I'm a bit short. Just tell him what's happened and he should be able to hook us up."

"Did you pay the tenner back you owed him from last week?"

Rachel shook her head and ragged her fingers through her thin greasy hair. She raised her eyes to the ceiling and sighed. "Argghh... Did I fuck! I forgot all about it. What am I like? I had the money there to pay him back too. It just slipped my mind." She was a lying cow and everybody who knew her – she was a full of shit. No loan man would touch her with a barge pole and even the neighbours had got wise to her now. Every night she was banging on a door for a bit of milk, a few rounds of bread, a cup of sugar – this woman had no shame.

Gary rolled his eyes and stared over at her. It was

pointless even going into it, she would always have an excuse to why she fucked up. "What about your mam then? Go and see if she'll do us a sub until next week."

Rachel snarled at him and punched her clenched fist into the sofa, a cloud of dust rising into the air. "Have you actually just said that?" She was up in arms and on the verge of throwing something at his big thick head. Rachel had a violent temper just like her son and once she was in the zone there was no going back. She had bad rage issues and in the past she'd had help in trying to control it. Gary was dicing with death, he just loved winding her up.

"Well, we don't have another option do we, it's either go and ask her for some money or we're fucked?"

Rachel's voice was choked and her eyes were bulging out from the sockets. "What! And you think I'd go and ask that old cow for a single penny. I'd rather stick hot pins in my eyes than ask her for anything. Fancy even suggesting that, you dimwit!" Gary sat back in his seat and knew what was coming next. He was sorry he'd even opened his mouth. "As if she would help me out anyway. For years she's just sat back and watched me struggle with our Mikey and never done a tap for any of us. I mean, what kind of mother watches her own daughter fall apart like I did and not offer to help out. An old battleaxe she is! I'll spit on her grave when she's six foot under! Just you wait and see! As far as I'm concerned, she's dead anyway, fucking dead!"

Gary started to read the newspaper and ignored her. She was pissing him off and he couldn't be arsed with her drama anymore. She would never let sleeping dogs lie. On and on she droned, never letting up for a single second. Her voice went through him. "I have nobody me. I was always the black sheep of the family. She always treated me differently to the others. If our Cath turned up for a tenner she'd be bending all the rules for her she would. Yes, it's always been different with me. She knows it and so do I." Gary looked up at her and nodded. He had to agree with her, his life wouldn't have been worth living if he said a single word in favour of Rachel's mother.

She looked at the clock on the wall and plonked down next to him running her thin fingers through his hair. Her dickey fit was nearly over. "Sarah said she was calling today. Perhaps she can lend us a few quid. I hate asking her though, she's a right toffee-nosed bitch. She just makes me feel so low when I ask her. You know," she raised her eyebrows. "She goes on like I'm below her or something. Like I'm begging."

Gary was sick to death of her now and tried putting her in her place. If she carried on like this he'd give her a back-hander, that usually worked for a short time. "Sarah has bunged you a right few quid in the past. She's never batted an eyelid when you've asked her before, so stop lying. I like her, it's just you getting on your high horse about her again. Face it, Rachel. You never think anyone's ever good enough for your Mikey?"

He was dicing with death now. This woman was a live-wire and any second now she could launch something at him. Rachel plonked back on the sofa and folded her arms tightly in front of her. She pointed over at him. "Whose bleeding side are you on here anyway, do you fancy her or something?"

Gary stood his ground and looked her straight in the eyes. It was time for a few home truths. There was no way he was backing down. "Every girl Mikey has ever brought home, you've always had something to say about them.

Face it, you'll never be happy with any of them. You always find fault in any bird he brings home."

Rachel defended herself. "I liked Susan Tilly. She was right up my street she was. At least with her I knew exactly where I stood."

Gary burst out laughing and held the bottom of his stomach. "You mean the same Susan Tilly you said you were going to knock out after she called you a daft bitch one night?"

Rachel pulled her face and flicked her hair back over her shoulder. "That was a misunderstanding, she was pissed and perhaps she was right in what she said. I should have kept my nose out of the argument. It was nothing to do with me really, it was between her and Mikey." There was an awkward silence and Rachel spat her dummy out. She hated being wrong and snarled over at him. Gary carried on reading the newspaper sniggering to himself as he hid his face away from her. Game, set and match.

Suddenly, Rachel jumped up from her seat as somebody hammered on the letterbox. She tiptoed to the hallway and stood with her back against the wall, her chest rising frantically. She'd been hiding from the loan men for months and every day they were trying to catch her at home. Gary was alert and already he was scrambling about on his hands and knees trying to locate the iron bar he always hid under the sofa. Anyone who knocked like this couldn't be trusted; once bitten, twice shy. Gripping it tightly in his hands he made his way into the hallway behind his girlfriend. His voice was low. "Who is it?"

Rachel swallowed hard and dipped her head around the corner, peeping. Her heart was in her mouth as she craned her neck. "Shut up big gob they'll hear you." She took a small step forward and let out a laboured breath. "I'll fucking strangle her knocking like that," she stressed. Rachel stormed towards the front door and unlocked the steel bolts from the top of it with shaking hands. Gary was edgy and held the bar up over his head, he was ready to strike, some cunt was getting this wrapped right over their head.

Seeing who it was, Rachel stood with her hands on her hips and growled. "What the fuck are you knocking like that for? We thought it was the dibble."

Sarah stood with her hands in her pocket and her cheeks were beetroot. She'd been there for ages and thought they were both asleep. "Well, you never hear me unless I knock hard. At least five minutes I've been stood here. Are you deaf or what?"

Rachel left the front door open and marched back into the living room in a strop. "False alarm Gary, it's only Sarah."

Gary lowered the bar and watched as Sarah walked past him. She shrugged her shoulders slightly and raised a soft smile at him. "Sorry, I just thought you couldn't hear me."

Gary shook his head and patted his hand on the top of her shoulder. His voice was quiet. "No worries, it's just her overreacting as per usual." Gary watched her enter the front room and he was definitely checking her arse out. A quick grab of his crotch and he followed behind her. Rachel flicked the TV on and sat down on the sofa. The room was well decorated and not what you might expect. Lime green curtains complimented a brown leather sofa. Big fluffy pillows were scattered over it and, in fairness, the place was clean. Mikey Milne loved a nice gaff. He would never live in a shit-tip and he always made sure that when he'd had a good earner he always bought something nice for his house. Nothing was bought on tick either. He hated the never-never and even though his mother had suggested going to "Bright House" for credit he told her straight that he would pay cash for anything he bought. There was no way he was bumping any company for furniture, how degrading was that when they came to take it back when you couldn't meet the payments? This was the only place Rachel had settled down in and he told her point-blank that she was staying here, no matter what. He was sick to death of moving about from pillar to post and when she signed the tenancy on this place he made sure his name was on it too. This was his base camp. All his belongings under one roof.

Sarah pulled her shoes off and stuck them at the side of the sofa. The carpet was new and every time she'd been here with Mikey he always made sure she took her shoes off. He hated muck on the carpet and he was forever picking bits of dirt from it. His mother always said he was a bit OCD and maybe she was right. Everything had to be in a certain place, Mikey could tell the moment he walked into a room if anything had been changed. He had an eye for detail. Mikey loved all the latest gadgets too; flat screen TV, PlayStation. It was all there positioned nicely around the room. This was a home to be proud of. "When do you think he'll be able to phone us, Rachel? Do you think it might be today? I've not slept for days worrying about him. My mam thinks I'm ill when in fact I think I'm lovesick. He's on my mind every hour of every day."

Rachel kept her eyes on the TV screen as she answered her. "He'll have to get some cash sorted first. He won't get his canteen until the middle of the week, so fuck knows when he'll be able to phone home."

Sarah was so behind the door when it came to the criminal world. She thought everything was pink and fluffy in her world and she'd never had to go without anything in her life. She wasn't streetwise either. "I can get some money together for him Rachel. I think he needs to be comfortable in there doesn't he. Can I send him a few DVDs? He loves 'Band of Brothers' and 'Fast and Furious'"

Rachel lowered the volume on the TV and pulled her legs up under her bum cheeks on the sofa. This was going to be fun, she was going to bring her back down to earth with a bang. Gary sniggered and he was listening with interest at the side of her. He covered his mouth with his hand so nobody could see his amusement. Rachel sucked on her gums before she delivered the blow. "He can't have films sent inside the prison, you dickhead. You need to realise a few things about being in jail. It's nothing like it is on the outside. Once you go through them doors you're treated as a criminal. Everything you get in there is what you've had to fight for. Only the toughest survive! And, as for posting DVDs, you need to take your head from out of your arse and give your head a serious shake. You can't send anything inside the big house unless the governor allows it. And that, my love, is very rare. In fact, it never happens."

Sarah's eyes were wide open. She hated violence and she hated crime. She had a lot to learn though, this was going to be no walk in the park. This was real life. "I know Mikey and he will stick to the rules and do what he has to do to get this over and done with as soon as possible. He told me this is the last time he'll ever go to prison. He wants to change Rachel. He wants to have a normal life without being scared of the police knocking on the door every single day."

Gary raised his eyes over at Rachel and knew she couldn't let this go. She twiddled her hair and sat facing her. This was her son they were talking about and she knew him inside out. Who was this tart trying to convince? She sat upright and looked her straight in the eye. "Mikey will never change. It's in his blood. Do you want him working a nine-to-five job? Because if you do, you need to give your head a shake and wake up and smell the coffee! Mikey is not one of them geeks who will sit down in an office all day long. Your family might be like that, but my son isn't!"

Sarah hated Rachel's negative attitude and she was sick to the back teeth of her putting Mikey down. He was intelligent, he had hopes and dreams. Perhaps, if his mother had ever sat down with him she would have realised he wasn't just a scally. He was lost in Sarah's eyes and the best thing he could do was to get Rachel out of his life as soon as possible. She'd ruined her own life and now she was doing the same with his. What chance did he have living with her every day? She was a lazy cow who thought the world owed her a favour. Not once had she tried to change or turn her life around. She never looked for work, she just sat on her bony arse all day moaning about the cards she'd been dealt in life. Bone idle she was. Every day was the same with Rachel; doom and gloom and negative thoughts. She was no role model for anyone. A waste of space she was, nothing more, nothing less. Sarah watched the TV and she was aware that Rachel was waiting on an answer from her. Thinking about her every word she smirked and knew she could outsmart this woman with her hands tied behind her back. Sarah was educated and knew a lot more than she was letting on. "Mikey said we're moving away when he gets home. We'll have a new start and by then my dad will have seen how much we love each other and give him a job. How cool will that be? My Mikey all suited and booted for work every day." Gary sat on the edge of his seat, this was going to be good. He'd underestimated this girl. She was a lot cleverer than he had given her credit for.

Rachel was chain smoking and popped another cigarette into her mouth. She let out a sarcastic laugh. Did this daft bitch just say "her Mikey"? No, there was no way she was having that. He was her son and nobody was taking him away from her. "My Mikey," she stressed as she continued, "would tell your dad where to shove his job! He knows what he's been saying about him and he's like me like that, he won't forget. Mikey is fine the way he is, so do yourself a favour and stop trying to meddle in his life. He is who he is – deal with it."

Sarah was on form today and giving as good as she got. "You must know a different Mikey than I do then because when we used to talk about this lying in bed, he was all set to meet my dad and tell him how much he loved me. He's not going to tell you everything we speak about is he Rachel? Come on, he's a man now, not a small boy. He told me he doesn't have a close relationship with you anyway!"

That was a killer blow and you could see the pain in Rachel's eyes. This war now and the two women were ready to scratch each other's eyes out. Gary had to step in and change the subject. He came behind Rachel and placed his hand softly on her shoulder as he spoke to Mikey's girlfriend. "Sarah, we're trying to get some money together for a parcel for Mikey, as you know, we're a bit short and we were hoping you could chip in?"

Sarah flicked invisible dust from the corner of her

jacket and looked Rachel straight in the eye. She wasn't scared of her, no way. "Yes, of course I will Gary. I don't agree with being part of anything illegal but I'm aware sometimes you need to turn a blind eye and this is one of them. I've got fifty pounds here, will that be enough?"

Gary rubbed his hands together and scratched the side of his nose. "Smashing that Sarah, that will help him right out of the shit, won't it Rachel?"

Mikey's mother was silent. She hated this rich bitch with a passion and the sooner she was off the scene the better. Mikey loved his mother, this tart was lying. The mobile phone started ringing at the side of Rachel. Gripping it in her hand she checked the caller ID. She was hysterical. "It's Mikey, I just know it is." Sarah moved closer and tried to get in on the call but Rachel twisted her body around and made sure she couldn't hear a word being said. "Hello, oh son, I knew you would be in touch with me. I've been out of my mind with worry." Rachel smirked and raised her eyes up to Gary. "Where have you landed, son? Is there anyone you know in there?"

Sarah was getting restless and she shouted out so he could hear her. "I love you Mikey, when can I come and see you?"

Rachel listened to the call and whatever Mikey said to her she wasn't happy about. She rammed the phone into Sarah's hand. "Here, he wants to speak to you. Hurry up, because I still need to sort stuff out with him." Sarah took the mobile phone into her hand and walked out of the room. Rachel stood and held her ear to the door. She twisted her head back to Gary and snarled. "Can you hear her? What a soft cow she is! She's crying down the bleeding phone. As if he needs to hear that when he's just landed in chokey."

"Just sit down and leave her to it. Give her a bit of space and stop interfering all the bleeding time."

Rachel paced the front room and growled over at him. "Listen, he's my son and I need to make sure he gets through this sentence no matter what. The last thing he needs is some daft bint giving him grief when he's trying to find his feet." Gary was pissing in the wind, she never took advice from him. She never would. Sarah came back into the room snivelling and dabbing her finger into the corner of her eye. She walked over to the sofa and plonked herself down. Her heart was low and she was struggling to hold it together.

"Rachel, Mikey wants you to book a reception visit for Lancaster Farms. He said make sure you sort him out too." Rachel understood what that meant and now Sarah was willing to cough up the cash she could start organising the parcel. "He seems alright. His spirits were high and he said he only had a short time on the phone because he was using his mate's mobile."

Gary felt her pain and unlike his girlfriend he actually felt sorry for her. He needed to show her some compassion. It must have been hard for her. He offered her some comforting words. "Once he gets into the swing of things he'll be on the blower all the time. Come on now, there's no need for tears. We're here for you aren't we Rach?" Gary sat down and cradled Sarah in his arms. Rachel was chomping at the bit and gritted her teeth tightly together. This girl was such a drama queen and she was doing her head in. She watched the way her boyfriend touched the young girl and her stomach churned inside. He fancied her for sure, he was all over her. He'd never touched her like that! She very rarely saw this side of him. She bit the bullet and spoke in an aggressive tone. "Pass me that money then, Sarah. I'll go and get what he needs. Gary, will you make a drink for Sarah to calm her down? I'll see you when I get back."

Gary was sat with his eyes wide open. How on earth was he going to cope with her? Rachel smirked at him as Sarah sobbed her heart out. She rolled her eyes and thought she would teach him a lesson for being such a soft arse. "Gary's a good listener, Sarah. You just sit with him for a few hours and you'll be fine. Won't she love?"

His face was bright red, he knew he'd been stitched up. Sarah dug deep in her pocket and passed the cash over. Rachel shoved it deep into her pocket. "See you later, Gary," she sniggered, "get the biscuits out for our guest to go with her cuppa and make sure she gets everything out that's worrying her. It's better out than in, that's what I always say, Sarah. Gary's got all the time in the world to listen, so you take your time."

Rachel was taking the piss now, she left the room laughing to herself.

CHAPTER FIVE

Mikey sat in the classroom with six other inmates, there were loud noises, rustling. The lads were fucking about throwing paper at each other and slapping each other around the side of the head. It was just like the old days in school and Mikey was the ringleader as per usual. He sat flicking small pieces of paper from an elastic band at the other members of the class. Each of them were sat at a desk and the teacher stood at the front of the room talking away to herself, oblivious to what was going on behind her. Education was big on the agenda in any jail and each prisoner was offered it when they landed in the big house. This was a chance for offenders to get their lives back on track and to try and make something of themselves. A second chance at putting the record straight and living a crime free life. This was a big ask – some of the inmates were past any kind of education and their minds were elsewhere. Who wanted to sit in studying all night long when they could be out on the street earning a few bob? That said, there were always a few prisoners who reformed and got their life back on track but they tended to be a lot older than this crew and at the end of very long sentences.

The only time most of the prisoners had done a day's work in their life was when they were in the big house. Anything to get them out of their cell really. To work in any jail was a privilege and something every inmate didn't take lightly. It was a chance to meet people, an opportunity to pass contraband around the jail, to stick a blade in someone if needed. Mikey planned to get a job inside the jail once he'd settled but as yet there were none available. Perhaps a shift in the kitchen or as a wing cleaner, anything to get him out of his pad for a few hours. He needed all the money he could get his hands on to get his empire up and running.

Brendan Mellor sat behind Mikey in the classroom and he'd lost a lot of weight already. His cheeks looked empty and his hair seemed to be thinning. The poor fucker was stressed out and his mind wasn't with it. He'd not slept properly either, just a few hours here and a few hours there was all the shut-eye he was getting. Potter was in the class too and the work he'd been given to do was child's play to him. He never once told the teacher how intelligent he was and he just let her carry on thinking he was as thick as pig shit like the rest of the students sat there. In his defence he could have probably taken the class. He was well educated and before he got nicked he had an opportunity of working at one of the top banks in the area. The other lads were lively and none of them were ready to learn. This was just another ploy to get them out of their cells for a few hours a day.

Mikey looked at the words in the book in front of him, his eyes squinting together tightly. His mouth moved but not a single sound come out. The teacher was by his side and she pulled up a chair next to him. She could see he was struggling. "Right, just read this paragraph for me and let me assess just how much help you need. It's nothing to be ashamed of, lots of people can't read properly." Mikey's ears pinned back and he hated that she'd put him on the spot. It was just like being back in school again, people making fun of him, calling him a thicko. The words started to roll from his tongue. He was doing well and he had the attention of the class. Suddenly, he paused. It just happened to him, his concentration went and his mind went completely blank. The words didn't make sense anymore. They were all jumbled up inside his head. There was an eerie silence and all that could be heard was his struggled breathing. Sniggering and whispering could be heard behind him. An inmate from the back of the class let his voice be heard as he chuckled loudly.

"Come on, we've not got all day. Derr…"

Mikey clenched his fist tightly and twisted his head back slowly. He shot a look at the prisoner and nodded his head. He swallowed hard and his nostrils flared. This wasn't good, it was about to kick off. Mikey's chest was firm and the vein in the side of his neck was pumping with rage. "Are you talking to me you clown?"

The teacher was aware Mikey was embarrassed and she tried to diffuse the situation. "Boys, boys. Come on, Mikey you were doing so well. Just carry on reading, you only have a bit left to read. Just concentrate." He was in a zone now and nobody would ever take the piss out of him and get away with it. In seconds the desk was launched and he threw the chairs out of his way as he sprinted for the lad at the back of the class. This kid was quick and he ragged him from his seat in seconds; head–butts, blows to the face and stomach quickly followed. It was over in seconds. A knockout blow put the inmate straight on his arse. He was out for the count and didn't have a clue where he was. He fell to the floor like a sack of spuds. Mikey stood over him and spat in his face. "Who's the thicko now? You fucking prick!"

Alarms rang throughout the jail; sirens, red lights flashing on the wall. The jail was on red alert. The screws were there in minutes. Five of them rushed into the room and twisted Mikey up. The teacher stood with her back to the wall, fanning her hand across her bright red cheeks. This was going to be messy, she hated any act of violence. Her husband had warned her about taking a job like this and although she hated to admit it, he was right. Every day she faced another challenge working with the dregs of society and more often than not she was always a witness to some kind of fighting or bullying. This woman thought she could change the world when she first started her job here but as time passed she realised that the world was such a dangerous place and all her good intentions went out of the window.

Mikey jumped onto a table and screamed at the top of his lungs. "Come on then you cunts. I'll bang you all out. Come on! Do you think I'm arsed. Let's see what you've got!" The security officers ran at him with force. They were all trained in this department and worked like a pack of wolves in bringing the criminal to his knees.

Brendan stood quivering. He covered his eyes with his hand. "Stop it, stop it," he mumbled under his breath. The other inmates jeered as they watched the action from the other side of the classroom. No one was getting involved. This was Mikey's beef and they all left him to deal with it. Punches were thrown, tables knocked over, this was a war zone. It took a while before the prisoner was restrained. He was having a good go. The screws had his head pushed to the ground. His mouth scraping along the floor, his arms twisted behind his back. Mikey was fighting a losing battle and even though he knew the game was up, he was still trying to shout the odds out as they lifted his body from the floor. Brendan chewed rapidly on his thumb and even though he was one of this guy's best friends on the out, he knew better than to get involved in this fight. He was weak and couldn't take the chance of getting into any further trouble. He was a shit-bag, a yellow-belly, a sell-out.

The rest of the inmates were hurried back to their cells. Education was over for today and the rest of the offenders would pay a price for Mikey's behaviour. The injured prisoner was helped to his feet and he was grey, he was still shell-shocked and unaware of his surroundings. Not so big with his mouth now, was he? That would teach him to fuck about with the big boys. The medical team led him out of the room. He was moaning and groaning and unsteady on his feet. He'd learned a big lesson today, one he would never forget: Never fuck with Mikey Milne.

Brendan stomped over to the teacher and stood quivering near her side. "Where have they taken him? They were a bit harsh with him, did you see the way they treated him. Are they allowed to use that much force on a prisoner?"

Mrs Edwards folded her arms tightly in front of her chest and raised her eyebrows. She was sick to the back teeth of the behaviour in her classes and stood her ground. "He should have respected the other people who wanted to learn. He acted like an animal. That poor lad is in a bad way. He was cut, his nose was pouring with blood. Nobody deserves that, no matter what they have done. I feel sick to the pit of my stomach. I need to go home for the rest of the day. I just can't take much more of this. I'd rather sit at home knitting than be in a room with this bunch of animals a second longer."

Brendan coughed to clear his throat. The teacher was old and her values in life were different than his. She wasn't right to work in a place like this, she was more like a private tutor. "It was just a one-on-one, Miss. It happens every day on the outside. If someone chats shit, you just one-bomb them and that's the end of it."

Mrs Edwards placed a single hand on her hip and took pride in putting this inmate in his place. "We're not on the outside though are we? And that behaviour is not accepted in life in general. What right does another human being have to strike another one just like that, for nothing? He's a menace and deserves everything that's coming to him." Brendan was bright red and knew he was fighting a losing battle with this woman. She had no idea of real life, how things were sorted out when two people had a gripe with each other. It was street law, it always had been. "Brendan, can you leave now and go back to your wing. As you can see I'm quite shook up with the whole experience. They don't pay me enough to go through this every day. I just want to be left alone."

The screw came into the room and clocked that the teacher was having a hard time. He whistled over at Brendan. "Oi, ginger balls, time to leave. Get back to your wing before you end up down the block too."

Brendan clenched his fist into tiny balls at the side of his legs. He walked a few steps forward and met the eyes of the security guard. Within seconds he'd gone from a shaking wreck to a young man who was willing to voice his opinion. What was the worst that could happen anyway? "You all took liberties with Mikey. How many of you did it take to bring him down, piss take if you ask me?"

The screw jumped down the back of his throat and

went nose to nose with him. "Nobody is asking you though are they? Do yourself a favour, ginger nut, and walk on. Keep back-chatting to me and you'll end up like your pal."

Brendan marched out of the classroom and Mrs Edwards was stood at the door watching him walk down the corridor. "These lads have no respect, none whatsoever. This job used to be enjoyable but how can you teach people basic literacy skills when they act like this?" The old prisoner officer knew exactly what she meant. He'd been in the job for over twenty years and he was nearing retirement age. When he'd first started out as prison officer, the inmates had respect for the rules in the jail, but not now, not any more. The young offenders were hardcore and would do anything to save face, even kill.

Mikey sat on the bed. This room was basic. The block was where inmates who couldn't adhere to the rules spent their time. No luxuries, no PlayStation, basic canteen and pure bang-up. His heart was banging like a beating drum in his ears and he was still raging inside. He knew how the jail worked and plonked down on his bed with his arms looped behind his head. He would be left alone now for hours. "Thinking time" the screws called it, time for him to calm down and realise what he was there for. He knew the ropes here and if these cunts thought he was licking arse just because he was down the block, they had another thing coming. The guy got slammed, nobody made fun of him about his reading skills, fucking nobody. Mikey jerked his head up slightly and spat on the door facing him. He watched the salvia drip down the door eagerly. They would never break him, never make him a soft arse who was scared of prison life.

Mark and Smithy stood on B-wing doing their rounds. There was noise on the wing but it was normal for this time of the night. Inmates were shouting out of their windows to each other, prisoners booting at their doors, abuse being shouted from one cell to another. It was the same shit, just a different night. Mark sat down in his office and his eyes focused on the computer screen. The new inmates had landed on his wing now and he was reading up on them. He liked to know what he was working with, get inside their heads. Each inmate had a personal officer and he'd been given Mikey and Potter to look after. Mark sniggered over at Smithy as he read over Mikey's personal file. "Have you read the script on this one? I've got my work cut out, I can tell you. This is that cocky cunt we met in reception. I knew he was trouble, fucking knew it from the moment I set eyes on him."

Smithy walked over and placed a hand on his shoulder as he started to read the inmate's previous criminal record. He sniggered and blew a laboured breath. "Good luck with that one, lad. Look at all the violence he's got on his track record, the lad's a nutter. Why have they sent him here? He should have been starred up and sent to the hairy arse jails. The men would have sorted him out." Smithy was talking about Strangeways in Manchester. Whenever they got a lad who was too much for them to handle, they always shipped them there. It was a man's prison and nothing like this place. Everybody knew about Strangeways and each inmate shivered at the thought of going there. There were a few older inmates at Lancaster Farms but they were mostly finishing off long sentences. This was a Cat C jail, it was more relaxed than other jails around the country.

Mark nodded and turned to face Smithy. "Why the hell do they give me all the fucked up ones? For once, I'd love an inmate who wanted to change, you know, the kind of lad who had actually made just one daft mistake."

Smithy agreed, he knew it was a big ask. Most of these lads were back and forth from the jail, they never learned. "Mikey's down the block already. He kicked off in education and put some prisoner on his arse. Mrs Edwards' report said it was a lethal blow too. A knockout one. The kid's on the hospital wing in a bad way."

Mark kept his eyes on the screen and sighed. "I'll go down to the block later and have a chat with him. Not like it's going to make much difference but I'll have to show willing won't I?"

Smithy sat at his desk and flicked through his emails too. He raised his head and studied Mark for a lot longer than he needed to. He was quiet, something was troubling him. "So, how's things with the missus? Has she stopped moaning yet?"

Mark went bright red. He hated talking about his home life and very rarely told anyone about his problems. Smithy was his pal though and they'd been friends for a long time. He had to get it off his chest, it was dong his head in now. He sat back in his chair and yawned. "It's shite, Smithy. On my life, all that woman does is moan, moan, moan. Twenty-four hours a fucking day she's at it! I can't be arsed with her anymore. Putting a ring on her finger was the worst thing I've ever done in my life. From the moment she got out of bed this morning, she's been on at me. I swear, it's non-stop. I was going to crack her one. On my life, she just presses my buttons. I'll be leaving her soon, then she'll see."

Smithy stretched his arm out and patted his shoulder. He was a married man himself and could identify with his pal. "Surely, she's not that bad, what's she whining over now anyway? Did you forget to put the bins out again?"

Mark's head sank and a wave of sadness came over him. He took a few seconds to answer. "No, I wish it was just that. I've fucked up with the mortgage payments again. You know what I'm like, I always borrow a few quid from it and put it back before she knows it's missing. But, I'm up shit-street now. I went in the bookies didn't I and blew the fucking lot."

Smithy was shocked. He knew his pal liked a bit of a gamble every now and then but he didn't realise how far he'd got into it. Smithy had a good heart and hated to see anyone with money problems. "I can sort you out until you get on your feet, Mark. Don't fuck about with your home payments mate. Imagine if you lost it, what then ay?"

Mark knew he was right and for the last few nights he'd been laid in bed asking himself the same questions. He'd be homeless and living on the street for sure. There was no way his mother would have him back home, no way in this world. And then there was his marriage; that would surely be over, although maybe that wasn't such a bad thing - every cloud had a silver lining. Deep down though, it would always be just one more bet, one last scratch card, one more spin of the wheel. This man would never learn. He was addicted to gambling, there were no two ways about it. Mark bit hard on his bottom lip and his pride was hurt. He hated admitting he was on his arse to anyone. He had no other option than to accept his mate's offer. He was fucked no matter which way he looked at it.

Mark chewed on his bottom lip and kept his eyes to the table. "If you could help me out Smithy, I'd be grateful. I've got no one else to ask, otherwise I would. I'll have it back to you by the end of next month. I'm keeping away from the bookies from now on. It's a fool's game."

Mark was lying of course. He even believed his own story. His mother had already told him that he wasn't getting another penny out of her, he'd fleeced her already, took her for every penny she had left. This was something he wasn't proud of. Once his father Jack died there was quite a bit of money left to Sheila. She'd never been used to money and it scared her. Old people were like that and if she had her way, she would have stuffed it under her mattress. There was no way Sheila was going to spend any of her fortune. The cash was just sitting there in the bank going to waste. She could have gone on holiday, spent time doing things she'd dreamt about but with her husband six foot under, all she ever spoke about was being in the grave next to him. Sheila had basically given up once Jack was gone and every day she just sat in her chair wishing her life away.

Mark had tried to help, he come up with the idea of finding an investment for her and double her money, he said. Sheila took him at face value and let him have over ten thousand pounds to put into something for her. What a daft sod she was! What planet was she on thinking this half-wit could ever manage money! Mark did look into making an investment for her at first and he even went to see her bank manager with her but that was just a cover for his gambling habit. It was all he could think of; the roulette wheel, the gee-gees and the poker table. He already owed thousands to the local loan sharks and to pay them off seemed his only option. It was a no-win situation. The people he owed money to had told him to pay up or his balls were getting cut off, simple as. And they meant it, too – there was no fucking about with these people. Mark had no other option so he used his mother's money to pay off his debts. After all, he treasured his balls. But now he was short and had to find Sheila's cash to invest and there was only one way he could get it back for her. For weeks he sat studying the horses and not once did he ever win a carrot, the plonker. The daft bastard blew every single penny of it, there was hardly anything left bar the odd tenner. He couldn't pay his old queen back. Sheila could read her son like a book and when the time was right she confronted him about the money he was supposed to have invested for her. She smelt a rat. Mark denied it at first but after hours of tears and arguing he finally admitted to her that he'd lost it all. He'd blown it, every single penny. Sheila collapsed when he told her the truth and she was rushed into hospital with an angina attack. He never told anybody about the money he'd had off his mother, not even his siblings. If they had known he would have been banished from the family circle, never to return. This was his secret and he'd pleaded with his mother never to tell anyone. Even to this day he pledged he would pay her back, but as yet he hadn't managed to give her back a penny of what he'd wasted and now he was heading into deep shit once again.

★

Mark peeped through the glass hatch and clocked Mikey lying on his bed trying to get some shut eye. He was still awake because he was flinching. If he could have his way he would have kicked ten tons of shit out of this smart-arse. He was in the mood to smash someone's head in right now and if this prick gave him any shit he couldn't promise that he would hold his temper. Mark had had a shit day and nothing was going right for him. It was just going from bad to worse. Slipping his key into the lock he opened the door and stood at the doorway with his notes stashed under his arm. There was no way he was going inside yet, he stood rustling his paperwork.

Mikey lifted his head from the pillow and clocked the screw stood there. Nodding his head slowly he rolled onto his side and scratched at his nuts. "What's up boss?"

Mark licked his dry, cracked lips and took a deep breath. This was one cocky cunt, who thought he was untouchable. "I'm your personal officer and I've come down here to have a chat with you. Procedure it is, nothing more."

Mikey rolled onto his back and yawned. He was at it again, he was doing himself no favours. "And, what, you think you've got the answer to all my problems do you? Do yourself a favour and fuck off and leave me alone. I've had all this head-fuck stuff before and it doesn't work?"

Mark hated this inmate with a passion. He had to hold it together though, be professional. His knuckles went white as he gripped his pen tightly and his chest rose at speed. Mark kicked his shiny boot against the bottom of the door slowly. There was silence. Mikey was on one and he was putting the world to rights. In his eyes he was never in the wrong and he was always right. "I mean, do you think I'm some kind of muppet who's going to let some twat talk to me like that. The prick got what was coming to him and when I see the wanker again, I'm going to waste him properly. He got off lightly if you ask me. I could have done a lot worse."

Mark scratched the top of his head and knew this inmate was going to take some hard graft if he was ever to get on board. Mark changed the subject and tried to calm him down. He'd already been on a warning about his work and didn't need his collar felt again. "I need a quick meeting with you. Just a few basic details to start with, just stuff so I can get to know you better."

Mikey chuckled, he was out to cause trouble. You could see it in his eyes. He lay with his hands shoved down the front of his pants. "Listen, fuck off out of my face and go and see some other cunt who will listen to you. Stop trying to be a do-gooder."

Mark gripped the paperwork tightly in his hand. He twisted his head behind him and checked nobody was listening and edged closer in the cell. He was on a short fuse and any second now he was going to blow. His expression changed and his teeth gritted tightly together. "Oi, fucking mouth almighty, cut the bullshit. Just let's tick the boxes and I'll leave you alone. Do you think I give a flying fuck if you change or not? You're just another number to me. Just another fucking head case who thinks they can beat the system." They locked horns and neither of them were budging.

Mikey sneered over at him. "Nar, sack it. I'm in no mood today. Close the door and fuck off out I'm getting my head down."

Mark sprinted over to the bed and gripped Mikey by his throat, he was choking him. Nose to nose they were. "I said, get fucking ready before I lose my rag with you."

Mikey was shaken. Never in his life had he met a screw

with balls like this. Usually they only give it the big one when they were team-handed but never when they were alone. This was a whole new ball game. Mikey had met his match. Mark backed off and stood at the door again. He was game and if this inmate gave him one bit of shit he couldn't be held responsible for his actions. Mikey flicked his body up from the bed and admitted defeat. He would have to watch this one, he was dangerous and could stitch him up given the chance. That's how it worked behind these walls, the officers could plant stuff on inmates and have them charged with it within a blink of an eye, shady bastards they were when their cages were rattled. Mikey bounced towards him. "Yeah, come on then, but if you start chatting shit trying to fill my head with goals and dreams I'm coming straight back here."

Mark watched the inmate walk past him and nodded his head slowly. He was confident now and knew he had the upper hand. Mark sat down at the table and joined the inmate. Usually, this kind of meeting took over an hour but he was sure it wouldn't last longer than thirty minutes. It was just a paper exercise in his eyes and knew he was pissing in the wind if he thought this lad would cooperate with him. Mikey rested his head in his hands and looked around the room, clicking his tongue against his bottom lip. Everywhere in the jail was more or less the same colour; pale yellow, supposedly a calming neutral shade. Mark opened his paperwork and picked up his blue biro. Twisting it around in his fingers he looked Mikey straight in the eyes. "So, tell me about yourself. How have you ended up in the slammer?"

Mikey gripped his chin in his hands and stroked a single finger slowly over his stubble. Why did everyone always think they could get inside his head and work him out? He was wise to them now, wary of what they were after. "I just have, haven't I? There's no real reason. I just got nicked. Wrong time, wrong place, you know the crack."

Mark knew his job was to get this criminal to open up. He'd had hours of training and course after course to make sure he got the results he needed. He reminded himself of the rules and sat back in his seat in a relaxed manner. "Do you think this is your life now? I mean, in and out of jail?"

"I'm not arsed to tell you the truth. Life is life and I have to do what's needed to get by. Stuff costs money doesn't it?"

Mark scribbled down on his notepad and continued. "You can change, there are people here to help you if you want it?"

Mikey had heard the same script all his life. His probation officer, school teachers, career officers, they had all tried to change him before. They could take a running jump if they thought he would ever lead a normal boring life. He was who he was and he was happy with that. Mikey was agitated and his patience was running thin. "I don't know what's written down on that paper there, pal. I'm just another number to you lot, remember that. I don't want any sympathy but don't judge me until you have walked a day in my shoes. Since I've been able to talk I've had to more or less fend for myself, nobody was there for me. I had to learn the hard way. Do you know how it feels to not know where your next meal is coming from?" Mikey was opening up, what was up with him? Mark was sorry he'd opened his mouth but the lad was right. How could he judge him when he knew nothing about his personal background? Mikey sniffed hard and for a split second his eyes clouded over but he switched in seconds and his guard was back up again. He wanted out of there. "This is a waste of time. Just write on my notes I said 'get to fuck'. I'm sure they won't be arsed."

Mark carried on writing, his head was down and every now and then he lifted his head up and shot a look at the convict. Mikey rocked back in his seat and stretched his arms above his head. The door opened and Smithy stuck his head inside and whistled over to Mark. "Are you nearly ready pal? I could do with your help on the wing. We need to spin two pads over. I've got a bit of information that there's a few mobile phones in there."

Mikey was alert, this was crucial information that he shouldn't have heard. Mark slammed the file shut and nodded his head. "Give me ten minutes and I'll be there with you. I'm nearly done here anyway."

Smithy closed the door behind him and Mikey sat forward in his seat. Here it was, time to test the water. "Someone's going to be gutted. A phone is like gold in here. Poor fuckers."

Mark knew the score with parcels being dropped in the jail and gave a cunning smirk as he rubbed his hands together. "Well, that's the way the cookie crumbles isn't it. You live by the sword, you die by it."

Mikey quickly twisted his head about and made sure the coast was clear, it was now or never. "There is good money to be made if you fancy earning a bit of extra cash. A mobile phone can sell in here for about seven ton. But if it's an I-phone you're talking more. Do you fancy it or what? Call it a business venture…" Mikey chuckled and watched him from the corner of his eyes. Mark swallowed hard and small beads of sweat were forming on his brow.

He knew more than anyone how much money could be earned if he was a bent screw, but did he trust Mikey? Mark stood up from the table and didn't answer him. There was no way he was letting himself get pulled in to this vicious circle, he had enough troubles of his own.

CHAPTER SIX

Rachel had tossed and turned in her bed all night long, she was restless, agitated. Police sirens could be heard outside, youths arguing and shouting at each other. She booted the blankets from her body and punched her clenched fist into her pillow trying to get comfortable. Something was lying heavily on her mind. Mikey's mother had been in bed smoking like a trooper for the last few hours. Nothing was making sense anymore, her head was mashed. Even the sleeping tablets she'd popped weren't taking effect. Her mind was in overdrive. The word was out now that her son was in prison and she knew sooner or later Davo and his boys would put two and two together and be booming her front door in. Mikey was a right nobhead fucking with these kind of people, he should have stuck to what he knew. But he just couldn't help himself, there was too much money there for him to walk away from. He'd watched Davo and his boys stash the cash after a big job and knew the moment they turned their backs he would have it away. Why should them lot have all the fun? He wanted a taste of the good life too. But, the idiot hadn't covered his tracks properly, he hadn't made sure there would be no comebacks. What a nerd he was! Martina Scott had seen him and she had the biggest mouth in the world. A right grassing bitch, she was - a proper gossip. It would only be a matter of time before she spilled the beans and put his name in the frame. She couldn't hold her own piss, she was a Judas.

Davo, real name Danny Davidson, was the main man in the area. An up and coming head the ball, everyone said. He was into everything and armed robberies were his forte. He was fucked in the head for sure and nobody messed with him unless they wanted trouble. Danny was older than Mikey and he never gave him the time of day. He wasn't in his league. Mikey was just a small time criminal in his eyes and nothing to worry about but he'd underestimated him. You see, Mikey was a sneak thief; crafty, cunning and he could smell a good thing a mile off. He wasn't scared of the main man and if push came to shove he would stand his ground. Davo would have leathered him if the truth was known but in Mikey's head he thought he was ten men and didn't realise his opponent would wipe him from the face of the earth if he needed to. Anyway, there was no point in crying over spilt milk. The deed was done and there was no going back. Mikey was that full of himself that he really thought that Davo and his boys had forgotten about the money. He never had an inclination that he was already a marked man. Of course, when the money first went missing he was questioned about it by the gang but so was every grafter in the area. They had fuck all on him and he knew it. As long as Martina kept it on the low they would never find out. There was no honour among thieves and each of them would lie to their back teeth if they needed to. All was fair in love and war and there was fuck all Davo could do about it. The money was gone and he hoped they would just take it on the chin.

Rachel glanced out of the bedroom window and folded her pillow under her head. Gary was snoring at the side of her, he was dead to the world. She hated his snoring and they'd had many an argument over it in the past. He made deep grunting noises and occasionally choking sounds. It did her head in every night. Usually, when she'd had enough of it, she'd just go and sleep on the sofa or kick him out of bed. Gary was bugging her lately, even when he was eating she wanted to smash his face in. He ate like an animal and commented on every mouthful of food he scranned. "Oh, this is mint Rach, lovely grub," she hated it. Rachel twisted her head slowly and waved her hand in front of Gary's face, double-checking he was still asleep. He was dead to the world. Slowly, she slid her thin body out of bed. She tiptoed out of the bedroom over creaking floorboards. The house seemed eerie, every noise seemed a lot louder than usual. Rubbing at her arms she made her way down the stairs. This house was freezing cold and no matter how high she turned the thermostat up, she could never get warm, she was a right frozen arse. Gary had always said she was anaemic or something because even when it was red hot in the summer she always complained she was cold. Flicking the main light on in the front room, her eyes shot about making sure everything was still in place. Burglaries were on the rise in the area and she'd been a victim of it before. The bastards took everything she had at the time, left her with fuck all. Television, stereos and anything that could be sold on the streets - jealous fuckers they were, scum of the earth. Rachel was a grafter herself but never in her life had she stolen from one of her own. She classed herself as working class and never pissed on her own doorstep. She robbed from the high street stores that would never miss the dint she put in their profits. Security was high on Rachel's list of priorities now and there were big steel bolts on the doors. Once bitten, twice shy. Rachel dragged the sofa across the room slowly. It was heavy and her expression changed, her neck stretched and her eyes widened as she used all her strength to move the piece of furniture. Stepping to the corner of the living room she paused and listened carefully. It was nothing, just the heating system, she was safe to continue. She tugged at the edge of the carpet, gripping it tightly. There was too much noise, she had to be quiet. Lifting the floorboards up, she bent down and tunnelled her hand down deep under the floor. She was concentrating as her hands moved about slowly. Eyes wide open.

Here it was; the hideout – the stash. Ever since the money had been hidden here she'd counted it nearly every night just to make sure none of it had gone missing. This was her son's money and if anyone tried taking it, she would stick a knife deep in their chest. She would die for her own flesh and blood, she'd happily do years in prison. Gary could never be trusted. She loved the guy but where money was concerned, she trusted nobody. The code of silence was something she adhered to and even when under pressure she would hold her own and never spill the beans. All criminals pissed in the same pot in her eyes and there was no loyalty where money was concerned. Not even with Gary. Rachel had noticed bits of things going missing from her personal belongings over the last few months; nothing major, just the odd tenner here and there. She had her beady eye on Gary, waiting to catch the fucker in the act. She never knew for sure but she had her suspicions that he was the tealeaf in her home. Every now and then she would set traps for him, but up to now she'd never caught him bang to rights. He was sneaky.

Rachel sat on the floor with her legs crossed counting the money, her fingers quickly flicked each note from

the pile. She froze as she heard a noise from outside the
room. With haste she dragged the sofa back to its original
place and hurried into the hallway to make sure nobody
was there. Her eyes scanned the area. Something wasn't
right, she took a few steps into the lobby and she could
have sworn she'd seen Gary running back up the stairs.
Standing on the bottom stair she held her ear to listen
for any movement. Not a sound, complete silence. Her
mind must have been playing tricks on her again. Rachel
backed off slowly and kept looking over her shoulder as
she headed back into the living room. She was spooked for
sure. Sitting down on the sofa, she sparked a cigarette up
with shaking hands. A fag always calmed her down when
her head wasn't with it. Rachel sucked hard on her cig and
blew a large puff of grey smoke out in front of her. The
nicotine was calming her down and the palpitations inside
her chest seemed to be receding.

Sat alone with her thoughts, Rachel started to go over
her life and ended up feeling sorry for herself again. Many
a night she would just sit there and torment herself about
the way things had panned out. The photo album always
came out at this time of the night and she'd always get upset
as she reminisced about days gone by. Her fingers stroked
a snap of her son when he was only a small boy. Mikey
looked so angelic and pure back then – he was unaware of
what lay in his future. Was she really to blame for the way
her son had turned out? Or was it just circumstances that
had led him down the wrong path in life? She always asked
herself the same question, night after night. She tormented
herself with it. Holding the snap in her hand she kissed
it and mouthed the word "sorry" as a single, fat, salty tear
rolled down her cheek.

Rachel had a good upbringing herself and she'd never really wanted for anything in life. Her family home was clean and both her parents worked all the hours God sent to make sure they had a happy home and food on the table. So how the hell had it gone wrong? Mikey's father, Dennis, had a lot to do with her downfall, she always blamed him, he was a no good bastard, scumbag and nobody knew the half of it. But, she could never tell Mikey the truth about him, it would break his heart. In her son's head his father was his hero and he could do no wrong. Many a time she had wanted to expose him for the dirty horrible cunt he really was but even in her drunken state she kept schtum to protect Mikey from any further hurt.

Holding the photograph of Dennis in her hand she spat at it and threw it back down in the album as if it contained some lethal disease. She'd always planned to burn her ex's photographs but Mikey would never let her. Dennis was his father after all and these photographs were the only real memory of the dad he loved and missed. He could rot in hell for all she cared, she'd dance on his grave. Dennis was the only reason she ever got involved with crime in the first place. Mikey's dad had been a good-looking man and in his youth he had all the girls around him like flies round shit. 'A fanny magnet', he liked to call himself and he was right, he could have had the pick of any female he wanted in the area. He had charisma, a great sense of humour and when he was in the room everybody fought to be in his company. Rachel was seventeen when she first bumped into Dennis. It was on a night out with her friends and she was very drunk – steaming to be precise – when she first set eyes on him. All her mates fancied him but he was too full of himself for her liking, he thought he was

God's gift. Rachel hated him with a passion to start with but after a few nights in his company at the local pub she began to see what the big attraction was with him. Dennis was a charmer and he could make her laugh at the drop of a hat. There were silly cheesy jokes he told her that weren't even that funny but still he made her chuckle. He never let Rachel buy a drink. No, he was always getting her beer in and making her feel special. He was a real gentleman, well, to start with anyway. Dennis ticked all her boxes and slowly but surely she began to fall for him, smitten she was, besotted.

Rachel was set to have a great career at this time. She was at college studying hairdressing and most of her assignments were A-star. She loved being creative. Her passion to stand out was for everyone to see. She created new hairstyles all the time and she wasn't afraid to think outside the box. All the clients who came there asked for her by name and she was popular among her tutors. Dennis was a bad apple though, a dead leg. He constantly smoked weed and was heavily involved in the crime world. He didn't know what day it was sometimes, he was twisted and couldn't even remember his own name. She didn't find this out until it was too late. He hid it all away from her and never once did he let the cat out of the bag that he was not the man she thought he was. He'd had her right over, pulled the wool right over her eyes. He hid a lot of things well, there were deep, dark, seedy secrets. That's how it all started really, her downfall.

Slowly but surely Dennis got Rachel smoking weed and her life just went downhill from there. Everything she'd ever dreamt about seemed to float away after that. She had no energy and her passion for life seemed to die.

Rachel was a like a plant that was never watered. Dennis soon changed his ways with her after she fell pregnant. The guy kicked off and told her straight that he didn't want any sprogs hanging around. He never came home the night she told him she was with child and from then on she was always hearing whispers about him sleeping with other women. She knew in her heart they were true but she always made up excuses for his infidelity and turned a blind eye. What a fool she was! Rachel started to lose any self-respect she had back then and even though she knew her man was shagging anything with a pulse, she still pretended everything was rosy in the garden.

Rachel's mother Agnes was devastated when she found out her daughter was in the pudding club and advised her that an abortion was the only way to solve her problem. Her daughter had no wedding ring on her finger and to be a single parent back then was frowned upon. "Get rid of the little bastard," her mother hissed. "Are you tapped in the head? He's a waste of space, he'll never do right by you, trust me I know his sort a mile off." Rachel would remember those words forever. Even though she hated admitting it, her mother was right. She always hit the nail right on the head especially with matters of the heart. Agnes always cared what people said about her and she knew without any shadow of doubt her daughter would be the centre of any gossip for months to come. Everyone had an opinion in the area and they were never afraid to voice it either. She could see it now, all the fish-wives gathered around outside the corner shop slagging her girl off. Rachel was never one to take advice though and she stood her ground and kept the baby. It was a big risk at the time but she thought she'd made the right choice. She was in love and just hoped that her and Dennis were going through a bad patch. What a bollock she'd dropped, her head was away with the fairies.

Motherhood was so much hard work and nothing like she expected. Rachel just presumed that having a baby would be a walk in the park and that it wouldn't really affect her life, how wrong could she have been? Sleepless nights, shitty nappies, constant crying – it was all taking its toll on her. She wasn't ready for anything like this. Agnes had never been the same with her daughter since that day. She told her straight that she'd ruined her life and she was washing her hands of her. Rachel had brought shame on her family name in her eyes and her mother could never forgive her for it. My God she tried, but it was there for everyone to see, she was gutted, heartbroken and completely devastated. So, there she was, aged eighteen living in a shitty one bedroom flat with a boyfriend who didn't love her anymore. The man she once thought was her Prince Charming soon turned into a horrible, violent woman beater too. At first it was just a slap, but as time went on the beatings began to got worse. Rachel never stood a chance. Dennis was a big fella and he was strong, too. He was an evil, sick, twisted bastard and once he'd had a drink the beatings went on for hours. He physically and mentally tortured her all night long. When Mikey was just one year old her abuser picked her body up over his head and flung her against the living room wall. Two broken ribs she had and other injuries as well – she was lucky to be alive. But, she never told a soul, she protected him and pretended it had never happened. How could she tell anyone what was happening, she would have been classed as a failure! People would have judged her and she would have had to admit they were right all along. Fuck happy ever afters, they didn't exist. Love was for fools.

The years went by and Rachel started shoplifting to try and make ends meet. There was no money coming into her household and her benefits were gone more or less on the same day she got them. After paying a few bills she was almost skint again. It was a vicious circle. The shoplifting started with nappies at first and a few tins of soup. She was desperate and had no other way of surviving. There was no way she wasn't feeding her son. She would have sold her body if she had to, sucked dirty old men off. There was nothing she wouldn't do for her boy to make sure he was fed and watered but, as time went on, she realised she was getting pretty good at this shoplifting lark and that's when her career took off. She took things to a whole new level. Money was power and slowly but surely Rachel began to stand up to Mikey's dad once she found her feet. This woman also found the courage inside her – she'd just got lost in herself, he'd sucked all the self-belief out of her, every last drop. Rachel vowed he wouldn't do that anymore!

The money she earned gave her the confidence she needed and she refused to be his doormat a moment longer. At last, she could see the wood through the trees. Their home was a war zone. Rachel and Dennis would fight for hours and each of them would walk away with injuries, bad gashes all over their bodies, deep purple bruises. She was just as bad as him now, she was like a preying lioness every time they fought. She'd sink her long talons into his eyes and she told him given the chance she would blind him for life, she hated him with a passion. The pair of them were lethal together; a car crash waiting to happen. Rachel was lucky to still be alive, she'd had a few near misses. Mikey loved his dad though, and in all fairness, it was safe to say Dennis loved his son back. Although he hated the thought of being a father to start with, he loved his son now he was here. They'd spend hours together playing games and talking about how when Mikey grew up he would be the best footballer in the whole wide world and he would make his father proud and play for Manchester United one day. Dennis loved football and on more than one occasion he'd taken his son to a few games. He never paid for tickets though, they both jibbed in and jumped the turnstile. Money was tight and lots of the local lads did it to watch their favourite team play. Dennis loved seeing Mikey happy and vowed that no matter what, he would never leave him. He was the apple of his eye and when he was spending time with him he was like a completely different person. He was gentle, kind and caring; nothing like he was with Rachel. How can somebody just change like that?

Mikey cried his eyes out for months after his father left him and in his heart he blamed his mother and her foul mouth for driving him away. He'd told her that, too. Any arguments they had after that, he would always throw it into her face about why his dad left. He never forgave her. "You made him leave, I hate you, I hate you," he'd scream after her. Rachel was on a road to disaster. She had to prove to the world that she could survive on her own. Her mother tried to offer her some help to start with but she told her straight she could shove her money right up the crack of her arse, she didn't need it! How dare she take an interest in her life now when she turned her back on her when she needed her most? She could fuck right off! Rachel needed nobody, she could fend for herself. Her shoplifting career was at another level now and she was travelling to different towns earning a good crust. Top notch swagger she was bagging too, not the cheap stuff. Leather coats, Armani jeans, perfumes – she was raking it in. The cash was flowing and she never wanted for anything, she was loaded in her eyes. Yet everything in life comes at a price and she let her son down big time. Mikey was shoved from pillar to post nearly every day and it was very rare he'd see his mother. She was out early in the morning and never came back until late at night. Rachel always seemed to attract the wrong kind of men too.

For a few years she was shagging anything with a pulse, there were some right mingers as well. Everyone was calling her a slapper and they were right. Her knickers were up and down like a yo-yo. This woman loved bad boys and John Pollock was just that. From the moment she set eyes on him she said he was her true love. Was she having a laugh or what? The guy was just as bad as Dennis, if not worse. She should have done her homework on him, checked him out. Rachel was fully aware that he'd got a few kids too; at least four, to three different women from all over Manchester, but she didn't bat an eyelid. He was hers now and there was no way she was ever going to lose him. He was just what she needed at that time in her life; a protector, a man who had made a name for himself. Rachel treated John like he was a king, she nicked all his clobber and dressed him up in the latest designer clothing. She bought his love. If she was being honest, she was scared to death he would ever leave her. Loneliness was a horrible feeling and she never wanted to feel it again in her life. This was the first time in ages that Rachel had really ever been happy. She was devoted to John and she'd grown up a lot in her mind set. She cooked and cleaned her house and Mikey was doing so well now that he had a role model in his life. Everyone seemed happy. Her son was doing well at school and the family home was something Rachel was proud of. Her mother could kiss her arse, she knew fuck all about being happy.

So, what happened? Rachel always felt teary when she thought back to how things had ended up. And it was a sad tale, one she could have avoided. John Pollock was a grafter and if the job would have come off, they would have been set up for years. If only life was that simple though, nothing ever worked out for her, it was like she was cursed. She'd begged him not to go on the job, pleaded with him, telling him if he left, their relationship was over. Did he listen to her? Did he fuck! He thought he was a smart arse. John was arrested for the crime he'd committed and the sentence he was given meant he was going to jail for a very long time. He'd nearly killed a man, left him for dead. He didn't set out to hurt the man, but it was a choice of losing the money or shooting someone. John Pollock made the wrong choice. Rachel's life just went from bad to worse from that day onwards and even though she vowed she would wait for him, it was never really going to happen. Don't get me wrong, she tried to remain faithful to her true love but each night she sat alone and craved the affection of a man holding her again, kissing her, lying beside her in bed. She was lonely.

News travelled and after a few flings here and there word got back to John that she was playing the field. This was bad, she was playing with fire. He wouldn't take this news lying down. The phone calls and the threats started then and he vowed on his mother's life that when he was a free man he was going to make her pay for her betrayal. Prison played with his head and he was not the same person she once loved, he'd lost the plot. The day of his release was looming and even though she was putting a brave face on it, she was shitting herself inside. She'd wronged her man and nobody would ever back her up. At the time it happened she lost a lot of friends because of it. John was liked by all who knew him and to hear he was heartbroken and rotting away in jail turned a lot of friends against her. To them she was a bitch, a dirty, filthy whore who couldn't keep her knickers on. The police were her only protection and all they ever said was that they would warn her when her psychotic ex-partner was due to be let out of jail.

Rachel continued shoplifting to support her family and she'd been imprisoned a few times. Her longest sentence was twelve months and that nearly broke her in two. Night after night she cried in her cell and she even tried taking her own life, she was at an all-time low. That's what turned her to hard drugs, smack in particular. The devil's drug. Just a few toots here and there to help her get through the hard times but before Rachel knew it she was addicted to heroin and came out of the jail with a raging habit.

By now Mikey was in and out of care and she was a lost cause. Her family turned their back on the pair of them and never once did any of them offer to give Mikey a home while his mother was inside. This lad was never the same after being placed in the care system. He was bullied, singled out and Rachel had a gut feeling that he'd been abused. He was just so distant when she spoke to him and something wasn't right in his head, he was always crying. She never mentioned it to him though, she turned a blind eye and couldn't bear to think her son had been fiddled with. Those were the darkest days Rachel had ever had in her life. She nearly died a few times, too. I suppose she might have been better off six foot under, at least that way she could never hurt anyone anymore. Mikey pleaded with her to stop using and this was the only reason she decided to sort herself out. Mikey watched her roasting and he saw things no child should have had to see at such an early age; his mother on her hands and knees begging him to let her die, numerous suicide attempts, pill popping and drinking until she collapsed. This kid had to be so strong, it's a wonder he wasn't in a mental asylum with what he'd been through. Rachel was on medication for her addiction and he made sure she stayed away from the dealers in the area. It was a big ask but he was always threatening the druggies and the drug dealers to stay away from her. He was only a kid at this time and even though he was no real threat to them, they all agreed not to serve her up or supply her with drugs anymore. Mikey was the one putting the bread on the table at this time and he'd done anything and everything to make sure his mother had all she needed to stay off the smack. It was such a crying shame - poor Mikey Milne, no wonder his head was fucked.

Sarah was in the back of the car complaining about Rachel chain-smoking in the front, thick clouds of smoke floated towards her face every few seconds. Sarah sat wafting her hands in front of her and broke out in a coughing fit. She was slightly overreacting. It wasn't that bad! "Do you have to smoke in the car? Can't you just wait until we get there? You're killing me here?" Gary looked at Sarah through the rear view mirror and sniggered. She was a non-smoker and hated that people were so inconsiderate of people who cared about their health.

This was never going to go down well. Rachel growled and clenched her fist together in tight balls at the side of her legs. This girl was starting to piss her off but she had to hold her tongue. She'd only been in her company for a few hours and her patience was wearing thin. She turned towards her and hissed. "For fucks sake, I've opened the window haven't I? You're just overreacting as per usual."

Sarah spluttered as she smashed her hand on her seat. "I'm going to stink of fags when I get to the jail. It's a filthy habit and you should think about giving it up. You're killing yourself you know! In fact, do you know how many people die of lung cancer each year?"

Rachel snarled and if she could have laid hands on her she would have ragged her all over the car. She was in no mood for this today, she was pissing her right off. "Get a grip, Sarah. Mikey is a smoker. I don't hear you giving him a lecture when he's sat smoking next to you puffing his head off, do I?"

Sarah shuffled about in her seat and casually flicked her hair over her shoulder. Who the hell did this woman think she was having a pop at? "I love Mikey though don't I, so it's different. And, if the truth be told he's trying to kick the habit, unlike you."

Gary choked and kept his eyes on the road. It was only a matter of time before Rachel punched her lights out, she was on a short fuse today and ready for trouble. She hated a smart arse and this girl was getting right on her fucking wick. She ignored her and spoke to her boyfriend. "Have you got the parcel, Gary, just double check before it's too late to turn back? Mikey will kick off if we turn up empty-handed." Sarah was half listening and watched with eager eyes as Gary patted his shirt pocket. "It's all sorted love. I've wrapped it all up tightly and he'll have no problems plugging it."

For crying out loud, she was at it again. She was bugging everyone for sure. "What's plugging?" Sarah asked.

Gary chuckled and raised his eyebrows. "It means you shove things up your shitter, love. Come on Sarah, you're not that daft are you? Everyone knows that!"

Rachel couldn't wait to add her two-pennorth into the mix. She held the bottom of her stomach and sniggered. "She knows fuck all, Gary. I can't even believe our Mikey has ended up with such a straight head. How the hell it happened is beyond me!"

Sarah's back was up now, she hated this woman more every day. She was a know-it-all. An interfering bitch who thought the world owed her a favour. She defended herself. "Rachel, keep your snide comments to yourself. It's not big and it's not clever to know all about crime. Just because you've been in prison it doesn't make you a better person than me. In fact, I wouldn't be shouting it from the rooftops, either. I would be ashamed! What a disgrace!"

Rachel spun around and squeezed her body through the small gap between the car seats. It was going off now, she'd had enough. She sank her fingernails deep into Sarah's knee cap and squeezed at it with force. "You've got a big mouth today haven't you? I'd keep it shut if I was you, unless you can back it up. Don't dare judge me until you've walked in my shoes! Do you get me bitch?"

Sarah wriggled about and tried to free herself. "Take your grubby hands off me. Don't you ever think you can hurt me like that! You just wait until I tell Mikey what you've just done to me and we'll soon see how smart you are then. He won't stand for that, no way on this earth."

Gary was in a panic, he knew the signs and he was aware Rachel was ready to steam into her. She was already starting to unclip her seatbelt. This was a nightmare, he was going to crash the car if they carried on. Gary used his left hand and dragged her back to her original position in the passenger seat. She was wrestling about still trying to get to Sarah in the back of the car. "For fuck's sake you two, turn it in. I'm driving here, do you want me to wrap the car up or what?"

Rachel wound her window down further and stuck her head outside the moving vehicle. She sucked in large mouthfuls of air and tried to calm down. Her face was blood red and she was raging inside. She pointed her finger in the wing mirror. "It's that daft bitch Gary. She just knows how to press my buttons. Go on, tell me it's me at fault and not her. Go on, you just say one word and I'm gone from here. You just watch."

Gary had a choice to make and there was no way he was siding with Sarah. He was the mediator now and spoke in a calm voice. "Sarah, you are out of order, love. You can't speak to people like that."

Rachel pulled her shoulders back and nodded. Her man had her back and he'd told the daft cow straight. This was a mess.

Sarah was tearful and as per usual she was blubbering. "I'm sorry but she's not treating me like that. I've had enough of her snide comments and it's about time I put an end to it. She's a bully and I won't stand for it."

Rachel kept her eyes on the road and replied to her in a sarcastic tone. "Sort your bleeding head out, girl. As if I'm a bully!" She raised her eyebrows as she continued. "You mean, I won't stand for any more of your bullshit. Just because mummy and daddy won't say a wrong word to you, it doesn't mean that I won't. It's about time someone put you in your place and told you a few home truths. You're a mard arse nothing less."

Gary blew a laboured breath and banged his hand on the steering wheel. "Can you both hear yourselves here? Just let's all have a breather for a few minutes. We're all stressed out and words have been said out of frustration. Mikey doesn't need to know about this either, he's stressed out enough without worrying about you two bickering all the bleeding time."

Rachel turned her head and growled at him. "Stop treating her with kid gloves, Gary. It's about time she knew that she's stuck up her own arse anyway. I don't care if Mikey loves her or not, she means fuck all to me." Here it was, the only way Rachel knew how to protect herself. Hurtful words; deep, soul-destroying sentences she could never take back. "Why don't you just leave our Mikey to it? Move on with your life, find one of your own kind. It will never work out with my son anyway. So just face it and stop kidding yourself." Rachel always had to have the last word, she could never let sleeping dogs lie.

Sarah wasn't taking it lying down though. If they were both putting their cards on the table here, she was getting things off her chest too. "We'll let Mikey be the judge of that. I'd be careful Rachel because if you make him choose, I'm sure I'll win hands down. He owes you nothing, remember. It's not like you have been Mother of the Year is it? In my eyes he's better off without you. You only bring him down anyway." Sarah had overstepped the mark, she dug deep and went for the jugular.

Gary could see Rachel bubbling with anger and reached over and stroked the top of her shoulder. "Come on Rach, don't be letting her ruin your day. If she wants to involve Mikey then let her do it. It just goes to show how inconsiderate and immature she is." Gary was clever with his words. He knew now Sarah would never tell Mikey about the beef between them. He carried on driving and turned the music up. You could have cut the atmosphere with a knife.

Lancaster Farms HMP looked like a modern jail from the outside. Made of clean, sand-coloured stone set in rural grounds, it was a bit of a contrast to Strangeways. This was the first time Gary had ever been to this nick and he raised his eyes as he drove into the car park. "Looks okay doesn't it, not like the shit-holes I've stayed in!"

Rachel had seen her arse, she was still in a mood. "It's a jail Gary, they're all the same to me. Behind them walls is nothing but tears and heartbreak. A jail is jail in my eyes. What do you want, a fucking circus."

Gary was in a world of his own, he was talking to himself. "It makes Strangeways look like a right dump. Look at all the modern shit it's got. I mean, take a butcher's at how clean it is." Gary parked up and unclipped his seat belt. "I'm just going to blast a cig before we go inside. I've been driving for ages and I need a fag to calm me down. You two have wrecked my head."

Sarah was quiet. She'd never been on a prison visit before and this was a whole new experience to her; a proper eye-opener. Gary opened the car door and twisted his body so his legs were hanging outside the car. When Rachel was in this frame of mind he knew more than anyone that she was better left alone, moody cow. She would come around without water or so his old gran used to say anyway.

Sarah pulled a cherry coloured lip gloss from her handbag. Mikey loved kissing her with this on her lips and always requested she wore it if they were having a date night. He was romantic in his own kind of way and deep down in her heart she understood him. This hard-man image he portrayed to the world was just his way of coping with stuff. Having led the life he had, he had to stand tall and never let anybody think that he was weak. Sarah had first met Mikey by chance. Fate she liked to call it… destiny. Her head was away with the fairies, it was just a party where he happened to be. It wasn't really her scene if she was being honest with herself. Sarah liked to have a few drinks when she went out at wine bars but she was never really into getting pissed like most of her friends. She wasn't a raver. She was a bit prudish really. The party had gone well and she'd had enough for the night. Her friends were still hard at it and all she wanted to do was to go home and get into bed. Standing outside the house to ring a taxi she realised she had no battery left on her mobile phone, it was flat. It was a complete nightmare.

Mikey Milne had always been a hit with the ladies and when he stood there watching her alone, he realised she was stressed out. He walked over with a cocky smile and full of confidence and made his move. "What's up pretty lady? Anything I can help you with?"

Sarah lifted her head and from the moment she set eyes on him her heart skipped a beat, she was breathless. She took a few seconds to speak. "It's this bloody phone. I need to ring a taxi and of all times for this to happen, the battery has decided to go flat."

Mikey pulled his own phone from his coat pocket and smiled over at her. "There you go, my lovely. You can use mine. Where are you going anyway?"

Sarah was shy and she'd not really had any interest from guys in the past. Her head was in her career and she had no time for them, they were more trouble than they were worth. Her future was way more important. "I live in Middleton. It's not far from here but it's too late for me to walk on my own at this time of the night. My dad will go ballistic if I did anyway. He's funny like that."

Mikey was never one to miss a chance to gain a new lady friend and he stepped up to the mark hoping he could be her knight in shining armour. "It's a nice night if you fancy me walking you home. It will save you a few quid too."

Sarah was gobsmacked, Mikey was so full of himself, she was stuck for words. "Would you really do that for me? You don't even know me and I don't know you?"

"So, let's take a chance and get to know each other then. You seem like someone I would like to get to know better anyway, so that's a start." There it was, the moment she would remember for the rest of her life, the night she became his lady. The two of them just hit it off from the word go and they looked as if they had known each other for years. He made her heart skip a beat every time she looked at him, she was smitten. It was love at first sight and no matter what anyone ever told her about him in the future, he could never do any wrong in her eyes. She was besotted by him. The pair were joined at the hip after that first night and Mikey was mesmerised by the new girl on the block. It didn't matter to him how posh she was or who her family were, he just knew he really liked her… a lot.

Love had never hit Mikey like this before – it was something he had always struggled with. Of course he'd banged loads of girls but they were just dirt-bags to him. They were little more than a jerk and a squirt; a sack emptier. He never loved them. Love was something that had caused him immense pain in the past and only seemed to leave empty holes in people's hearts and Mikey never wanted to open his heart again. All the things he'd ever loved had gone. He had loved his dad and he left, he loved his family too but they just got off and left him to rot. No, love was something that he struggled with and as of yet nobody had ever got into his heart. Of course, Sarah's family went ballistic when they found out who their daughter was dating. Some big mouth from the estate let the cat out of the bag. Her parents told her point-blank to end the relationship before they did. They didn't understand the passion they shared and they were doing everything in their power to make sure their daughter got as far away from this dead leg as she possibly could. Sarah's brothers were livid at the thought of their sister mingling with the riff-raff in the area. They had done their homework on Mikey and they had him down as a scumbag, a grafter and a liar. And, it didn't take long before they paid someone good money to warn him off. They would break his neck if they had to.

Mikey Milne shit himself when it happened. They Shanghaied him right out of the blue, with no warning whatsoever. There he was just minding his own business walking down the street when from out of nowhere he was dragged into the back of a white transit van. A pillowcase was rammed over his head and he was in no position to fight back. His body was numb and he was light-headed after the first blow was struck. They went to town on him, kicked fuck out of him and nearly killed him. His attackers took him to a deserted area and that's when he could see their identity for the first time. These men were the real McCoy, gangsters, head the balls and, his heart was in his mouth the second the ordeal began. Malcolm Jackson was a well-known head around the area. He was getting on a bit nowadays but he could still put the fear of God in someone if he wanted to. He pulled out a silver pistol from his jacket and stuck the cold steel barrel in the side of Mikey's face. There were another two men there too and they watched as Malcolm began his torment. "I'll blow your fucking head off if you ever go near Sarah again. Do I make myself clear, laddo?"

Mikey was shaking like a leaf and he swallowed hard. All he could do was nod his head. His eyes were wide open and he felt his windpipe tightening. He was in a bad situation, one he'd never found himself in before. Malcolm was a sick bastard and he was well known for the way he attacked the people who'd wronged him. He grabbed some rusty old pliers and stuck them deep into his victim's mouth. Mikey was wriggling about but there was no way he was moving. They had him pinned down. Malcolm rammed the pliers inside Mikey's mouth and attached them to his teeth. He had a firm grip on one and let out a menacing laugh. "Fuck me, these are like donkey's teeth." He pulled and tugged inside his mouth. A metal taste oozed onto Mikey's tongue, there was blood dribbling down his chin. This mad cunt had pulled one of his side teeth out. Writhing in pain, Mikey was sucking up the dribbling blood and watched as Malcolm examined the bloody tooth still lodged firmly inside the pliers. "This is just a reminder, kid. If I ever see you again it will mean you didn't listen to me. And trust me I'll pull every one of them gnashers out one by one! I'll make a fucking necklace out of them!"

Mikey had feared for his life that night but he didn't say a word about it at the time. He tried his very best to cart his new girlfriend but she kept coming back and after days of sobbing her heart out, he knew he couldn't let her go. He had to face the consequences of his actions and when the time came for Malcolm to pay him another visit he would just have to be ready to defend himself. Mikey Milne was tooled up every day after that attack. He was always looking over his shoulder and waiting for the next beating. The missing tooth on the left side of his mouth was a constant reminder that death was only a whisper away and now he was a target, he valued his life more than ever. In truth, prison was a good place for him to be at the moment and while he was locked up he knew Malcolm and his boys couldn't get their hands on him. In his own way he'd tried to tell Sarah how bad things were but she wasn't the sharpest tool in the box and even if he spelt it out to her, she would never have believed her family could have contemplated having him wiped from the face of the earth just so she wouldn't date him anymore.

Gary stood inside the visitors centre and booked in for the visit. It was such a malarkey and things had changed so much since he'd last visited someone in the nick. It gave him the creeps. They were given bright green wristbands to wear and it was the screw's job to make sure they were fitted securely on the visitor's wrist. Every last detail had to be followed; passports, proof of address, utility bills – it all had to be produced before a visitor was allowed inside the jail. Rachel sat tugging at her wristband, she was still in a mood. "What the fuck is this all about? Look how tight mine is, it's irritating me already. I'm going to rip it off."

Gary was distraught and kept a low voice as he tried to calm her down. "Just leave it alone! They won't let you go over to the main prison if you're not wearing one. Please, for me, just chill out." He was sweating, small beads of sweat forming on his forehead. The parcel had to be stashed yet and his arse was twitching knowing the time was nearing to go into the main prison.

Sarah was fidgeting, she'd had enough of the atmosphere. She shot a look over at Rachel and gasped her breath. "Can we just start again? I'm sorry for my part in all this but you have to understand where I'm coming from. Day after day I take all the insults from you and I just keep quiet. But, it does my head in, it really hurts my feelings."

Rachel folded her arms tightly in front of her and bit hard on her lip. She was a ticking bomb and if they would have been anywhere else, she would have dragged her hair all over the place and kicked fucked out of her. But they were in public and she knew she had to curb her anger and try and sort things out, not for her, for her son. "Just forget about it now, I can't be arsed anymore. It's happened and we both said stuff. No point in going over it all is there?"

Sarah was never one to be quiet. She wanted to explore the reason why they argued now and she tried dissecting every part of the dispute. "We're just different me and you. You have to accept me for who I am. It's not my fault if I come from a good background," she paused. "And, I know you don't really mean all you say anyway, it's just your way of trying to release your frustration. I've read up on things like this and it's a sort of defence mechanism. The best form of defence is attack."

Rachel flicked invisible dust from her black leggings. They were cheap and cheerful and something she picked up from Primark when she was in Manchester last. You could see her scabby knickers through the thin black material too; her skanky underwear was ready for the bin. There was no way she was giving her the time of the day anymore, she was doing her head in. Rachel's voice went higher. "I said it's over didn't I! Just be quiet and let's get this visit over and done with. Our Mikey loves us both, so for now just let's keep him happy and not stress him out." Sarah sucked in a large mouthful of air and her chest expanded. She nodded slowly at Rachel and the war seemed to be over for now.

Rachel smirked as she watched Gary go to the toilets to conceal the parcel. The visitors centre was clean and bright, which made a big change from what she was used to on previous visits. Usually, these places were a shit-tip with stinking toilets, scruffy chairs and snotty kids running around crying their eyes out. Rachel clocked her surroundings. There were children's toys in the corner of the room and a flat screen TV secured firmly on the wall. This was one of the best centres Rachel had ever visited and she felt at ease knowing she was warm and sat in a nice place before she went to see her son. Reaching over to a table nearby Sarah picked up a newspaper written by HMP inmates. It was distributed throughout the country and most criminals read it to pass a few hours. Opening the pages, she started to read the news inside the prison world. Her eyes were wide open as her expression changed.

Rachel snarled over at her and shook her head. What did this girl know about her world? Fuck all! She didn't have a clue what it was like to suffer.

Sarah wiped her eyes as tears started rolling down her cheek. She lifted her head up and choked up as she passed the newspaper over to Rachel. Her finger pointed at a piece in the paper. "Please read this poem here that an inmate has written. It's heartbreaking, just read it and you'll see. Honest, it's really pulled at my heartstrings." Rachel knew what kind of poems were inside this paper. When she was doing her time she used to read it religiously. Everyone did. The poems were written by inmates and some of the verses were really good. It's amazing how people can find the words to describe their pain when they are locked away from their loved ones. Rachel used to cry reading this newspaper back in the day. There was one piece in particular that still stuck in her mind and it was about an inmate writing to her children back home asking them for forgiveness for the life she'd led them in to. Each criminal locked away behind prison walls always had regrets about the choices they'd made in life. Prison life broke them and all that was left for some inmates was raw emotion that made them feel weak and vulnerable. Rachel had written a few articles whilst she was doing her time too but she never showed them to anyone. These were her private thoughts and nobody was ever getting inside her head to see the real her. She'd been hurt too many times in the past to ever expose her inner feelings again. Rachel cast her eyes over the verse. She was just reading it to be polite, she didn't digest any of the words. Passing it back over to Sarah she raised her eyes. "Life, innit. Words said inside a jail cell mean nothing on the outside love. It's just jail talk. Ask a few of the girls sat here about it," she jerked her head forward at the girls sat waiting in the corner of the room. Rachel continued in a low voice. "They'll tell you all about it. I'm sure they've probably heard buckets of it. Meaningless shit it is, a load of crap. I should know, I've been there and got the t-shirt so to speak."

Sarah held her head to the side and whispered over to Rachel. "I do want to learn about how you lived your life if you will let me. I won't judge you. You just have to trust me. After all, we're family now."

Rachel nearly choked. Was this girl on this fucking planet or what? How on earth did she think she could say something like that? Rachel was just about to give her a bollocking when Gary came back into the room, he saved Sarah from a mouthful of abuse. All it took was one look over at him and she knew the job was done. The drugs were stashed, plugged right up his arsehole. The officer in charge started to shout out inmates' surnames and the visitors made their way over to the exit. They were all nattering and straightening their clothes. Some of the younger girls were dressed up to the nines; their arses hanging out and tits popping out of their bras. Sarah got excited as they started to walk over to the main prison. Her eyes were everywhere. "Is he in there, what part is he in? How many prisoners will we see today? Are there any criminals doing life sentences?" Sarah was doing everyone's head in. Even Gary, who was usually laid back, was getting sick of her now. She was hard work. He had to keep a straight head and she was spooking him out with all her questions. Sarah latched on to some other visitors and they could hear her waffling on behind them as they all entered the main prison. The security checks now began. All the doors were locked and each of them were being watched eagerly, there was CCTV and officers all over the joint. Once the visitors came through the main doors it was time to be searched. This was the point of no return, there was no going back. Everything the visitors had in their possession had to be put in a small grey dish and placed on a table. No notes were allowed inside the jail, just loose change. There was a vending machine in the centre and visitors were allowed to buy drinks and chocolates for their loved ones. Mikey loved chocolate. He had a right sweet tooth and when he was craving sugar he could eat loads of it. He loved thick, creamy chocolate, a Mars bar was his favourite. He always said the chocolate bar had everything he needed in one bite. Rachel often treated him to his addiction when they'd had words. All she had to do was place one on the table near him and he knew she was sorry for whatever havoc she'd caused. Rachel and Mikey knew each other inside out. They didn't have to say a word to each other. All it ever took was a look to know how the other was feeling.

Sarah huddled in behind Rachel as their turn came to be searched. Mikey's mother knew the script inside out and her spine tingled at the memory of her stretch inside a similar big house. She stretched her arms out ready to be frisked, her face was frozen. Gary licked his dry cracked lips, his head was spinning. His eyes were all over looking for the sniffer dog. If that scruffy mutt came anywhere near him he was going to boot it right up the arse. He'd concealed the drugs well but there was always that small chance that they would be detected by the hound. Rachel smiled at the female officer. "Am I all done now, love?"

The screw nodded. "Yes, just go and wait at the other door until the rest of the visitors are ready."

Rachel picked up her loose change and shoved it back inside her pocket. "Fucking miserable lesbian," she growled under her breath. Mikey's mam stood with her back against the wall and chewed the side of her fingernail. She clocked the female screw and wondered how many times she'd actually found something on a visitor, probably none. It was just a basic search, a pat down. Sarah was chuckling as her body search began. This girl couldn't keep her big trap shut for a minute. This was a big adventure for her and she was taking in everything around her. "Do you ever find anything when you're searching the visitors?" The female officer raised a smile but there was no way she was getting into a conversation about it. This was confidential information and she wasn't willing to discuss it. Rachel let out a laboured breath from where she stood and shot a look over at Sarah. She was so on top, a fucking busybody. She was bringing attention to them.

Gary walked past and stood with his arms out as the male officer began to search him. He knew the script and tried to get it over as soon as possible. If this screw would have suspected anything he would have sent him into another room where they would examine him with a wand. The wand was the nickname of a device they used to scan visitors for any trace of drugs. This included people who smoked weed, or who had recently been in contact with it. These visitors usually had their visits cancelled at this point if any evidence of drug use was found on them. This was a zero tolerance jail and the officers were all on the ball. Nobody was trusted. The price on the outside to bring a parcel inside any jail was about two hundred quid, usually the junkies would take the chance to take stuff in. They were desperate for some extra cash and would do anything for it, even risk their own freedom. Jail meant fuck all to them; it was three meals a day and a roof over their head. It was more than any of them had on the outside. But money was short and Rachel's boyfriend's neck was on the line this time. He hated taking chances but Rachel had pressured him into doing it. Fuck Mikey Milne! He needed to sort his own shit out and man up. All of a sudden now Mikey was banged up he had his mother running around after him. She never usually gave a flying fuck and now she was acting like the mother of the year. It was a joke.

Gary finished his body search and gave the security guard a shifty look as he walked away. The coast was clear for now and everything was going to plan. Rachel gasped as he made his way to her side. "Thank fuck that's over," he whispered under his breath. Sarah was taking everything in, her head was all over the show looking at every detail. As they walked through another doorway they could see the grounds of the prison from where they stood; thick metal fencing with sharp jagged blades of metal sticking from the top of it. Sarah was mesmerised by it all and Gary had to give her a gentle shove to keep her moving. She was at it again. "I can only imagine how hard it is for Mikey in here Rachel. I never really thought of prison in this way. It's shocking, it's really opened my eyes."

Rachel pushed her in the small of her back and hurried her along. "Will you turn it in? Honest to God, give me strength! Just move your arse and let's get up to the waiting room." For the second time today Gary agreed with his girlfriend. He wanted this parcel passed over as soon as possible. He knew he'd put his freedom at risk and he was starting to regret the risk he'd taken. But it was too late, there was no turning back. Drug smuggling into any jail carried a heavy sentence. Three years, sometimes more. It was no walk in the park, this was serious shit.

Gary sat down and stared at the grey door facing him. He knew that any time soon he would be in the main visiting centre and Mikey would be there waiting for him. Looking about, he clocked the other people sat there and nudged Rachel in the waist. "Look at the state of her, fuck me she looks as rough as a bear's arse. Wouldn't you have thought she would have made a bit of an effort to come here? I bet she's got a right sweaty arse crease?"

Rachel pulled her jacket around her body and dipped her head, she smiled slightly. She was just as bad as the other woman and realised now how scruffy she looked as well. Scraping her hair back from her face she tucked it behind her ears. She was paranoid about her appearance and started to pull the white pieces of fluff from her leggings. Sarah was in her element. She was watching everything that what was going on. This was another world to her and she was fascinated by it. Her mother had spoken to her about people less fortunate than themselves and whenever she saw a charity box she always put spare change inside it. There were small children crying and everyone was eager to get inside to see their loved ones. The mothers were getting frustrated and one woman ragged her son about on the spot to calm him down. "If you carry on fucking about I'll slap your arse, just turn it in," she whispered at him as she squeezed at his hand. Then they could hear the sound of keys jangling. Everybody was on edge, eyes fixed firmly on the door. The visitors stood up as the door opened fully. It was a stampede of bodies rushing to get inside the room.

Sarah moved quickly and stood next to Rachel to

avoid being crushed. She was excited. "Is this it, is he in here?" Sarah flicked her eyes about the large room. There were men sat at tables wearing red bibs over their clothes. A group of officers were situated at the front of the room. They were higher up than the rest of the tables, enabling them to get a good look at what was going on. And stuff would go on too, lots of illegal contraband would be passed about. There were women wanking their boyfriends off and inmates trying to get a quick grope of the Jack and Danny when nobody was looking. Sarah screamed out at the top of her voice. People were looking at her, she was behaving like a right dickhead, she had to calm down. Then, through a sea of faces, there he was, her Mikey - her heart's desire. With a shrieking tone she ran to his table.

"Mikey! My Mikey!"

Rachel shook her head and turned to Gary at the side of her. "Is there any need for her big gob? She's a bleeding embarrassment. It's the last time I'm coming here with her I can tell you now. She's been a nightmare. What a daft bitch! He needs to cart her and get someone bleeding normal because she's up it." Gary's head was in the game now and he wasn't really listening to a word she said. He swallowed hard and made his way to sit at the table. Sarah hugged Mikey and as predicted she broke down crying. She was drawing attention to them and Rachel snapped. She gripped the top of her shoulder and sank her fingers deep into her shoulder blade. "Sarah, just sit down, you drama queen. We spoke about this before didn't we? Mikey doesn't need to see you in this state does he?" Mikey prised her fingers from around his shoulders and asked her to sit down facing him. The screw was at his table and he had a sour expression. He had a job to do and no one was pissing on his parade. "Can you sit down, Miss? You're not allowed on the same side as the inmate. If it happens again your visit will be over."

Sarah held a puzzled look. "I'm his girlfriend. Surely I'm allowed to comfort him?"

"I don't care if you're Princess Diana, sweetheart. You still stay on the right side of the table or you'll be removed from the visit."

Gary was white and the stress was starting to show. He gave the eye to Mikey and let him know the goods were on his person. Mikey quickly diffused the situation. "No worries boss. She'll stay on that side for the rest of the visit. She's just a bit upset that's all. You know how these women get when they see us for the first time."

The officer sniffed hard and moved along to the next table, shoulders held high. Mark and Smithy were at the main desk and it was their job to make sure all the rules were adhered to during visiting time. They'd seen some things during this shift in the past, things that would make your toes curl. The room was like one big orgy. Some of these men hadn't had sex in years. They were like dogs on heat. If they got a whiff of fanny on the visit they were buzzing for days. This was what it was like and each inmate would discuss what they got from their partners. For some lucky criminals they got the stink finger. To delve a finger into a warm wet pussy was heaven for them. The finger was sacred after that. They never washed it for days and they forever had it stuck under their noses, licking at it and tasting it at every given opportunity. Some prisoners even shared it too. Yep, if someone had the scent of a hairy beaver they would always let other less fortunate inmates have a whiff of it too. Pussy was pussy and no matter who the smell belonged to, it was all fair game behind the prison walls. They always hooked each other up.

Mikey looked over at Sarah and he knew that no matter what, he wasn't getting a bit of finger-pie today. He'd be lucky to even get a touch of a pubic hair, never mind sticking a finger up her. She was proper like that Sarah was, fucking frigid. She was nothing like the girls he'd had in the past. They were game for anything and didn't care what name they got for themselves.

Gary fanned his fingers across his mouth and whispered. "I've got your shit when you're ready pal."

Sarah was bright red and her heart was in her mouth as she realised what was going to happen. She was clever this girl, a lot more intelligent than she'd been given credit for. She stood up from the table. "I'll go and get you some chocolate and a drink Mikey, what do you want?"

"Get him a Mars bar," Rachel butted in, "he loves them, don't you son?"

Sarah growled at her and now Mikey was by her side she had no fear of Rachel whatsoever. He'd never just sit there and let his mother speak to her the way she had been doing. He would have put her right in her place, told her straight. Sarah was playing a dangerous game now, she knew exactly how to wind this woman up. "I think we should let him pick what he wants to eat himself. I bet he's sick to death of the same bar of chocolate all the time, he might want to try something new. What do you want Mikey?" she asked.

All eyes were on him, watching his every move. Rachel reached over and touched his hand softly. "A Mars bar son, you know they're your favourite?"

Mikey chewed on his bottom lip and stretched his

arms above his head. He was unaware of the beef between them both. "Get me anything you like, sexy. I'm not arsed to tell you the truth, just don't get anything with nuts in. I hate them and they get stuck in my teeth."

Sarah gave a little giggle and made her way to the vending machine on the other side of the room. Rachel could kiss her arse now, there was no way she was getting him a Mars bar. He was her man and she would pick something new for him to try. Sarah left with a bounce in her step. Now she was gone it was the ideal time to pass the parcel without her being there. Mikey moved his head to the side and clocked her shapely arse as she wiggled over to the other side of the room. "I've got a mint bird me," he chuckled.

Gary was getting restless – it was now or never. In a low voice he whispered over to Mikey again. "Just say when and I'll pass it over. I'm sweating my nuts off here. I just need to get it over with."

Rachel gave a cunning smile over at her son and covered her mouth as she spoke. "There's enough stuff here to keep you on the go for a while. Make sure you make the most of it because you know money is short don't you?"

Mikey rubbed vigorously at the end of his nose with a flat palm. Whenever he was ready to do something shifty he always tweaked the end of his conk. The noise inside the room was loud, people were laughing and kids were screaming as they ran about the small floor space. Mikey shot a look over at Mark and Smithy and he was aware they were watching him like a hawk. He had to pick his time wisely. One wrong move and these cunts would have had him twisted up in seconds. He knew his card was marked and nobody trusted him as far as they could throw him.

Mikey was a security risk, it was all over his prison file that he was a bad apple and if they had an inclination he was up to no good, he would be dragged off the visit before his feet touched the floor. Nobody fucked about on their watch, or so they thought.

Mark sat at the desk and scanned around the room. He was making sure all the inmates' hands were on the table and nothing untoward was going down in the visiting room. He was alert and ready to strike at any second. Parcels were passed at the drop of a hat and if he blinked, he knew he could very well miss it. Smithy was by his side and he nudged him in the waist. His voice was low as he tickled the end of his chin. "Keep your eyes on Milne. He looks like a right cunning fucker. I've got his card marked already. I know his sort. I'm sure he's on a drop today. Don't ask me why, I just have a gut feeling about it. Get a butcher's at him, he's flapping."

Mark looked over at Mikey. "I'm all over him, don't you worry about that. He keeps looking over at me so he knows I'm onto him." Smithy coughed to clear his throat and made his way over to the tables near him. Just his presence made the inmates jittery and only the brave would test him in trying to get a parcel into the jail. Smithy had seized lots of drugs from the visiting room. He knew the signs of something going down and he was rarely wrong when he had a gut feeling that somebody was up to no good. As he paced around the room he stood tall and held his hands neatly behind his back. Every step he took he was vigilant and aware of his surroundings. The smell of perfume was overpowering, the females had hammered it and it was choking him. Mark twisted the blue biro in between his fingers, rolling it, chewing it at the lid, he was ready to pounce at any second. Mikey was looking over at him and he was agitated, fidgeting. There was definitely something that had unnerved him. Smithy paused on the spot. There was shouting and screaming from the back of the room. All the officers were ready to go. This was a code red. Smithy was the first there to see what was going down. There was shouting, screaming and objects being flung about. A female visitor was going sick at her boyfriend, livid she was, she was ready to attack him.

Smithy grabbed her by the arm trying to control her. "He's a cheeky fucker. I've stayed in for months and not been out partying once and that daft bastard has been writing to other girls. He's a cheeky twat, a liberty taker." Smithy gripped her again and started to pull her away from the inmate. She was strong and was fighting back with all her might. Tears ran down the side of her cheeks and she was heartbroken. The rest of the room were buzzing with all the commotion. Sarah was in her element.

The dumped inmate dropped his head into his hands and he knew there was fuck all he could do about it. He'd been caught bang to rights. He pleaded with her. "Alison, it was one letter. It was ages ago when me and you were on a break. She means fuck all to me. Come back and let's sort it out."

Smithy paused as Alison turned on the spot. "Do you think I want you now after this? Everyone told me you were a lying, cheating bastard but I always told them they were wrong. What a nobhead I look now! You can get to fuck if you think I'm ever coming here to see you again. Get that slut to come and see you." Mikey saw the moment was right and quickly plugged the parcel from Gary. They were quick and nobody seemed to notice. Mark was at Smithy's side and they assisted the angry woman from the room. Just before she left, she turned around and made sure she had her boyfriend's attention. She yanked her bright pink top up and revealed her breasts. "See these you wanker, you'll never touch them again. I'll show you what it means to take the piss out of me. I'll have a man in my bed before the week's out. A real man too and not one with a two inch cock." Everybody was pissing their sides. What a character she was! That would teach him to play the field when he had a girl already. Serves him right, he had got what was coming to him.

The commotion was soon over and the room was swarming with officers. The inmates were laughing and shouting over to the dumped prisoner. "You've fucked that one up, mate. You better start writing your begging letter now. Give me her number I'll try my luck with her." The banter began and the inmate smirked. There was no way he was losing face in front of the boys, he took it all on the chin. The prisoner left the table and was escorted back to the landing. His pride was hurt and he knew after a long phone call later with his woman she'd be back to see him. He was such a cocky fucker and it would have served him right if she moved on and left his sorry arse on his own; that would have showed him, wiped the smile right off his face. Mark calmed the situation down and sat back down at his desk. Mikey was chatting and he never looked over at him once. Had he missed something? Had the drugs already been passed? He wasn't sure. His head dropped as he concentrated on his computer screen. Every now and then he peeped over at Mikey just to see if he could catch him in the act. Nothing.

Sarah held Mikey's hand and stroked every finger slowly. She looked deep into his eyes and her sweet warm breath tickled the end of his nose. "This is the last time you'll be in here isn't it? Our life can be so much better if you just turn your back on the crime world."

Rachel sniggered under her breath and Gary kicked her under the table. Mikey shot a look at them both and snarled. "I'm going to do what I have to Sarah. I'm trying to change but shit happens doesn't it and I'm not making any promises that I can't keep."

Rachel just blurted it out, she had no shame whatsoever. "That's what I told her, she's a dickhead even thinking you can change. I told her straight. I said my son will always be a grafter, it's in his blood."

Sarah dropped her head. This wasn't what she wanted to hear. Mikey could see she was upset and his mother was just rubbing salt in the wounds. "Mam, can you leave us alone for a bit. I'll try and ring you later. Just give us a bit of time on our own, we've got stuff to sort out."

Gary was on his feet as quick as could be. There was no way he was sticking around longer than he needed to. His job here was done and he'd never be doing a drop again. It wasn't his style, it was too on top. Rachel was shocked. "But son, I've not even told you about stuff yet. I've hardly spoken to you."

He cut her dead in her tracks. "I said I'll ring you later. I need to sort me and Sarah out. Stop moaning, fuck me."

Gary walked to the corner of the table and hugged Mikey as he stood up. Mark and Smithy were watching every movement and they were eager to uncover anything being passed over. Mikey gripped his mother in his arms.

She was much smaller than he was and she looked lost in his firm, toned arms. He knew she was upset but just ignored her. Fuck the drama today, he was in no mood for it. "See you soon. Thanks for coming," he shouted after them both. Rachel barely managed a wave and you could see her and Gary having words as they made their way towards the exit. Mikey touched his girlfriend's cheek with his finger. "I'm trying Sarah. It's hard in here, remember that. You don't know what it's like in here. There are some dangerous bastards about who will stick a knife in me the moment my back is turned. Just let's get this sentence over with and see where we go from there."

Sarah raised a smile and kissed his hand. "You're so lovely. I see so much in you that's good. You just need to believe in yourself and put all this behind you. You're better than that. You can be so much more."

Mikey was listening to her and even though she was talking out of her arse she did make sense sometimes. Sarah lived by the law of attraction and she honestly believed that the way people thought made a big difference to the way they lived their life. In her bedroom she had photographs of the things she wanted in life. A big house set in the hills and a nice sports car parked on the driveway. Mikey had never got his head around it all and thought it was a load of mumbo jumbo most of the time. "You make your own luck in life" is what he'd told her. "Does any of your family know I'm in here?" he said after a pause.

Sarah swallowed hard and even though she wanted to lie she just couldn't do it. She always thought he knew when she was hiding something, she just couldn't look him in the eye. "My brother knows. He'd heard it from one of his mates. He's happy about it and told me he hopes you never get out. In fact, he said he hopes you're raped and bummed senseless. He's a right idiot sometimes."

Mikey gritted his teeth tightly together. Who the fuck did her family think they were? His fist tightened and he bit the edge of his knuckles as he spoke. "It bugs me you know. They don't even know me, yet they think they can judge me. Your brothers and your dad are daft twats too. Do you know they tried having me done in? Look," he stretched the side of his mouth open wider. "This is what your old man had done to me. I bet he never told you that did he?"

Sarah's mouth was wide open. Her nostrils twitched slowly. "What, say that again so I can get this right in my head. You're saying my father had someone do this to you to warn you against seeing me?"

Mikey nodded. He knew he should have kept this to himself but they'd pissed him off big time, he couldn't help it. They were no better than he was, they just had money, nothing else. Sarah rolled her eyes and sat staring at the wall behind Mikey. He clicked his fingers in front of her eyes trying to bring her back down to earth. "Forget about it now. I'm sorry I even said anything. It's just... Oh, I don't fucking know. They wind me up. Don't mention anything to them. It will just make thing worse."

Sarah slammed her flat palm on the table. "That's not happening. If my father has organised some idiots to come and give you a good going over then he's getting a piece of my mind. How dare he dictate to me when he's doing underhand stuff like this?"

Mikey was sorry he'd let the cat out of the bag. Sarah was never one to let things go without thrashing it out first. There was a silence between them. They sat in deep thought. Smithy was doing his rounds and he tapped Mikey on his shoulder as he stood next to his table. "Start to finish your visit off now. Five minutes left, son."

Mikey shuddered as he felt the warm palm on his body. "No problems, boss," he replied. Mark was doing the same thing on the other side of the room and all the officers knew that this was an ideal opportunity for drugs to be brought into the prison. At each table inmates kissed their loves ones. Some lovers were going for gold and if the screws weren't there they would have had sex right there on the spot. These women had no shame, they had to get the most out of their men before the time was up. Hands rubbed over each other's bodies, necks were being bitten, bodies pressing firmly against each other. These lot were dying for a quick leg-over.

Sarah looked at a couple on the next table and held a sour expression. "There's no way you would get me doing anything like that in a public place. Ewww… she's touching his private parts."

Mikey had to quieten her down. She was so on top and bringing attention to them both. Mikey gripped her head and planted his warm wet ripe lips onto hers. She was quiet now, not a word. Sarah was lost in the moment and for a split second she would have let Mikey do anything he wanted to her, she was passionate and ready for sex. Mikey heard the final call and after a few more seconds he pulled away from his chick. "Can you write me some letters? It's boring in here and it will give me something to read."

Sarah smiled and gripped him closer to her body with desperation. "I'll write to you every day. I'll start tonight. I love writing. I can tell everything that's been going on outside and, just how much I love you." The visit was over and each inmate had a look of sadness in their eyes. Each of them sat at the table and watched their loved ones leave. Kids were crying, mothers trying to reassure them that daddy will be home soon. Girlfriends were blowing kisses and trying to get the last look at them before the door closed.

The inmates lined up to go back to their wings. First though, they were searched to make sure they didn't have anything they shouldn't have on their person. Mikey bounced up towards Smithy with his arms stretched out. He was confident and showed no signs of concealing any drugs on his body. Mark was at his side and he watched eagerly as his workmate did a body search. Nothing, the lad was clean. The officers looked at each other with a blank expression. Had they got it wrong, were they barking up the wrong tree? Mikey started to walk onto the main landing and he whistled as he walked along. What a result!

"It must be up his dirt box," Smithy growled as he continued. "I swear he's got something. Look at the smarmy cunt laughing at us. Let him get settled and we'll spin his pad tonight. We'll show him who's boss."

Mark was by his colleague's side and usually he was game as fuck to catch a drop that had just landed but today he was more laid back. Smithy nudged him in the waist. "What's up with you today? Usually, you're all over it. Don't tell me you've gone soft in your old age." Mark headed back into the room and carried on frisking the other inmates. Nothing was found here today, nothing, zilch.

Mikey slammed his cell door shut. It was bang up time and the door would be locked any second now. Potter sprang up on his bed and he looked like he'd been crying his eyes out, the fucking fairy. Trying to hold his tears back, he spluttered as if he had to get something from his chest. His hands were all over his body, itching, scratching hard. "I'm struggling today, Mikey. I hate this place. I'm never going to get used to it. I think I'm losing my marbles. Honest, some serious shit is going on inside my head at the moment."

Mikey ran his fingers casually through his hair. He'd seen this a hundred times before, cabin fever. Prison life was daunting at first and if you didn't know the crack it was a bad place to be, it sent men under, broke them down. This convict had to man up and learn quickly if he was ever going to survive in this joint. This was no place to show any weakness or to start to fall apart. Mikey jumped onto his bed and kicked his shoes off, casually scratching at his nuts. He kept his eyes on the door and fidgeted about trying to get comfortable. He was confident and thought he knew it all. "Listen our kid, I'm not here to hold your hand. You're a nice lad and all that but you're fucked in the head if you think I'm babysitting you. Life's hard enough without a tag-along. I've told you before, I'll sort you out but you need to shake this shit off. We'll be running this wing soon and I want you by my side not quivering under your bed sheets. Stop being a pussy. You need to grin and bear it."

Potter wiped his eyes and replaced the glasses back on the end of his nose. "I'm soft as shit, who's going to listen to me on this wing? Don't add this to my worries. I'm alright as I am." Mikey froze as he heard the key locking the door from the outside. The hatch lifted up and he looked the screw straight in the eye. Jumping up from his bed, he held his ear to the door and placed a single finger over his mouth at his pad mate. Was the bastard still outside or was he gone? After a few seconds he made his way back towards his bed. The coast was clear. Mikey pulled his strides down and squatted down. Potter croaked and covered his eyes, his jaw dropping down. He spoke in a distressed tone. "My father told me about the gay men in the jails and there is no way I'm giving you oral sex. You're going to have to rape me. Do as you must but I'm not consenting to any of this."

Mikey screwed his face up as his hand stretched behind him and he wiggled his fingers about up his back passage. Mikey pulled the drugs from his arsehole and rushed towards the sink to wash his hands. Potter could hear him moving about and shouted after him. He was distraught. "Did you hear me, I said there is no way I'm doing anything with you. I will report you if you so much as lay a finger on me? I'll take a beating, you can kill me but I'm not having anal sex with you."

Mikey turned around and held the bottom of his stomach laughing his head off. "Stop it, you're killing me. No way did you think I was going to stick one up you?"

"Well, you pulled your pants down and why would you do that if you wasn't planning on bumming me?"

Mikey sat on the side of his bed with his legs apart and couldn't help but chuckle. "I was getting this lot out of my dirt box you dick-head." He fanned his fingers open and revealed the drugs. They were all tightly held together with clingfilm.

Potter looked like he'd had the cares of the world lifted from his shoulders, he let out a laboured breath and started to see the funny side of things. "Oh, so sorry about that. Where the hell did that come from? I told you, my head's fucked. Potty I am." Mikey jumped to his feet and looked at the light fitting over his head. He shook it rapidly. It was loose and with a bit of pressure he was able to lift it up to plant the drugs there. He never planned to keep them there, no way, they were getting shifted as soon as possible. Nothing was ever in his pad long enough to get a nicking. He knew the system like the back of his hand and every second he had them in here, he risked another charge.

Potter was eager to talk. He'd been alone for over an hour now and he was keen to get some things from his chest. "Mikey, do you really think I can fit in around here? Can you teach me to be like you?"

Mikey walked to the small window and stuck his head up towards the bars. He sucked in the night air and shivered as a gentle breeze filtered his body. "Potter, you don't want to end up like me mate. I'm fucked in the head. If I had my chance again, I'd be like you."

"What? A boring, specky geek who has no friends? No, no one wants to be like me. I'm a nobody."

Mikey was stood in the same position and he let his guard down for just a few seconds. "Life's been hard for me and if I could have my time again I'd probably be more like you. I never really stood a chance with my mother but ay, you play the cards life has dealt you don't you?"

Potter stood up and paced slowly behind Mikey. Dropping his hand on his shoulder he patted it gently. "That bad was it?"

Mikey realised what he'd just said and dropped his hands from the ledge. What was he thinking acting like this, he had an image to portray. Shaking the moment off he quickly changed the subject… "Right, let's talk about business and see how this is going to work out. I know you don't have a clue about jail life yet but in a couple of days of watching me, you'll get the gist of things around here. You keep your gob shut and you never tell anyone fuck all without talking to me first." Potter swallowed hard and watched Mikey land back on his bed. "Let's get some money flowing in this wing and once we get an iPhone under our belt we'll be laughing. Have you got a woman on the out Potter?"

His pad mate plonked down on the bottom bunk and rubbed his hands together with excitement. "I've not got a woman as of yet but I have felt some boobs before, warm, squidgy they were. I nearly got a mouthful of one but she put a stop to it before I could."

Mikey screwed his face up and kicked his foot playfully into his waist. "So, you're still a virgin, right?"

Potter blushed and nodded. "It's just never happened. There was a girl I liked very much and I was even going to ask her to marry me but I lost my nerve."

Mikey covered his mouth and burst out laughing. "Fuck me, mate. You're going to have to up your game if you ever want to pop your cherry. You just wait until I get a blower in here and we'll get you some birds going on Facebook and Instagram. Are you on Facebook already?"

"I was for a short time but I only had twenty friends and it was very rare I spoke to them so I tended not to go on it very often." Mikey was alive and just the thought of being on social media again sent a shiver of excitement down his spine. He'd been such a player in his day and Facebook was like one big fanny pot. Fuck-book he liked to call it. The girls on the site were gagging for it and many a night he'd sat up talking to birds from all over the country on it.

Potter was alive and his eyes were wide open. "Do you think any girls would like me?"

"They might do if I sort you out. You need some lean muscle on you first. I need to fatten you up a bit too. I've seen more fat on a chip you bony fucker. We can start to smash the gym and all that?" Any troubles Potter previously had seemed to be of no relevance any more. He was calm and getting his head around his new life in the jail. Mikey's head was working overtime though. The drugs needed to be distributed, this shit just got real.

CHAPTER SEVEN

Rachel queued up at the post office to collect her Jobseeker's Allowance; a poxy one hundred and thirty pound to keep her going for a fortnight, what a joke this was. What did the government expect her do with that amount of cash? It was a pittance, a drop in the ocean. Fuck all really. Once her bills were paid there was barely enough left to buy any food never mind anything else. It was a piss take, a fucking joke! These big wigs in authority needed to try and live on this amount each week, then they would see how hard it was. They didn't have a clue about modern society. This was the same for many people in the area, no wonder the crime rate was so high in Harpurhey. What chance did anyone have of making something of their lives when they were confronted by poverty every single day? No money to pay the bus fare for job interviews, no money for new clothes or luxuries, just basic rations every bastard day. Rachel chewed rapidly on her gum, she stank of stale tobacco and her greasy hair was just tied back as per usual, she was a soap dodger for sure. There was no colour in her cheeks and this woman looked like death warmed up. Rachel very rarely ate a full meal and when she did it was never healthy, nothing that would help her immune system fight off the illnesses she was always getting.

The door to the post office opened rapidly and a young man stuck his head in through the doors. He was dressed in black and his hood was pulled tightly over his head. The male clocked her and seemed to look at her a bit longer than he needed to. Rachel double-checked behind her to make sure he was looking at her and nobody else. Her body language changed, she was agitated. He was definitely weighing her up. What the hell did he want with her? She'd not ticked any drugs, she owed nobody as far as she knew. Rachel was sweating, her arse was twitching. She moved forward in the line of people and started to chit-chat with the woman next to her, trying to ease her rapid heartbeat. "Freezing isn't it?"

The old lady was more than willing to talk to her, she was bored shitless and she started to gossip about things going on the area. "I've not slept a bleeding wink all night, love. The little fuckers around here torched a car last night at the side of my house. Three hours it took to put the fire out, sirens blazing, police all over the show. I'll tell you something for nothing. This area is going to be the death of me. I hate it here. I can't wait to bleeding move."

Rachel chuckled, Harpurhey had gone downhill for sure. Years ago it was the place to be but of late, the council had re-housed some of the lowlifes from other areas and planted them in this community. The crime here was booming and even in the newspapers they had it down as one of the most deprived areas in the whole of North Manchester. Single mothers, junkies, armed robbers, yes, they all resided here. There were some good people who still lived here though and it was a shame they were tormented by the up-and-coming gangster wannabes. Money was power and each gang did whatever it took to line their pockets. They had no shame, few morals, and little respect for anyone. Most of all they didn't give a fuck about the police.

At last, Rachel reached the front of the queue. She pressed her head against the glass that separated her from the assistant. "Morning Hamid, can I have all my money out please." Placing her Post Office card in the machine, she kept her eyes wide open waiting for the amount to be displayed on the screen. There was always hope in her eyes when she looked at her balance, hope that maybe the benefit agency had got her claim wrong and transferred extra money into it. Today wasn't that day though, she hadn't been that lucky. It was just the amount she always got, she was on a downer. "Thanks Hamid," she said to the smartly dressed Post Office clerk, "I'll go and buy that car now, and the mansion I've always wanted." She chuckled and raised her eyes. Shoving the cash in her pocket, she went over to the counter on the other side of the shop. Londis was a convenience store as well as a Post Office and most of the residents shopped there for their bits and bobs. It was the place to be if you wanted to find somebody too. Rachel picked up a loaf of bread and a packet of cigs. She was gasping and couldn't wait to get outside to spark a fag up. Her last cigarette had been late last night and now she was craving nicotine.

When she got out it was still pissing it down and the wind was howling through the streets. It was depressing really and it did nothing for anybody's mood. Everyone looked pissed off and there was no positive energy about, it was all doom and gloom. Rachel chugged hard on her cigarette and started to head home. Gary would still be in bed and there was no way he would raise his ugly head for at least another few hours. He was a right lazy bastard and he always complained that he never got enough sleep. You see, Gary was a stoner, a pothead. Every day he was wrecked and he couldn't function without a few spliffs in the morning to set him up for the day. He was bone idle. The word 'work' made him get a sweat on. He was on sick benefit at the moment suffering from depression. Well, that's what his sick note said anyway. Who was he trying to kid? There was fuck all wrong with him; nothing that a few weeks of hard work wouldn't sort out. Most people in the area had blagged the benefit system in one way or other into believing they were unwell. Some of them even believed they were too sick to work, too. Gary always told everyone he wanted to find work but nothing ever came up. Even with his depression he told the doctors he would love to work, to get him out of the house, to get his life on track. What a lying bastard he was. He'd never looked for a job. Even when his pals asked him to do a few days labouring for them he always found a reason why he couldn't, the money was cash in his hand as well. Gary was stuck in a rut. Why work anyway when he could earn whatever money he needed doing a few grafts here and there. He was his own boss and nobody told him what to do. He lived by his own rules and worked whatever hours he wanted. A lazy bastard he was.

Head down, coat zipped up fully, Rachel cut across the grass verge at the side of the shop. It was quiet and not a single soul was about. As she walked along she could hear gravel crunching behind her. "Oi, a word please," a voice shouted behind her. Rachel turned slowly and she screwed her eyes up to try and get a better look. Her eyesight was shocking lately and even though she was as blind as a bat she'd never been to get her eyes tested. Rachel carried on walking and hoped the man would leave her alone. There were always junkies hanging about here begging for a few quid or a hot meal and she just thought this was one of those days. She was in no mood today for mither from anyone. If they shouted her again she was going to tell them to fuck right off. She had her own problems and couldn't be arsed with anyone else's today. Suddenly, a car door opened behind her and as she looked back over her shoulder she could see two males sprint to the side of her gripping her under each arm. They dragging her up against a brick wall. Two piercing blue eyes looked at her now and they were wide open, menacing. She feared for her life and she had every right to feel threatened, this was bad, very bad.

"It's Mikey Milne's mam, right?"

Rachel's eyes were wide open and she swallowed hard as the man's warm breath circled her face. She wriggled about but there was no way she was going anywhere, her body was pinned to the wall. This man was strong and even with one hand he was controlling every movement she made. This was serious and nothing to be taken lightly. "Your fucking son owes me some money. You tell him from me if my cash isn't back by the end of the week he's a dead man walking."

Her eyes twitched rapidly and she licked at her dry cracked lips. Nothing was registering, her head was all over the show. "What the fuck are you going on about? Take your hands off me you prick."

Why didn't she keep her big mouth shut, these were not the kind of men you messed with? The man choked back and spat in her face. Green and yellow spit right in her eyes. "You little rat. Tell Mikey, I want my money back. He's going to get leathered when I get my hands on him. Who the fuck does he think he is, having me over?"

Rachel was white, the penny had dropped. The other man at the side of her was in her face now and he was as aggressive as Davo. He chipped in adding his two penn'orth worth. "We know all about the lying cunt. We've been told he had the cash. He had his chance months ago to come clean and he never. Listen, you slut. You know how things work around here and if the money isn't back in the next forty-eight hours shit will go down. You get me?"

Rachel's chest was rising frantically, and she was struggling to get her breath. The man at the side of her was nose to nose with her. His hand was raised and she knew she wasn't leaving without getting a good going over. Closing her eyes she felt a fist pound into her cheek. Her head crashed to the wall and for a moment she was unaware of her surroundings. This bastard was laying into her now. His foot swung into her legs as she melted to the floor. He made sure she wasn't getting back up in a hurry. Rachel curled into a tiny ball and tried protecting herself. She'd had beatings in the past and knew all about protecting her face and teeth.

Davo stood over her and his voice was chilling. "You tell your son to find me before I have to find him."

Rachel was in a bad way and blood was seeping from the side of her mouth as she lifted her head up. "He's fuck all to do with it. Mikey's in the big house, how could he have had your money away when he's in there?"

"Since when has he been in jail?" Davo asked.

Rachel tried to explain and hoped she convince these two that her son was innocent. Davo looked at his pal and inhaled, nostrils twitching. "Did you know he was doing a rip?"

"Nar, Davo, I'm as much in the dark as you are."

Davo bent down and gripped Rachel's cheeks again. His fat fingers digging deep into her flesh. "Which jail is he in? And, don't fucking lie to me because I'll find out. Your son owes me and I'll make sure he pays every single penny back. Does he think people don't talk around here?"

Rachel sat up and dragged her knees up to her chest, she was quivering and her lips were shuddering, she had no choice but to grass him up. "He's in the farms, Lancaster Farms."

Davo had connections and he was sure to know someone who was serving time at the prison too. The man nodded slowly and stroked the end of his chin. Standing to his feet he chuckled. "Either way, if my money doesn't land soon I'll be coming back for you. You make sure you tell him that right?"

At that moment Rachel would have done anything to save her bacon. She knew the script and nodded her head slowly. "Davo, Mikey has enough shit of his own going on. I think this is a big misunderstanding but I'll make sure he knows what you've said." The two men started to walk away but she didn't move an inch. She was in total shock.

Davo and his wing-man dived into a silver Vectra and screeched out of the car park. She kept her head low as they passed her and didn't make eye contact. Her hand pressed firmly against the ground, she used every bit of strength in her body to get up from the floor. A few people were there now and they were whispering about her. Rachel was limping as she passed them. She was fuming. "You could have given me a lift you fucking cowards. Fancy just standing there watching a woman get attacked by two men. Where is your backbone, no wonder this world is in the state it is." The onlookers watched her walk by but stayed silent. They huddled together and in their own hearts they knew she was right but who would ever step up at a time like that? They knew the code of conduct around these parts and have a go heroes never came out of it too well. Once you opened your mouth, you were involved. You were a marked person too. Yep, one wrong word and your home could be petrol bombed, your family beaten up or worse… the list was endless. Nobody ever got tangled up with anyone else's beef.

Rachel wiped her mouth with her sleeve. Her teeth were gritted tightly together as she dodged the cars as she crossed the road. She just wanted to get home now, away from any danger. This woman was a target, a sitting duck and she knew it wouldn't be long before they came to her house to smash it up. Her step quickened and she didn't even go to get Gary a weed from the dealer. He was going to go berserk, but her life was in danger, she was living on borrowed time. He could get to fuck.

Rachel's hands shook as she tried to place her key into the front door. At one point she booted the door thinking it was stuck or something. She was shrieking at the top of her voice, hysterical. "Gary, get the fuck out of that bed, shit's going down. We need to tell Mikey! We need to let him know he's not safe." Rachel slammed the front door behind her and staggered into the front room. She was screaming at the top of her voice and collapsed onto the sofa.

Gary sprinted into the front room, he was still half asleep. Rubbing his knuckles deep into the corner of his eyes he could see her properly for the first time. She was bleeding, bruised and in a right state. "Rachel, what's happened? Fuck me, you're cut. Babe, take a deep breath and tell me what the hell has happened."

She was hyperventilating, her teeth chattering together. Gary twisted his head around the room and ran to get a blanket. He wrapped it around her shoulders and cradled her in his arms. He was rocking her, trying his best to comfort her. "Sweetheart, come on. Just tell me what's gone on. Just take your time. Do you want me to light a cig for you?" Rachel nodded slowly and her breathing was starting to calm down. Gary sparked a cigarette up and sucked a few long drags of it before he passed it over to her. "Here, get that down you."

She held the fag like it was a piece of gold. Pushing it into her mouth she inhaled deeply and closed her eyes. The nicotine filtered her body and it seemed ages before she blew the smoke out from her mouth. "Davo knows about the money. Gary, we're not safe here. He'll be coming through our front door soon. He's tapped in the head, he's a fucking lunatic."

Gary blew a laboured breath and sat back on the sofa. "How do you know, who's said that?"

Rachel snapped and smashed her hand against the arm of the chair. "Look at the state of me Gary, we're not talking about any little dickhead here who we could sort out ourselves. Davo is a gun merchant and he wouldn't think twice about coming here and knocking the living daylights out of us. Look at the state of me. And this is just a warning."

Gary sniffed. His arse was twitching, he was by no means a fighter. Yeah, he could throw a few punches but when push came to shove he was a shit bag. He liked to big himself up as a bit of a street fighter but the fact was he was a nobody. He couldn't fight his way out of a paper bag.

"Well, say something then," Rachel stressed.

Gary was shell-shocked and he knew in his own head that when they came to the house they would leave him for dead. He was a man and what they done to his girlfriend was just a taster of what was to come in the future. Licking his dry cracked lips slowly, he sat in a deep trance. Rachel punched him in the arm and she was in no mood for him to be having second thoughts about being with her. He was like that Gary. Any real sign of danger and he was on his toes until it all calmed down. "Fuck that Rach. I mean, they'll fucking murder me if they come here. What was Mikey thinking when he got involved with them? Davo is a nutter we both know that right?"

Rachel clenched her fists tightly into two rounded balls. She knew he was getting ready to bail and leave her to it. She bolted from the sofa and stood facing him. "Don't you dare leave me to deal with this on my own Gary. I swear to you now, if that's your plan you can fuck right off. Every time this happens you're always the same. You're a shitbag. Go on, if you're going, fuck off now and save me the trouble of binning you."

Gary was fidgeting, he was trying to defend himself but he was struggling. "Rach, I'm going nowhere," he said unconvincingly, "It's just that I don't need all this shit in my life. I'll stand by you. Come on give me a bit of credit. As if I would just get off and leave you to deal with this on your own." Rachel shot a look over at him and knew he was chatting shit as per usual. He was never there when she needed him, he was a yellow belly. Rachel plonked down on the floor and Gary joined her. "If you know where the money is just give it him back. Simple isn't it?"

"No fucking way. Mikey would go ape. If we give the

money back then they'll know for sure he had them over. He can't win. I need to speak to Mikey, he'll know what to do."

"Where's the money. Please tell me it's not in the house. If they come here and find it we're fucked."

Rachel rubbed vigorously at her skin, she was itching at it, dragging it. For a split second she forgot who she was talking to and told him about the stash under the floorboards. Gary's eyes were wide open and he ran to the corner of the room. He was quickly bent over and his hands seemed eager to get his fingers on the money. Rachel grabbed him from behind just as he was about to pull the cash from under the floorboards. "Shift out of the way. I'll get it." Gary moved back slowly and he was watching her like a hawk. As the money was revealed he rubbed his palms together. "Rach, let me stash it somewhere safe. Let's face it, where can you hide it that's secure? If you leave it here they will find it for sure."

Rachel wasn't born yesterday and there was no way she trusted Gary. He was her boyfriend yes, but she didn't trust him as far as she could throw him and he was a right fat twat. "Just leave it with me, Gary. I know where I can put it. I'm not going to leave it in here, I'm not that daft. Do you think we should even be staying here with all this going on? It's only a matter of time before they're knocking on our door for the money," her voice went higher. "Fucking hell, when it rains in this house it pours."

Gary wasn't listening to a word she said, his eyes were fixed on the cash and he was watching every move she made. "Come on babes, let's get you cleaned up. Look at the state of your lip. It looks like your eye's going to be bruised. It's already swelling up."

Rachel placed the money on the table and walked to the mirror. "Bloody hell, you're right. I'll tell you what Gary, they had no qualms about giving me a crack either. The two of them set about me in the car park with no mercy whatsoever. God help you if they get their hands on you, they'll destroy you." He swallowed hard and blew a laboured breath. What the hell was she doing to him, he was as white as a sheet!

The mobile phone starting ringing and Rachel was in a panic looking for it. Gary found it first and looked at the caller ID. "It's Mikey, it's the number he rang from the other day."

Rachel answered the call and dispensed with the pleasantries. "Mikey, they know about the money. Davo and his mate give me a good hiding this morning at the post office. I swear to you son. This isn't going to stop here. I had to tell them you were in prison. He was going to kill me." Rachel held her ear to the blower and every now and then she gasped. Gary was sat on the edge of his seat and he was puzzled at what was being said. The phone call continued. "Right, son. I'll do just that. Don't you worry about me I'm as tough as nails when I need to be. Ring me later and I'll know a bit more." The call ended and Rachel stood thinking for a few seconds. "I'm going to get a shower to sort myself out. Put the kettle on and I'll be down in ten minutes." Gary nodded and watched as she left the room, he could hear her footsteps bouncing up the stairs.

Rachel stood looking in the bathroom mirror. She was a mess and Gary was right, her eye was swelling up. Touching her skin with the base of her finger she frowned as the pain filtered through her body. There was dried claret around her mouth and her chin was dark red as she scraped at it with her fingernail trying to remove it. The bathroom was clean and tidy and even the colour of the walls was pleasing to the eye; a soft yellow, a warming neutral colour. Rachel peeled her clothes from her haggard body. She must have only weighed about seven stone. Her ribcage was visible and her collarbone stuck out from the top of her chest. With every movement she made she moaned and groaned. Usually, Rachel only had a quick wash in the morning but today she had no other choice than to get a shower. Turning the dial on the wall, she made sure it was piping hot. Standing in the shower cubicle she scrubbed every inch of her skin. A bit over the top really, but she was making sure every bit of blood was gone from her body. The room was full of mist and she didn't notice Gary come into the bathroom. He was in and out at the blink of an eye. Once she was cleaned up she wrapped the bath towel around her head and stood in front of the mirror. There were deep purple blemishes all over her skin that looked sore to touch. There was a loud knocking at the front door and she froze, eyes open wide. Tip-toeing out from the bathroom she whispered down the stairs. "Gary, somebody is at the door." Her body edged down the staircase and she was doing her best to make sure she wasn't spotted. She tried again but a bit louder this time. "Gary, I said there is somebody at the bleeding door." There was still no reply. Rachel took a deep breath and peered around the corner in the hallway. Were her eyes playing tricks on her? She couldn't be sure if it was a man or a woman. The letterbox lifted and she recognised the voice.

"Rachel, it's Sarah."

Mikey's mother looked relieved as she opened it. She

was shivering and she was still wet. "Go in the front room. Gary must have fallen asleep. I'm just going to shove some clothes on and I'll be down in a minute. Tell him I hope he's brewed up. I'm gagging for a nice cup of tea after the morning I've had." Rachel ran back up the stairs and Sarah walked into the front room.

By the time Rachel was cleaned up there were two cups of tea on the table and Sarah sat smiling at her. "I've made us both a nice cuppa."

Rachel snarled and shot her eyes around the room. "Where's that lazy bastard, I asked him to do it for me ages ago!"

Sarah shrugged her shoulders. Rachel turned her head towards the kitchen. "Gary, bring some biscuits in with you. I think there are some chocolate ones left on the cupboard."

Sarah was confused. She'd been in the kitchen only a few seconds ago. There was no sign of Gary. "I think he must have gone out Rachel. He wasn't here when I came in." The words worked through Rachel's brain and all of a sudden she was running around the front room like a headless chicken. She stormed into the kitchen, doors could be heard being opened and then slammed shut. Rachel was screaming at the top of her voice. "Gary, Gary where are you?" Sarah sat on the sofa and seemed oblivious to what was going on. Rachel raced past her and headed upstairs, Sarah could hear her feet stomping about in every room. Rachel came back into the living room and her body folded in two. She was sobbing and holding her head in her hands. What the hell had happened? "He's done it. He's took the fucking money. I left it right there on the table and the dirty horrible twat has had me over. I knew not to leave it near him. I only went upstairs for a wash. Why has he done this to me?"

Sarah was used to these two arguing all the time and tried to brush it off. Mikey's mother always had a drama going on in her life and today was no different. She had to look concerned though, she couldn't just sit there and watch her crying like that. "Rachel, come on, get your drink. Gary will be back soon. I bet he's just nipped to the shops or something. Has he belted you too? Oh my God, look at the state of your eye."

She reached down into her handbag and pulled out a wet wipe. What she thought she was going to do with that, God only knows. Rachel pushed her away. She was livid now. "He's took all of it. Mikey's money has gone."

Sarah looked puzzled. Mikey always said he was potless, she must have heard her wrong. "I'm sure it's a bit of a mix up. How much do you think he's taken? I'll lend it you until he comes back if you want?" Sarah reached over for her bag and pulled out her brown leather purse. "Here you go, there's twenty pound. You can give it me back once he comes back."

Rachel pushed the money back at her and growled. "You barmy cow, you don't understand do you? Put your money away, I don't need it."

Sarah gasped, what was this woman's problem? "Why are you so nasty to me all the time? I was only trying to help. I don't know why I bother sometimes. Honest to God, you are such hard work."

Rachel realised that she had to explain further. She reached over and held her hands in hers. This was a first and never in her life had she seen Mikey's mother so weak. "Sarah, it was Mikey's money. The money for his future."

Sarah's ears pinned back and she listened carefully before she spoke. "Rachel, you need to explain because I'm not with it. What money are you talking about?"

Rachel grabbed her cigarettes from the table and knew she would have to come clean. Sarah would never tell anybody anyway, she knew that. "Mikey did a graft before he got sent down. It was a daft stupid thing... but you don't need to know the ins and outs of it. What's done is done. All you need to know is the trouble it's caused." Rachel was deflated, her son had been caught bang to rights and there was no way she could save him. Gary always called her son 'Goldenballs' and he would have been laughing somewhere now about his downfall. He was a no-good bastard and when she got her hands on him he was going to get a mouthful from her. She didn't need him in her life, she would move on and find someone who would stick by her through thick and thin. He was history in her eyes now, a dirty no-good sell-out. "Sarah, he's dropped a right bollock and these men aren't plastic gangsters, they're the real McCoy. Honest, they'll chop his balls off if they get their hands on him. Slice him up."

Sarah wasn't sure if this was some kind of sick joke. Rachel was always telling her things that weren't true and she didn't know whether to believe her or not. "Rachel, I never know when you're telling lies. If this is your way of trying to scare me off then you're doing a good job of it, let me tell you. I'm scared to death."

Rachel was in no mood for games and now Gary was gone there was no time to make enemies. She was alone and nobody had her back. "Sarah, you have to help me. They'll be here soon. They had hold of me today and told me they want to string our Mikey up. Ten grand's a lot of money and Davo won't stop until he's got back every penny that he's owed."

"Ten bleeding grand! Mikey nicked ten grand from this guy and now he wants it back?"

"For crying out loud, yes. I had hold of the money but Gary's nicked it just now. Bleeding hell, what aren't you getting here? I've told you how many times."

Sarah sat back in her seat with her arms folded tightly against her body. She looked over at Rachel and her face was bright red. "What the hell are we going to do? They'll find out I'm his girlfriend and then what? Oh my God, they could kill me too. I'm too young to die." Rachel gripped her by both arms and shook her with force, she was hysterical and going way over the top. "Mikey is sorting it out but until then we've got to keep a low profile. Is there anywhere we can both go until this blows over? I swear, Mikey's going to go sick when he's heard Gary has nicked his money, this is all going to go from bad to worse."

Sarah was the one in control now and for the first time Rachel listened to her. "My gran has a bungalow on the other side of Manchester. She's staying with us at the moment and it's empty. We could go there, we would be safe."

Rachel was relieved and for the first time she spoke to her with some respect. There was no attitude anymore. Sarah looked at her wrist watch. She had an idea. "Get some clothes ready. Just take all you need for now. This is a complete nightmare. Rachel, if they hurt one bone on my boy's body I'll kill them myself." The two of them started to run around the house gathering clothes together. They were sitting ducks now and the clock was ticking.

CHAPTER EIGHT

Mikey stood on the landing looking down at the main prison. He saw himself as a predator. Things happened at the blink of an eye in this place and he needed to be vigilant; everyone was up to no good - whispering, looking round corners, ducking and diving. This was a bad place to be in, nobody could be trusted. These bastards would have your eyes out and come back for the sockets if you weren't careful. Mikey's jeans hung low and the top of his boxers were on show. Not his usual Armani make though, these were prison issue ones that somebody else's knackers had been floating about in at some point. They were itchy and he was sure he'd caught something from them. His eyes shot down to a few inmates playing pool and socialising. It was his job now to suss out who was who. There had to be a main man, someone they all licked arse with, someone who called the shots. Each wing had one and he knew before bang up he would have located his target. This wing was full of hard men and he'd heard the name Frankie Warren being dropped a few times from a few lads he'd already spoken to. Mikey stood back from the landing as a man approached him from below. There he was, he knew it was him just by his presence on the corridor. Inmates stood with their backs against the wall and let him pass in silence. Mikey clocked Frank and stood close to the banister. He was a big cunt and he looked like he could have a go, probably a sted head, he thought. Mikey watched carefully as his wing men strolled at his side. Something was going down, he was sure of it. His neck stretched out. "Come on you bastards, nicely does it," he whispered under his breath. There it was, the switch. He nodded and sucked hard on his gums. He had all the information he needed now, this shit was going down. With a bounce in his step he walked downstairs to meet the others on the wing. Potter wasn't far behind him. He was pulling his jumper over his head and trying to look half decent. He'd had a crap night's sleep and was still uneasy in here. Mikey sat near the pool table and shouted over to the inmates already playing. "Put me and Potter down for the next game, lads. I'll whoop his arse and show him who's boss."

Within minutes the banter stopped and there was an eerie silence as Frank Warren arrived at Mikey's side. His warm breath tickled the side of his neck. He didn't know this kid from Adam but already he'd taken an instant dislike to him. Who the fuck did he think he was coming onto his turf and shouting the odds like that? This kid needed to be put in his place before he got ideas above his station. Frank's voice was deep and he was ready to cave this prick's head in if he gave him any back chat. "Oi, I'm on here next." All the other prisoners were watching now, each of them knowing that Frank was a crafty cunt and he could one-bomb Mikey at the first opportunity. This guy was ruthless and when you least expected it, he'd strike a blow. Mikey raised his eyes to meet Frank's, his ears pinned back slightly. There was no way he was letting this cock talk to him like this. He'd didn't give a fuck who he was or what reputation he had made for himself. Mikey had nothing to lose and everything to gain. There would be a new sheriff in town from now on and they were all just about to find that out right now...

Mikey cleared his throat. "Is that right? Have you put your name down?" This was the best action any of the inmates had seen for months. Frank Warren was a bully and if he was put on his arse today there would be a lot of celebrations going on behind closed doors. Each convict knew if Mikey knocked this fucker out, all their debts would be cancelled. No one would pay a second prized wanker. Frank would be shipped out for his own safety and never seen again. Good riddance to bad rubbish. Mikey had support now, allegiances turned in an instant as the tide suddenly changed. Frank didn't sense this change, or if he did he ignored it. He chuckled, trying to laugh off this imposter and made sure everyone could hear him. He still thought he was untouchable. Mikey was in the zone now, he was focused and already looking for his target's weakness.

"Listen up lads," Frank started, "have you heard Braveheart here asking me if I've put my name down for pool. Somebody word him up please before I lose my rag with him, fucking idiot."

One of Frank's acolytes walked over to Mikey, "Frank runs things around here," he said nervously, "he doesn't put his name down for anything. That's just the way it is." Mikey was far from impressed. What was up with this bunch of fairies? Why didn't someone put a pool cue over the prick's head? Warren needed to be put in his place – there were enough of them here, they should have wasted him but they were all shit scared. Was he that big and hard that nobody had ever tackled him before? Mikey Milne would show them how it was done. He'd never back down to this clown. Mikey smirked as Potter arrived at his side.

He knew he was dicing with death but he didn't care. The inmates were whispering now, side bets were being placed. It was going to go off, they were sure of it; a real fight, a one-on-one, a battle that could determine the new boss of the wing. This was a show not to be missed. An inmate whistled up the landing to a few others stood talking, no-one wanted to miss this.

They checked the coast was clear and put a look-out on the end of the corridor. The circle of men started to close in around them like a pack of wolves. If this was going to kick off, their job was to make sure no screws got to them before the beef was over. Mikey stood and went nose to nose with the main man, teeth clenched tightly together. Their foreheads touched, their eyes were locked. They were touching heads now, it was a test of strength. Potter stood with his back to the wall. What was he supposed to do? He didn't have a clue. Should he be preparing to jump Warren and help his mate if he was getting leathered? Potter looked confused. Should he stop the fight, whack the kid over his head with a chair? He'd seen stuff like this before on the TV and he knew a few moves he could throw into the mix if he needed to. For now though, he was frozen to the spot.

Frank's eyes were bulging from their sockets and he knew this inmate wasn't backing down. Mikey had balls and he was willing to go all the way. There was no way he was having the piss taken out of him. It wasn't his style. He had a name to protect, a wing to run. Winner takes all. Frank sank his fat fingers into Mikey's cheeks, squeezing at them, his warm stale breath on the end of his nose. "Fuck off nobhead before I put you on your arse in front of this lot. Don't ever think you can chat shit to me. Go on, do one." The other inmates were on edge. This had to happen fast, the screws would be here soon. Someone needed to throw a punch. The prisoners were sneering now, placing bets on who would knock who out.

"Fucking waste him Frank," his wingman yelled.

Mikey freed himself from Frank's grip. They were all looking at him now, he had to come back with something, make his mark. Potter was trying to support his mate and before he knew it he was shouting too. "Bust his nose Mikey, give him a dead leg." The inmates sniggered at Potter. Where the hell did he think he was? This wasn't a bleeding youth club scrap for fucks sake! This was serious shit. This was jail life. Mikey flicked his eyes rapidly and clocked a weapon near him. But, this was a one-on-one, no weapons were allowed; a bare knuckle fight. He might have bitten off more than he could chew, he'd not thought this through. He was going to get wasted if he didn't think quickly, he needed to pull something out of the bag. Here it was, Mikey reached the point of no return. He was ready to rumble. His fists curled into tight rounded balls at the side of his legs and his nostrils flared. It all happened so fast. Mikey steamed into Frankie and twatted him. The pair were going for it now; punches, kicks and head-butts were exchanged. Potter moved closer, he was steps away from the pool cue. Was this the right time to pick it up and steam in as well? He wasn't sure. If he moved in, Frankie's mates would as well...

Frankie was like a gladiator, he picked Mikey up and slung him against the table. His head crashed against it and it looked like it was all over. No, wait, Mikey was back up and his eyes were menacing as he ran at his opponent at full pelt. He was rapid and each punch connected with his opponent. The inmates heckled and some of them started to bang objects on the walls. "Fight, fight, go on, kill the fucker." Potter chewed on the end of his fist. Mikey wasn't giving up without a fight, he was giving it all he'd got. He was a crank, he was biting and mauling his victim, he fish-hooked his mouth at one stage, it was a superb move that hadn't been seen for a long time in the big house. The inmates were alive, they were ready to kick off and smash the wing up. What did they have to lose? Frankie might have been bigger than Mikey but the younger man was fit as a fiddle and agile, he dodged Frank's punches and stung Warren with his own. Inmates gathered around the pair of them, this wasn't going to last much longer. Mikey had Frankie on his arse in minutes and was kicking fuck out of him, pummelling his fist deep into his face. "Go on Mikey, give it him," Potter screamed at the top of his voice. His eyes were dancing with madness, his head was in the game. He'd never felt excitement like this before, he was alive and part of something.

Alarm bells were ringing now. The footsteps of the screws pounded ever closer. The inmates backed off. The show was over anyway and there was nothing much left to see. With one final kick Mikey took his role as the main man on the wing. Frank was out for the count, sparked. Mikey growled and let out a roar from the pit of his stomach as he banged his fist onto his chest. He'd earned his stripes now, they now knew what he was all about. He wasn't all mouth. He was a hard fucker. Who'd have thought it? What a result, there was no way in this world you would have backed Mikey against Frank. Gasping for his breath Mikey was quickly rugby tackled to the floor by two screws, he fell like a sack of spuds and was soon pinned down. The screws were eager to get the cuffs on to restrain him; there was shouting as inmates hurled abuse at the officers. It was kicking off now on the wing and it might take hours for it to calm down.

Potter was up in arms and ran to Mikey's side but he didn't get a word in because the screws pushed him out of the way and started to drag them down to the block. The pair of them were forced down the corridor at speed. The poor fucker, he was done for. Mark was on B-wing now with Smithy by his side and they were making sure all the inmates were back behind their doors. There could have been a riot; chairs smashed, windows going through. It was a struggle at first but with a bit of extra manpower they were getting there. At last the prisoners were doing what they were told. Frank Warren was still on the floor receiving urgent medical attention. He was coming round now and his eyes were twitching slightly, he was fucked up. What a disgrace he was, he'd been beaten by a newcomer, his empire was in tatters. How could he ever come back from this? He was a laughing stock now. His reign was surely over. From this day forward nobody would listen to a word he had to say anymore, he was just another wannabe. There was only one option for him, he had to be shipped out. He would go on the vulnerable prisoner's wing, what a disgrace this was.

"Fuck me, loosen the cuffs, they're digging into me," Mikey howled at the top of his lungs. He was right too, his skin was starting to bleed and the colour of his skin was changing.

The screws at the side of him were not listening to a word he said, they were ragging him about. "Shut it Milne, let's see what kind of a big man you are once you're down the block," one growled at him. This convict was a trouble causer and they knew the moment he had landed in the jail that their work was cut out for them. Mikey was cut on the side of his cheek and bright red blood was seeping from a deep gash but what did that matter now, he was a winner. He'd taken the big bastard down and made a name for himself in the jail. Cuts and bruises were the least of his worries. Mikey was flung into a cell and the door slammed shut behind him. It was just something he was used to nowadays. The screws were stood outside and he could hear every word they were saying about him. "He needs sorting out. We should put his name down for a ship out, who's his personal officer? I need to have a word with him. I can't be arsed with all this shit again. We've only just got the wing sorted out and that prick in there thinks he can mess it all up. Look at the state of me, I'm sweating my nuts off."

Mikey smirked as he held his ear to the door. He was used to people talking behind his back and didn't give it a second thought. He'd done what he had set out to do and that was all he was arsed about. Mikey started to calm down and licked the blood from the end of his knuckles. Was he really fucked up in the head or was he just misunderstood? It said on his personal file that he was a violent prisoner but didn't most of the inmates have an evil streak in them? It was the environment they were living in, it changed men forever. There were only two charges of assault on his criminal record and, could you really call them violent crimes when he had slapped a youth around his head and took his mountain bike from him? They had it marked down as assault and robbery on his notes but not a word was said that it was nothing more than a slap, he had just clipped the kid and got off with his bike. Yeah, he robbed the bike but he'd wanted one for ages and this rich toffee-nosed kid was riding one about without a care in the world. He even left it outside the shop when he went inside, he didn't care about his possessions. His family had more money than sense. Mikey lay down on the bed. The block was getting to be his second home now. No sooner had he left there than he was back again. It didn't faze him, it was what it was, pure bang up and more thinking time.

Mark sat with his colleagues around a table in the cafeteria. Their shift was over and they were just finishing off a coffee. Barry, the one who'd nicked Mikey earlier, marched to the table and gasped. "Mikey Milne, he's your lad isn't he?"

Mark hated this tosser's attitude already and snarled at him, "and what?"

"Either sort him out or get him out of this jail. Two minutes he's been here and he's fucked everything up. Frank Warren is on the hospital wing in a bad way. A broken nose and ribs they think. He's not with it at all, he's still in shock." Mark was sick to death of this smart arse. If ever there was a problem on B-wing this shit-stirrer was always there knocking at his door about how he should control the inmates on there.

Smithy sniggered and looked away. He was aware of the beef between these two and didn't want to get involved. Mark could hold his own, he didn't need any help from him. He folded his arms tightly across his chest and watched the fun and games begin. "Listen Barry, crack on with your own shit and stop sticking your nose on my wing. I will sort Mikey out, so just back off. And, if I remember rightly pal, am I right in saying Frank Warren was on your wing first before you carted him over to me?"

Barry stuttered and loosened the collar on his shirt. "He was, but it was none of my doing why he was moved. Talk to the governor about that, he was the one who made the decision on that one not me." This guy was lying through his teeth. Everybody knew Barry was a smacked arse and if any bit of trouble came his way he was banging on the main man's door asking for help. Barry was too old for the game now. Like a lot of the other officers who worked there he was waiting out his final years here before retirement and a fat pension. He didn't need the aggravation, the fights, the endless rows and banter between inmates. He wanted a quiet life.

Mark knew he had him where he wanted him and he turned his head slowly towards Smithy. "Isn't that right mate? Everybody knows about Barry's snide meeting with the governor. You'd better be careful, people will start getting the wrong idea about you. Nobody likes a suck-up."

Barry was up in arms. He'd never snitch on his work mates and he was more than willing to put his neck on the line to prove it. His cheeks were bright red now as he rested his body on the wall behind him. How dare anyone blacken his name in this joint? He was a team player, there was no way in this world he was a Judas. Mark knew just by looking at him that Barry was backing down. His tone changed completely and he sat next to Mark patting him on top of his shoulder. He backtracked. "No offence meant, Mark. All I'm saying is can you have a word with Mikey? He'll listen to you. You have a way of getting through to anyone with a chip on their shoulder."

Mark smirked and licked his lips in a cunning manner. He could tell a brown-noser a mile off and Barry was that far up his arse it was untrue. His workmate was right though, in his time as a prison officer he had been able to reach out to some of the most notorious criminals inside the jail. He had a knack of getting them to drop their defences to reveal the real person inside. But that had been many moons ago when he was a bit wet behind the ears, when he was new to the job and still had a faith in people that told him everyone deserved a second chance. His finger stroked the scar on his cheek, touching the deep crease, remembering how he had been scarred for life. He had been a good screw in his day but the constant dramas in this place had worn him down and made him hard on the inside. He could never be soft again, it was too dangerous but who would help these sick twisted fuckers if he gave up on them? He was fighting with his own conscience and a part of him was realising that just because one convict turned on him in the past, he couldn't take it out on the rest of the youths who came through the door. He needed to think this through, he'd sleep on it and address it in the morning.

Smithy stood to his feet and put his coat on. "Clocking off time guys. I don't know about you two but I'm ready for the knacker's yard. This shift has written me off."

Mark reached his hand out towards Barry, he'd been a bit harsh with him and was regretting his foul mood. This man was harmless and he didn't deserve the way he'd spoken to him. "Don't worry Barry. I'll have a word with Mikey. You're right, it's my job to see what's going on with him. I'll crack on with it tomorrow."

Barry was relieved, he hated a bad atmosphere in the

workplace. He shook Mark's hand and walked out of the cafeteria with them both. Another day, another dollar. The shift was over.

CHAPTER NINE

Rachel gazed out of the window at Sarah's gran's house. It was a nice compact bungalow out of the way in a respectful rural area. There were so many plants in the garden, a bloom of bright colours. This was nothing like her garden - that was a jungle. Fuck all grew there except weeds and the odd dandelion. Rachel had never been into gardening, although sometimes she wished she had green fingers. It looked so calming when she watched other people doing it and thought it could be the answer to her stress levels. It was too much like hard work though, a headache in her eyes; cutting grass, pruning flowers, feeding the lawn. No, she was alright with her barren garden. The cycles and old motorbikes in her front garden added culture onto her lawn, at least that's what she told everybody who commented on it. The housing were always onto Rachel about tidying it up but she never listened, she told them she'd do it when she was ready, she never did. But today, for some strange reason, she was fixated on every flower and petal she cast her eyes on. She loved flowers and the scents from them, sweet calming aromas. The last time anyone had ever bought her flowers was longer than she could remember. They were all tight cunts her former lovers and they wouldn't part with a fart, buying her flowers was the last thing on their minds and they would much rather have shared a spliff with her instead of giving her a romantic gesture. Gary had given her the odd bunch but he never paid for them. He was a right tight arse. I mean, proper tight. The kind of guy who would do anything rather than put his hand in his pocket, he was as tight as a fish's arse. At first Rachel thought that he was a romantic guy. Every night he was coming home with a new bunch of flowers for her, and we're talking huge spray of flowers here, not just a few stalks. She thought he was madly in love with her. Nobody had ever showed her love this way before. It was only when she read a card shoved down the side of the cellophane wrapper that she uncovered what a low-life sly sad bastard her boyfriend really was. She had to laugh when she thought back about it though, he'd pulled the wool right over her eyes. What a hard-faced fucker he was. "Rest in peace, Auntie Mabel. We love and miss you. Love Janice and family," it read. That night she steamed right into him and whacked the dead woman's flowers right over his napper. She knew it was too good to be true. He was a scruff with no morals or respect for the dead.

Rachel thought about the next time she would ever receive any flowers. It would probably be when she was six feet under. Who would turn up to her funeral anyway? Everyone she had ever loved had turned against her. They'd probably spit on her grave, never mind place flowers on it. Rachel was feeling sorry for herself again and sniffed hard as she scratched the end of her nose. She turned and looked at Sarah. "It smells of old people in here. You know like pensioners pissing everywhere."

Sarah's jaw dropped low. Was she hearing her right or what? She was getting told. How dare she call her gran's humble abode? "You cheeky cow, you can go back home if you say stuff like that. My gran does not smell of urine. Are you sure your nose isn't too near your own arse."

Rachel realised what she'd just said and tried to backtrack. "No, I mean, well, it smells a bit stale in here that's all, just saying."

"My Gran hasn't lived here for over two months so it probably needs a bit of a spring clean. If you're that concerned you can help me freshen things up. I'll open the windows and let some air in."

Rachel sniggered, she never did know when to keep her mouth shut and she'd dropped a right bollock here. Sarah opened the windows in the front room and the morning air circled in; a crisp, fresh breeze. It was summer time and just a few white fluffy clouds hung in the blue sky. Rachel loved clouds, there was just something about them that mesmerised her. She would stand watching them all day if she could. She liked to watch them move about in the sky and sometimes she was sure she could see faces inside them. As a small child she always thought that the clouds were the stairway to heaven. Silly, I know, but that's what she believed. Rachel imagined in her head that after she passed away she would bounce on every white fluffy cloud until she reached the white pearly gates to meet her maker. Part of her still believed that was true and it gave her inner-peace to know there was another life after death. Perhaps, her next life would be better than this one, she wouldn't be rotten to the core anymore. And, that's what people said about her you know, rotten. Her own mother had said it on more than one occasion to her so it must have been true.

Agnes was never one for holding anything back and she'd told her own flesh and blood that she would be better off dead. Sad but true. Rachel touched the windowpane with the tips of her fingers as if she could move the clouds in the sky. Her finger glided about gracefully and she seemed lost in the moment as Sarah came back into the room. "So, what now? You can't stay here forever, somebody will find out. My gran's neighbours are very observant and they will report any strangers at the house to my father as soon as they see them." Rachel was still in a deep trance and her finger was still moving about on the window. Sarah shot a look at her and raised her voice slightly higher. "Rachel, did you hear me. I said you can't stay here for long?"

She shuddered and turned slowly, hairs on the back of her neck standing on end. "Yeah, I've heard you. I'll sort something out. I just need a few days to get my head back together, that's all, them bastards don't scare me."

Sarah plumped the cushions up on the sofa and sat down for a few minutes. "What are you going to tell Mikey? Do you think it's best that you try and find Gary first and see what he has to say for himself?" Sarah was eager to hear her answer and sat playing with her fingers.

"That prick will be miles away from here now. He's not daft. He won't show his face in Manchester again for a long time. I should have known better. He's always been a shady cunt." Sarah watched Rachel carefully. She was quite attractive under all that untidiness. Her deep blue eyes held so much sadness, Sarah knew this woman had suffered but could she ever change? Was she too long in the tooth to ever turn her life around? Rachel was a bag of rags and you could tell her hygiene level was minimal. She was the sort of woman who would have body odour and a sweaty biff, you know the sort.

Sarah pulled a sour expression and let out a laboured breath. In her own head she thought she could save the world and help people, but how can you help someone who doesn't want to be saved? Rachel would rather spit in her eye than admit she'd failed in life. Sarah cringed a little and tested the water. "Shall we have a girly day, Rachel? I mean, a day of me and you bonding? We've not really spent any time getting to know each other have we and this could be a blessing in disguise for us. We can paint our nails, have a manicure, a facial and I can style your hair for you."

Rachel nearly choked. A fucking beauty day! Was this girl on this planet or what? Did Rachel really look like one of these women who gave a flying fuck about her appearance and how she smelt? She was a soap-dodger, a sweaty skank. Sarah rubbed her hands together and before she could get a word out in protest she was by her side holding her hand, examining her nails. "Eww, these have never been touched for years? Look at your cuticles growing over your nails."

Rachel cast her eyes down to her digits and watched as Sarah started pushing some skin from her thumb downwards. "Ouch, you barmy cow that hurts. Just leave me alone. Look, you've made it bleed now."

Sarah smirked and wasn't giving up that easily. "Just relax will you. I've got some products in my car to sort you out. Why don't you go and have a shower and wash your hair and I'll sort the rest out?"

Rachel wasn't sure how to handle this situation. The girl was only trying to be nice and she knew that her heart was in the right place and she was only trying to win her over... but a bonding day! She wasn't really sure about that. Sarah left the room and headed down the garden path towards her car. Rachel lifted her arm up and whiffed the edge of her hairy armpit. This was the bog of eternal stench for sure. What a skank she was! She hummed, she actually smelt like the crack of a homeless person's arsehole. Her cheeks were beaming and for the first time ever she admitted to herself that she needed a good scrub, jet washing even. Rachel wasn't one for soaking in the bath but today she was going to make the most of it and pamper herself. She was a walking disgrace.

Sarah had been ages and she'd decided to nip to the shops to get some treats. She was stood over the stove melting a block of thick creamy chocolate inside a bowl over a pan of boiling water. She clocked Rachel coming out of the bathroom and sniggered. "You just take a seat in the front room. You're going to love what I've got for us. It's going to blow your mind."

Rachel was dressed in one of Sarah's grandmother's housecoats and her cheeks were bright red. She'd heard what Mikey's girlfriend had shouted after her and wondered what on earth she was going to bring into the room. It needed to be some strong shit if it was ever going to blow her mind. Was she forgetting her drug use in the past or what? Rachel smirked to herself and plonked down on the sofa. For the first time in ages she actually felt clean. She'd even trimmed her private bits too. Her big hairy beaver was now nicely shaped and half the size it used to be. Sarah was in a fluster as she came into the room with her hands full. "Ouch, it's boiling hot. Quick, get hold of this before it burns my fingers off." Rachel sprung up from her seat and grabbed a few packets from her grip, ducking and diving and scared she might drop it. The melted chocolate was now neatly placed in the centre of the table with steam coming out from the top of it. Sarah shoved a wooden stick through a pink marshmallow and dipped it deep into the bowl. The chocolate oozed from it as she passed it over to Rachel. "Try one, go on, it's pure heaven."

Rachel was unsure, it looked so sickly and not her usual cup of tea but she had to try it just to be polite. Her mouth was wide open as she shoved the food into her mouth. The corners of her mouth started to rise. With a gob full of chocolate she gave the thumbs up to Sarah. "This is heaven, what's it called again. Get me another ready, these are bleeding lovely." Sarah was over the moon, at last the old hag had raised a smile. They both sat munching and Rachel was going for gold, what a greedy cow she was, she devoured at least ten of them one after another. Rachel fell back onto the sofa and rubbed at her stomach. "I'm done in now, look at the size of my gut." She pressed down on her housecoat and there it was, a little pot belly. Rachel had chocolate all over the sides of her mouth. She looked like a little kid. "All I need now is a bifta. Do us a favour and just pass me my fags from the table queen. I honestly can't move."

Sarah smirked, had she heard her right, did she call her queen? This was a breaking point for sure. Without hesitation she got her fags. Rachel popped one in the side of her mouth and slung her feet up onto the sofa. Her head fell back and she closed her eyes slowly as she sucked hard on her cigarette. Smoke hoops oozed from her mouth and her jaw clicked slowly. "I love a fag, I do. I know I'm not supposed to say stuff like that because it's unhealthy for you to smoke but it really chills me out."

Sarah raised her eyebrows and sucked on the corner of her lip. Mikey smoked too and she hated the smell of it if she was being honest. She would never kiss her boyfriend if he'd just had a cig, no way, she always made sure he brushed his teeth. It was a hanging habit and she couldn't see why people would choose to pollute their bodies with so many toxins. Sarah sat on the chair facing Mikey's mother. Once the food had settled in their stomachs she was going to give her a makeover. Rachel was still puffing her head off on the sofa. Sarah was such a nosey cow and she just couldn't help herself. "I know it's none of my business but why don't you try and make friends with your family. It must be so lonely for you with nobody to back you up when you need them, especially at times like this?"

Rachel twisted her body and lay on her side. She was in no mood to go over her life story and she tried to keep it simple. "No point, been there and done that over the years. Our Cath still speaks to me a bit but that's only to be polite. I can see it in her eyes that I repulse her. She's not said that to me directly but I know. It's my own fault really, what can I expect?"

Sarah was thankful she'd not told her to fuck off and thought she'd crack her one for being nosey. "But, that was then, maybe things have changed now. I mean, your mother must miss you and Mikey."

Rachel was getting agitated, she hated talking about stuff like this and her blood started to boil. This was her weak point and whenever anyone mentioned her mother's name it always got her back up. "Turn it in will you. That old trout has never given a shit about our Mikey. For crying out loud she let him go into care. I was locked away in that hellhole and the selfish bitch let him be taken from his family. I'll never forgive her for that. I swear on my life." Rachel's eyes began to cloud over and for a second it looked like she was going to burst into tears. Her tone lowered and she sat playing with her fingers. "He was a kid for crying out loud. She must have known what those places were like. And yet, just to have a go at me, to prove her point, she sold her own grandson out. Fucking bad news that is! I don't care what anyone says, it is."

Sarah was fascinated by the way this woman had lived her life and delved deeper. She wanted to get inside her head and see what made her tick. She was playing with fire and Rachel could have switched on her at any time. "But, your sister, you even said yourself that she still speaks to you. At times like this you need to build bridges and forget the past. Why don't you make the effort to go and see her? You can't turn back time but you can make a better future."

Rachel sat thinking, twiddling her hair. If the truth was known she did miss her sister. They used to have a right laugh when they were younger and they had each other's back. Nobody fucked with them. Okay, she'd hurt her, stolen from her and said some things that she could never take back but was that really the only reason she'd never made contact with her sibling? Sarah was on her high horse now... "Family means everything to me Rachel and without them I don't know what I would do. My dad's a bit irate sometimes but he means well. I love all my family warts and all."

Rachel was hiding something and it was on the tip of her tongue, whatever it was she wasn't ready to disclose it just yet. There was a silence and Rachel sat thinking. She closed her eyes slightly as she started to remember the days gone by. "Our Cath blames me for what happened. She never listened to my side of the story. It was all him. He was a dirty bastard and I just told her he was a wrong' un from the start. It's not my fault she ended up marrying the tosser. Our Cath said it's all in the past but she watches every movement he makes when I'm in the same room as him."

Sarah's eyes were wide open and she was on the edge of her seat. This was better than any other gossip she'd heard in ages. Families always held secrets and it was only when the shit hit the fan or when they were pissed that the truth came out. She was bursting with excitement, she couldn't hide it. "So, are you saying you had a fling with your sister's husband?" Rachel hated to admit it but yes, she did have a bit of slap and tickle with Cath's fella. A passionate few dates it was, where he fucked her brains out for hours and this all happened while her sister was working. She was a dirty slag and she should have never crossed the line. Sisters before misters it should have been.

Rachel was opening up now. Well, she was once Sarah cracked open a bottle of red wine. She topped her glass up and passed it over to her, she was fuelling her up, loosening her mouth. "It was him who come onto me. Our Cath was out working and he was sat waiting for her at my mam's. He was always flirting with me and if I'm being honest, he was a dirty rat. But, he got me at a really bad time in my life and the drink didn't help either. John was a charming fucker. Honest, he was drop dead gorgeous. He had the body and the gift of the gab. I was putty in his hands."

Sarah sipped at her vino and stroked her neck. This was a passionate affair and the more she was hearing, the more she was aroused. She'd heard from friends before about having affairs, secret meetings, the forbidden fruit, the fantastic sex, but as of yet she'd never had one herself. It wasn't right, people got hurt. Sarah had always declared she was a one-man woman and liked to think her loyalty to any man she dated was something special. Rachel was getting down to the nitty-gritty now, the real reason her sister had disowned her. Her head dipped as she stared into the bottom of her glass, slowly running her finger around the rim. "I was pissed out of my head. And, there he was, ready for the taking. I was fed up and just wanted to feel good about myself. I only wanted a kiss, nothing more. Someone to show me they cared. But, we just got carried away and before we knew it we were having sex. None of us heard the door opening and there she stood... I will never forget the look in her eyes," Rachel choked up and it took a while for her to compose herself. "I'd hurt her so badly, done her right in. Cath just looked at us both and closed the door behind her and left the room. It would have been easier if she battered me, kicked fuck out of me, but all she did was give me the silent treatment." A chill passed over her and goose pimples started to appear all over her arms, she was spooked. Her back was up now and her grip tightened around her glass. "Of course that twat blamed me for it all. He's dead smarmy and one of these days he'll get what's coming to him. She'll see what he's all about. Cath thinks he's innocent but he's a dark horse. I've heard loads of stories about him with other women but if I told her, she'd just turn a blind eye to it all. She's like that, our Cath, she just likes to think she has the perfect life." Sarah was caught up in the whole episode now but Rachel switched the subject so quickly that there was no going back. "You're right, you know. I should try and fix stuff with them all. I'm not getting any younger am I?"

This was just what Sarah wanted to hear, she loved a happy ending and hoped in the future that Rachel would have her family back onside. She jumped out of her seat after she swigged the last bit of wine from her glass. "Come on then, let's get you sorted. You can't let them see you like this, let's get you all dolled up." The makeover began and the two of them were actually laughing together for a change.

★

Mark Fulton sat alone in his front room. The TV was on low and in his hand he held a letter from his mortgage provider. The idiot had done it this time, he'd blown the money Smithy had given him to pay the arrears. What a complete dickhead he was! How on earth was he going to get out of this one? This was serious, he was going to be homeless. The clock on the wall ticked loudly in his ear and as he stared at the debt letter his eyes filled up. Dropping the piece of paper from his hand he plonked onto the sofa and let out a laboured breath. Mark froze, there was noise coming from outside the room. He could hear her coughing. It was his old ball and chain stood at the door. This woman had a face like thunder and no wonder, every time he looked at her he wanted to slap her, she was so cocky. "Are you coming to bed or are you staying down here all bleeding night again?"

Mark twisted his head towards her and snarled. He could easily have jumped up and strangled the moaning cow, stopped her breathing, ended the misery of her constant moaning. He turned over to his side and plumped the pillow behind his head. "I'll come up when I'm ready. I'm just going to watch a bit of football."

Tracy came into the room with a hand fixed firmly placed on her hips. "Don't you mean you will be watching more porn like you always do? I'll tell you what Mark, I didn't sign up for all this crap and if you come home one night and my bags are packed, don't be surprised."

Mark bolted from the sofa and ran at her with clenched teeth. She was getting it now, he was sick to death of this moaning bitch and he was telling her how it was. Night after night she was pecking his head and he was ready to blow. "What are you saying? Me, come to bed with you. And what, watch you sleep, fucking snoring your head off like a fat pig. Yeah, I will be watching some porn tonight just for the record. I've got to get my kicks somewhere haven't I? It's like shagging a wet lettuce, having sex with you." Mark used his flat palm to push her away from him before he punched her lights out. He snarled at her. "What happened to you ay? You used to like sex, every night we used to have a bang and now I'm lucky to get a feel of your tits. A frigid bitch you are! Oh, what was is it you always say to me? I've got another fucking headache. I'm just too tired, let's leave it tonight Mark."

Tracy's eyes were wide open, she was gobsmacked. How dare her own husband talk to her like this? Her eyes filled up and she pointed her finger deep into his chest. She was livid. "Oh, so it's like that is it? And, for your information Casanova, I bleeding hate having sex with you too. You're like a mad, crazed animal, there's no tenderness, no kissing, just wham bam thank you mam. Sex is crap." She took a deep breath and looked him straight in the eyes Tracy looked him up and down in a disgusting manner. Silence. Go on girl, she was holding her own now and going to put him in his place. She walked further into the room and sat on the edge of the sofa and smirked. She was the one calling the shots now and he was getting a mouthful. Why should she have to listen to his bullshit anyway? Two can play that game, she was giving him a taste of his own medicine. His face dropped. He'd opened a right can of worms now. She continued. "Why are we even together? We don't do anything anymore. We're like two pensioners. All the things we used to do, you hate now. So, come on, you tell me what you want from me, because I don't have a bleeding clue. I know what I want," she paused and sucked in a large mouthful of air before she delivered the killer blow. "I want a fucking divorce."

Mark went bright red and he marched around the front room like a headless chicken. "Yeah me too. There you go, I've said it now. You make my skin crawl and that fucking droning voice of yours goes right through me. And I tell you something for nothing should I? You've turned into your mother." This was below the belt, he knew how much she loved her mother. Tracy stood up and picked up the piece of paper from the table, she hadn't read it yet, she was too busy telling her husband what she thought of him. "Go on, call my mam like you always do. I'm used to it by now, call my sister too and our Simon. You can't hurt me anymore. I'm immune to you."

Mark stormed into the kitchen to get a cold drink. He was sweating and ready to burst. Tracy blew a laboured breath and started to read the letter in her hand. Her jaw dropped and she was speechless. She yelled after him. "So, this is what it's really about. What the hell have you done with the money? Oh, don't tell me. The fucking bookies again." Mark was back in the room and he was white. He'd seen the letter in her hand and his head dipped, his secret was out. He was calming down now and as per usual he started to regret his words but she'd wound him up, she knew what he was like once his temper blew. There was no forgiveness this time, there was no going back. "Go on you tell me why the mortgage hasn't been paid? Don't lie. For once in your life just tell me the truth." Tracy's body folded in two and she was sobbing. Her home was everything, she thought she would have lived here until the day she died.

Mark sat near her and dropped his head into his hands. He was stuttering, ashamed. "I'm sorry. I need help, I just can't help it anymore. I try so hard to stop the gambling but it's got a grip of me."

Tracy looked over at him and her fingers started to unfold from the clenched fist, she loved her husband so much but he was just a dickhead sometimes. Her hand reached over and touched his knee. "We can't lose the house, Mark. It's our dream, it's all we ever wanted. If the house goes then there's nothing left." He lifted his head up and a single tear ran down the side of his cheek. Yes, she was a moaning cow but deep down he did still love her. If she left, what would he have then? Nothing – fuck all and plenty of it. His head was all over the place and he was panicking. "I'll get the money, somehow, some way. I'll make it right. Don't leave me, just give me a bit of time. If you go I'll end it. I swear. You're all I've got." Here it was, the real Mark, not the big man he to liked to portray. He was just a weak man who wasn't coping.

Tracy kissed the top of his head and ran her fingers through his hair slowly. "I don't know if we can fix it anymore. I'm sick of worrying every day about the next payment. We need a miracle."

Mark was desperate and he held his hands on her cheeks. "Baby, don't go. Just give me a bit of time. I'll sort it out. We won't lose the house. Honest, trust me, just give me a chance to make things right." The two of them held each other tightly. The pressure was on now, he had to get the money from somewhere otherwise he'd lose it all. His wife, his home, everything he loved.

CHAPTER TEN

Mikey Milne was back on his landing; he was the man now, the top dog. He'd proven what he was all about and at last these muppets on the wing were going to give him the respect he deserved. The battle with Frank let them all know he was game as fuck and if they wanted a piece of him, all they had to do was ask. As he held his personal belongings in his hand, he marched along B-Wing like a soldier returning from war. Head held back, chest pushed forward, smirking. The other inmates nodded respectfully towards him and each of them knew, without asking, that things on the landing were about to be turned around. This new kid was sly and cunning and none of them fancied getting into any kind of beef with him, he was a dodgy cunt who was capable of anything. They'd whispered to each other behind his back as he strolled past them. None of them was ready to challenge him yet.

Potter came out of his pad and smiled as he spotted Mikey returning. He was a soft fucker and you could tell by his body language that he'd missed his pad mate's company. Being banged up alone was bad news, no one to talk to, no laughter, just pure silence. Of course Potter had tried to amuse himself and he even tried to make a few new friends on the wing but without Mikey, no one gave him the time of the day. He was a prick in their eyes. Why the fuck should they bow down to him just because his pad mate could swing a few punches; no, they owed him fuck all. Since Mikey had been down the block, Potter had had a lot of thinking time on his hands and he was more than ready to fight to the death for this guy. It was an honour in his eyes and he would take the role seriously. So what if it was against his morals, this was prison life and he was going to do what he had to in order to keep his head above water. Never in his life had he ever been part of anything like this, he had always hid in the background like a shivering wreck. With Mikey as the daddy on the landing he would earn the respect of the prisoners. No longer would they look at him like he was a big nothing. From now on they would respect him and bow down to him, kiss his arse and do as he said.

Brendan Mellor ran to Mikey's side and casually punched his fist into his chest. This prisoner looked like he had just come from a concentration camp, he was so thin, at least half the size he used to be. "Fuck me Mikey, I'm glad your back. Shit's been going down on the landing and I need to word you up about a few things when you get settled back in."

Potter heard the conversation and chirped up. He was the sidekick here, nobody else. "I'll word him up Mellor. No need for you to be involved. I've got his back." Brendan shot a look to Mikey. Was he hearing this kid right or what? The plonker better keep his mouth shut before he decked him! Brendan's friendship with Mikey went back years, not a few weeks like this runt. And, if anyone was pulling rank here, he was. Brendan was fuming. This arsehole was getting told, he was holding nothing back. "Mikey, have a word with this specky cunt will you? Tell him me and you are running the shit on here now, not him." Potter looked puzzled.

They watched Mikey for an answer. Here it was; whose camp was he in? He had to decide. He took a deep breath and scratched the side of his nose. "Brendan, chill out will you. Potter is my pad mate and I need someone who's watching my back twenty-four-seven. You're over the other side of the wing. What good are you to me if it kicks off?"

Brendan choked up, what a fucking sell-out his mate was. All the promises he'd made about looking after him had gone out of the window. There was no way he was taking this lying down, he was getting told. "Mikey, we're a team me and you. Don't give me all this shit about somebody watching your back around the clock. If you're picking that bean sprout over me then just say it. I'd rather know."

Mikey started to enter his pad and both of them followed closely behind him, hanging on his every word. Mikey Milne stepped inside the cell and smiled as he looked around. He was glad to be back. But what was this, white paper hanging from one side of the room to the other. Potter had made him a welcome home banner out of toilet roll. His heart was in the right place but you didn't do shit like this in prison, what the hell was he thinking? Prisoners would get the wrong idea about their relationship and the banter would start. There were lots of gay relationships formed behind the prison walls, some that were never ever spoken about. Nobody would admit it but even a few of the straight lads would have a suck from the landing slag when times were hard. Most of them just covered the guy's head with a towel or a blanket, anything, so they couldn't see the man's head sucking hard on their cocks. It was well known every landing had someone to give oral sex out.

Nobody batted an eyelid either, it was just the done thing. Mikey had never had a crunch off another man but he'd said it in jest in the past that if ever he got a ten-year stretch or more, he'd seriously consider a bit of oral sex with a gay inmate. He wouldn't have anal sex though, no way. No matter if he was the one giving it he would never do that, it was sick and twisted in his eyes, memories of a past he was trying to forget.

Brendan covered his mouth with his hand as he clocked the welcome home banner. He was giggling and making sure everybody heard what he had to say. "What the fuck is all that about? Mikey are you slinging one up Potter or what?" Mikey turned slowly and growled, the vein at the side of his neck pumping rapidly. So what, Brendan was his pal on the outside, there was no way he was listening to stuff like this, it made his stomach churn. This was how rumours started and he wanted to nip it in the bud before all the lads started to think he was a poo-poker. "Brendan, sort your fucking head out will you. Potter has just done it to show he's missed me that's all. He doesn't mean anything by it, do you our kid?"

Mikey rubbed his hand over his the inmate's hair and messed it up. Potter was bright red and you could tell he'd not thought this through. He was caring like that. If it was somebody's birthday at home he would always decorate the room for them and make them feel special. It was just the way he was. His dad had often doubted his sexuality and on more than one occasion he'd even asked him if he was gay or not. Potter was stuck for words, he was on the spot and had to make sure he had Mikey back on side. "Yeah, it was for a laugh, a piss take nothing else. I just thought you could do with cheering up that's all."

Brendan saw his arse and this was the second time today Mikey had picked this new lad over him. Brendan cupped his hands together and slid them across each other. "Anyway, Mikey, what's the script now you're back on the wing? Is Potter getting carted and I'm moving pads with him. Me and you know each other and you know I've always got your back. No disrespect to you specky but that's just how we roll, isn't it Mikey?"

There was an eerie silence as Mikey jumped onto his bed and looped his arms over his head. He knew he called the shots on the wing now and he only wanted people in his team who he could trust with his life. Brendan was a yellow-belly and when they were on the outside, there had been a few occasions when he suspected that Brendan had set him up. It was only a feeling but his mate was not all he seemed. He studied him for a few seconds and his mind was made up. "Brendan, you can tag along with us if you want but Potter is staying put. I promised I'd look after him and that's what I'm doing. You're big and daft enough to look after yourself. You don't need me behind you."

Brendan screwed his face up, he was spitting feathers. "Nar, seriously though. You said you would look after me but since we've landed in this place I've seen fuck all of you. What happened to sorting me out? I've been having a bad time too if you'd even bother to ask me."

Mikey licked his lips. His mind was made up and no matter what Brendan said here today, he wasn't selling Potter out. Brendan stood waiting for some sort of answer but as he looked around the room, he realised he wasn't going to get one. He went nose to nose with Potter, who was stood near the door and pushed him slightly. Mikey was alert and if he needed to, he'd put this bully on his arse.

Brendan shouted behind him as he stormed out of the room. "Fuck it, I'll do my own shit. You stay here and look after a lad you've only known for a few weeks. I can see now that our friendship means fuck all to you."

Before Mikey could say a word, Brendan slammed the door and left the room. Potter was a bit shell-shocked and even though he was trying to act hard, you could see he'd been unnerved. He stood on the same spot for longer than he needed to and it was only when Mikey spoke to him that he moved back onto his bed. "Don't let him rattle you. Brendan's just a bit annoyed that's all. He won't lay a finger on you while I'm around. Just keep away from him and you'll be fine."

Potter digested the words and he wasn't happy that he'd made an enemy already. "It's not my fault I'm padded up with you, so why is he taking it out on me? I don't make the rules in this place, do I?" Mikey just wanted a bit of peace and quiet and now he was back from the block, he had to get things moving.

Potter reached over to the small table and grabbed a pile of letters. "Here you go, they came earlier today. That one smells of perfume. I think it's from your girlfriend. I've been smelling the envelope all morning it's a gorgeous smell, it smells like fresh daises."

Mikey snatched the letters from his hand, he was eager to open them. Letters from home were like gold dust; news from loved ones, gossip from the outside world, the promise of wives waiting forever for their missing partners were held inside letters from home. Mikey's time down the block had been hard and he had not one letter from his family during this time. Rachel was never one for writing to her son. She struggled with any emotion and she could never write what she really felt in her heart. Even when she was slammed in prison herself, she struggled to tell anyone how she truly felt, it just wasn't her style. Mikey unfolded the white piece of paper and studied the words on it, his eyes flicking from side to side. All of a sudden his expression changed and he sat up on his bed, gritting his teeth together. "For fuck's sake. I'll rip his fucking head off." Mikey's cheeks were blood red and the grip on the letter tightened, knuckles turning white. Potter never said a word, he just sat quietly watching him. Mikey bolted up from the bed. He sprinted to the window and gripped the cold metal bars in his hands, shaking at them rapidly. "I'll rip his fucking head off. I swear to you, I'll find him and torture the cunt. What the fuck was she thinking, leaving my money about with that low-life around." Mikey roared from the pit of his stomach and pushed his head through the small gap. He sucked in mouthfuls of air as his temper boiled. This kid was going sick and he looked like he was losing the plot. This wasn't normal behaviour and somebody should have spotted this uncontrollable rage a lot sooner.

Potter didn't know what to do for the best and he looked uncomfortable as he watched Mikey pace around the cell in some sort of trance. His voice was low and he wasn't sure if he was doing the right thing. "Is there anything I can do to help?" Potter whispered with his eyes closing slightly, afraid of his reaction.

Why didn't he keep his big trap shut? Mikey was going ape and he was ready for fucking somebody up. He launched a book across the cell, just missing Potter's head. Objects were being flung at the wall. "The bastard has taken my money. I'll string him up. I swear, I'll cut his balls off and make a necklace out of them. Who the hell does he think he's messing with? I need a phone. I need a blower as soon as. I have to sort this mess out before he spends a penny of it." He stormed out of his cell. Potter didn't know what to do, should he follow him or stay where he was until he'd calmed down? He sat fidgeting. Curiosity eventually got the better of him and he made sure Mikey was gone by popping his head outside the door. Reaching over for the letter, he sat down on the edge of the bed and started to read it quickly. It wasn't his mail but still, he needed to know what he was up against. If Mikey was upset, he needed to know what had gone down. The letter was written in some sort of code and it took a while to crack it. It was all written in riddles.

Mikey sprinted down the landing and he knew where he was going. Word travelled fast around the jail and he already knew who had mobile phones on the landing. He'd smash their head to bits if they denied it. The mood he was in, nobody was safe, he was a liability. Mikey needed a connection with the outside world and he would do whatever it took to make sure he was in contact with his family during this stressful time. Eyes all over, checking he was safe, Mikey boomed a pad door open and ran straight up to Lee Jones. Taken by surprise, Jones didn't have a clue what was happening. Attacks like this usually happened in the showers or just before bang up at night, never at this time of the day. Inmates would use anything as weapons, most of the time it consisted of putting a few tins of Tuna in a sock and whacking fuck out of their victims with it. There were some gruesome attacks that went on inside. Stabbings, boiling water being thrown over each other, that was just the tip of the iceberg. The nonces were the ones who got the most stick. The attacks made on them were enough to make your toes curl. The kiddy fiddlers were kept away from the main prisoners but there were times when they were vulnerable. If an inmate got a grip of one it was Goodnight Vienna for them. Skulls were smashed, faces slashed with cold metal blades, their injuries were endless.

Mikey gripped Lee by the scruff of the neck and pinned him up against the wall, his warm breath right in his victim's face. "Phone! Now! Don't make me snap your jaw. Just hand it over. I'm in no mood for shit today."

Lee was stuttering, the colour draining from his face. He had no other option than to go to his hideout and give up the mobile he had. Lee could have denied having a blower but what was the point in taking a beating when he could avoid it? Shit like this happened every day and sometimes you just had to take a loss on the chin. Lee closed his door slowly and rolled his body under the bed. His heart was racing and he knew his life was in danger. There were scraping noises, struggled breathing and rustling. Mikey dipped his head down and spotted the loose brick in the wall behind the single bed. This was a top hideout and somewhere he would never have thought of stashing something. The prisoner was taking ages, fucking about trying to put the brick back into the wall. Mikey dragged him out by his leg and wrestled with him slightly. He dusted the iPhone off and nodded his head. Lee feared for his life and sat near the wall with his legs drawn up to his chest. He was bricking it, shitting himself. Was it over or was he going to get wasted? Mikey looked over at him and just for a split second he felt sorry for him. He could see the fear in his eyes. He knew how it felt to be the underdog and hated himself for putting someone else through it but what choice did he have? Mikey reflected back on days gone by. When he was in care horrible things had happened to him, things he would never tell anybody, things that sometimes kept him awake at night. His voice was low as he slid the phone down the crack of his arse. Mikey offered his hand out and helped pull Lee back up from the floor. "I'll sort you a basher out when things get rolling. I just need one for an emergency at home, you know how it is. No hard feelings, ay?"

Lee's eyes were wide open. Unsure of his safety, he quivered. "No, sorted bro, just remember to get me one back if you can. I'm not arsed what type it is either. I just need one to ring my daughter each night and tell her a bedtime story."

Mikey cringed. What the hell was up with him? Was he going soft or what? His eyes closed slightly and he remembered when he used to wait for a phone call from his own father when he was in nick. He'd also called him a few times after he got out but as time went on, the contact between them just ended. It was like his father had disappeared off the face of the earth. He'd tried finding him a few years ago but nobody knew anything about him. Or maybe they did, but they were just keeping schtum. It seemed like his father was a taboo subject that nobody was willing to talk about. "Leave it with me," Mikey said at last, "like I said, I'll sort it out as soon as I can."

Mikey took a deep breath and got on his toes. As soon as he came out of the pad he dipped his eyes and made his way back down the landing. He didn't spot Mark watching him like a hawk from above. He knew this kid was up to no good and he started to head down the stairs to get a grip of him. Mikey stood talking to a few prisoners outside his door. From the corner of his eye he could see the screw bouncing towards him. His cheeks were beetroot and he clenched his arse cheeks tighter, making sure the phone stayed in the crack of his arse. Mark stood tall, he was in no mood for any confrontation. "A word now Milne!" he shrieked.

Mikey had to keep his cool, not give anything away. His neck was on the line here. "What's up boss?"

Mark's eyes were wide open and he could have punched this hard-faced fucker right out given the chance. "Come down to my office. We need a chat… I mean now! Not in fucking ten minutes!"

Mark had a face like thunder and it was only when the inmate started to walk slowly down to his office that he began to relax. Mikey stepped into the room and slumped into a chair. He leaned back and was balancing on two legs as Mark entered the room. The door slammed shut and the screw sat on the edge of the table facing him. Mikey was a pain in the arse and no matter how much he tried, he just couldn't break him down. Mark kept his cool and never took his eyes from the prisoner. "I've just seen you coming out of Jones's pad. What's the crack there and don't feed me any bullshit, or else I'll have you strip searched and you'll be on another nicking. The choice is yours, mate."

Mikey's heart was beating rapidly, did this cunt know he had a phone stashed or what? He wasn't sure. The last thing he needed was a strip search, he had to think on his feet. His voice was confident as he answered him. "I don't know what you mean, Boss. I was just sat chatting with him, he's being having few problems lately with his missus and needed a bit of advice, that's all. You know me, I like to listen sometimes, help people out." Mikey sucked on his bottom lip – was he buying it? He wasn't sure.

Mark gasped his breath and spoke in a sarcastic voice. "And, since when have you been a counsellor? Listen, don't take me for a dickhead. We both know what goes on in this joint, so cut the crap. I'll tell you what, I'll get the boys in here and we'll see if you're telling me the truth. One last chance, tell me what's going on."

Mikey wasn't sure of his next move, he was backed into a corner and knew he had to come up with something fast. This guy was on the ball and there was no pulling the wool over his eyes, he knew the script better than he first thought. "If I tell you the truth are you going to nick me for it?"

Mark scratched the side of his nose. What a result this was, he never expected this in a million years, a breakthrough at last. He thought he was going to have to do this the hard way. Things happened inside this jail and to give a convict a good arse-kicking when nobody was watching was something everybody turned a blind eye to. "I'm listening, just tell me what's happened and then I'll decide what I'm going to do with you."

Mikey had to pull this one out of the bag and his voice was low. He was such a lying bastard and deceiving people was second nature to him. His expression changed and he was putting on a show any actor would have been proud of. He sat forward in his chair, legs apart with his hands dangling down. Here it was, his attempt at getting off with his crime. "Lee needed a phone to ring his missus. I said I'd sort him one out. You know me, I'll do anything to hook a brother up," he looked the screw straight in his eye and never flinched. "Lee was ready to string himself up, honest, he was in a bad way. So I sorted it for him," he licked his lips as he continued, "I know a few lads had mobiles on the wing and I just sort of lent him one for a while," he smirked. "Okay, I never borrowed it, I taxed it."

Mark sniggered. Did this kid think he was born yesterday? What a load of codswallop this was; pure lies. He delved deeper. "Mikey, give your head a bleeding shake and just tell me the truth. I've had a hard day and all I want to do is get home and get my head down. I've got enough shit going on in my own life without having to fill out paperwork for you, every bastard day. Why don't you turn it in and just get your head down and do your time. It's not rocket science is it?" Mark twisted a pen between his fingers and his stress levels were rising. His cheeks were on fire. "Every wing meeting I have in this place it's your name that keeps popping up. You just attract trouble wherever you are, don't you?"

Mikey was defensive. So what if people thought he was trouble? He was in prison, what did they expect? "It does my head in you know. I never, ever, get a second chance. As soon as anything is going down, it's always my name that's thrown into the mix, even if I've got fuck all to do with it. My card has been marked for as long as I can remember, so what's the fucking point in even trying to change? I'm used to it now." He watched the screw from the corner of his eye. He knew when he'd used this story in the past it had always earned him some brownie points and, judging by Mark's expression, he was ticking the boxes yet again. Sympathy was a great emotion and it was something he'd learned how to manipulate. Everyone wanted to help a lost soul; save them, put them back on the right track. Meddling bastards they were, fucking know-it-alls who knew nothing about the real world and how people lived.

Mark's voice changed as he sat on the chair facing Mikey. He knew exactly what he meant by his words and he could identify with the prisoner. Nobody ever gave him a second chance either. Nobody really trusted him anymore if he was being honest with himself, not even his wife. Looking up to the ceiling, he began to speak. His tone changed now and he was actually feeling sorry for the lad. "Mikey, you're a young man with your whole life set out in front of you. You've just had a bad start that's all. My job is to help you try and change. All the help is here for you, you've just got to let people in and stop pressing the self-destruct button all the time."

Mikey was a cunning fucker, he smirked and ran his fingers through his hair. All he needed to do now was to tell him a few things about his life and he would have him eating out of the palm of his hand. This one always worked, got them onside. "Blah, blah fucking blah. Don't you think I've heard all this shit before? Nobody can help me. I'm a lost cause. My life has been shit, my own mother was a smackhead and I've been in the care system for as long as I can remember." Mikey was blurting it out now, he was holding nothing back. He was telling him things he should have kept to himself. "My dad fucked off when I was a kid and I've looked after myself for as long as I can remember. So don't give me that 'we can help you' story. My head was burnt out ages ago, nobody can do fuck all. It's gone too far."

Mark rolled his sleeve up slightly and checked his watch. He had a bit of time left before his shift ended and he really thought he'd crossed a bridge with this inmate. He was ready to do anything to try and help him. "Everyone has shit in their lives mate. Even me. I know you think I probably have it all but trust me, you don't know the half of it." Mark should have stopped right there but for some reason, today his problems at home were there for everyone to see. He folded his arms tightly across his chest and seemed in a world of his own as he confessed how fucked his own life really was. "I'm in debt up to my eyeballs lad and if something doesn't give soon, I'll lose my wife and my home." Mark was giving out confidential information now and had clearly forgotten who he was talking to.

Mikey was listening carefully and he was never one to miss an opportunity to challenge somebody. "Stop lying to me. You have a good job that pays well. You must be stacking the cash, how can you have money troubles, don't make me laugh!"

Mark dipped his head and cupped his hands together, playing with his fingers. "You don't want to know pal… anyway," he gave his head a shake and realised he was revealing too much about his personal life, "let me help you out and see how it goes. I promise I won't judge you and I will give you a second chance."

Mikey chuckled. What a load of bullshit this was, these were just words – the same words every Tom, Dick and Social Worker had said to him over the years. Mikey was listening and looked at the screw more closely. But then perhaps this Mark wasn't that bad after all, perhaps he'd got him all wrong? "Yeah, let's see. I can't think as far as tomorrow at the moment, never mind the future. Just let me stew over it for a while and I'll get back to you. There's no rush is there. It's not like I'm going anywhere, is it!"

Mark looked puzzled and went to his computer screen. He sat at his desk and it was clear that something had unnerved him. "What did you say your dad was called?"

Mikey shrugged his shoulders. Why was he asking that? With caution, he sat forward in his seat and answered him. "Dennis, my dad's called Dennis."

Mark scrolled down the screen and he seemed to be reading something on one of his files. The keyboard clicked rapidly as he punched at the keys. Mark sat reading again. The colour drained from his cheeks and he lifted his head up slowly. Mikey was uneasy and although he didn't speak, he knew something was going on. The screw sprang to his feet and changed the subject quickly. What the hell was going on? "Right, erm. Let's talk again tomorrow. I'll have a word with the others and tell them to back off for a while."

Mikey sniggered, he'd done his job. He wasn't getting a strip search. He stood to his feet and looked the officer up and down. Perhaps, these two could work together after all, they could help each other out, scratch each other's backs. Mikey whistled as he left the room. "In a big-un."

Brendan Mellor sat in his pad and punched his fist into the pillow. He'd show Mikey Milne what he was about. How could he just sell him out like that? Somehow, someway, he was getting what was coming to him. Everybody was right about him, even his own father had told him that Mikey was all about himself. He'd argued and defended his mate and called his old man a liar but, not now, not anymore. Now he saw him for the self-centred prick he really was. It was every man for himself from this day forward and he was going to bring Mikey down the second he got the chance. His mate had ruined his life, taken his freedom away, and all for what? It was payback time!

Mark finished his shift and made his way to the car park. The van containing more prisoners being shipped to the jail was pulling up inside the grounds. The officer stood watching from a distance as he popped a well-deserved cigarette in his mouth. Smithy came to join him and shook his head as they heard the shouting and screaming of an inmate being dragged from the van. This criminal was hardcore and even as they watched, they knew the new inmate would land on their wing. All the troubled convicts somehow ended up on their blocks. Mark chugged hard on his fag and shook his head. "Fuck me, like we need any more shit on our turf," his eyes shot back to the commotion opposite them. "Do you think we should give the lads a lift with that one? It looks like he's overpowering them. Three of them are on him and they're not moving him an inch."

Smithy shot a look over and patted Mark on the shoulder. "You finish your cig. I'll just run over and lend a hand." Mark watched as his work colleague sprinted into action. Smithy would sort this new guy out, he was a master at restraining even the hardest of criminals, he would take him down in one move, put him on his arse. Mark flicked the butt from his cigarette and listened to the loud noises coming from the van. He sniggered to himself and craned his neck. The situation was under control now and just as he had thought, Smithy had helped them get the new prisoner inside the jail. He would have given him a good hiding no doubt, ragged him about.

The wind was howling and the cold night air was tickling his ears. Blowing warm breath on the palms of his hands, he rubbed them together trying to get warm. Smithy was on his way back. As he reached him he was gasping for breath. "Fuck me, he's a big bastard that one. I swear, I'm losing my touch. I need to train a bit harder."

Mark started to walk to the car park and smirked. "Tell me about it. I've not got the motivation to train anymore. It's this job stressing me out. Who was it anyway, is it anyone we know?"

Smithy started to take his coat off before he opened his car door and gasped his breath. "I'm not sure who he is. One of the other thugs called him Davo though. Anyway, tomorrow's another day, fuck speaking about work now, we've clocked off. We'll deal with it when we have to."

Smithy jumped inside his car, fastened his seatbelt and started the engine. Mark walked to his vehicle not far away. He paused before he got inside. Turning his head slowly, he looked back at the prison and seemed in a deep trance as he took in his surroundings. This place was getting to him now and the sooner he was out of there the better. Smithy honked his horn as he drove past him. Mark was still in a world of his own and raised his hand up slowly to say goodbye. He was alone now and there was nobody else in the car park. As he listened closely he could hear the disturbing voices from the inmates locked behind bars; swearing, whistling, singing, screaming. They were all off their rockers. Not one of them was anywhere near normal. Mark opened his car door and turned the radio on. He needed to get as far away as he could from this place now. It was wearing him down.

CHAPTER ELEVEN

Rachel was quivering. She rubbed vigorously at her arms as she hovered about, looking at her mother's house from the other side of the road. "Just go and knock on the door… no, wait, think about it." Her head was all over the show. This woman had most certainly bitten off more than she could chew. Her heart was in her mouth. Rachel peered out from near the bus shelter like a sniper, she shot her eyes one way, then the other as she ragged her fingers through her hair. This was a bad idea and she didn't know how she'd let herself come this far. It had all seemed a good idea when she set off but now she was facing her fears, she was flapping. Rachel slid down the wall at the side of her and dropped her head into her hands, "Fuck, fuck, fuck," she whispered. This was all Sarah's fault; she'd filled her head with that much shit regarding family values that she let her think she had no other option than to go and see her mother.

Rachel stood up and paced one way then the other. She looked different today; clean and tidy and not her usually scruffy self, she had scrubbed up well. These last few days had been horrendous for her and it was only when she heard that Davo had been lifted that she started to relax. The local gangster had been caught bang to rights on a job he was involved in and had broken the conditions of his parole; word on the street was he was getting the book thrown at him. He was a twat and getting what he deserved. Davo had done some bad things to the residents in the area and a lot of them would have been relieved behind closed doors. Good riddance to the prick. Let him rot in hell! The threats he'd made to Rachel had really unsettled her, he said he was going to set her house alight with her in it and he would have as well, the guy was a sick, twisted bastard who liked to see his victims suffer. This was one of the first days Rachel had set foot outside her front door, she'd had the shits for days and her stomach was churning constantly.

Mikey had been belling her nearly every night after bang up. He was worried about her safety as well. His head was done in and anytime he got the chance he was on the blower to his mother checking she was alright. He'd told her straight that he'd left her in charge of the money and it was her job to make sure she got it back. This was a bit unfair and a big ask but he was right, he'd left her in charge of the cash and she'd lost it. It was her problem to deal with. Mikey had accused her of being part of it. Yes, in his own head he actually thought his mother had a part to play in all of this. He might have been paranoid but his mind was working overtime and he didn't know what to think anymore. Mikey's words hit her deep in her heart and she'd tried to make him believe that she would never double-cross him like that but she had history - she was a thief and a liar, her track record wasn't great. What did she expect? She'd done similar things in the past and where earning some extra cash was concerned, she didn't care who she had over. A ruthless bitch she was with no morals.

Rachel's spirit was low and she had nowhere else to turn in her time of need. She'd felt loneliness before in her life, isolation, but it never hit her as bad as it did now. There was an emptiness in her heart, a dull aching pain that never left her. Sarah was helping her out but she couldn't be with her twenty-four hours a day. In fact, if she was being honest, Sarah was doing her head in most of the time, she was a right boring cow and they never really had anything in common to talk about. Chalk and cheese they were. Her heart was in the right place she supposed, but fuck me, Rachel thought, she could talk a glass eye to sleep. She just never shut up chatting pure bullshit. Who on this earth wanted to know the latest news about politics and how much a Mac foundation cost? Rachel knew full well that crime didn't pay in the long run but she had no other choice than to start shoplifting again, even if it meant risking jail. Somehow, some way, she had to make sure the money was back for her son. It was his nest egg, his chance of a better future. She owed him that much, she couldn't let him down. She was trying to change but it was so hard for her. It was like she was banging her head against a brick wall. Rachel had lived in this kind of world for as long as she could remember and to be a straight head was something she would always struggle with. Where was the excitement in going to work every day anyway? It was boring and not her cup of tea. She had no real qualifications, the best job she could ever hope for was a cleaner or a lollipop lady.

Rachel craned her neck and watched the house across the road. Her sister's black car was parked up outside her mother's house. A smart top-of-the-range BMW it was, her husband's pride and joy. His fanny magnet, or so he thought. Rachel knew that, at this time of night, her family would be sat around the kitchen table sharing a bottle of red wine. Cath had always thought she was a cut above the rest and liked to think she was posh. She ate lots of foreign dishes and travelled to exotic holiday resorts hoping to learn more about different cultures. Rachel had never got as far as Blackpool. She had no urge to ever travel either, she was a home bird and liked what she was familiar with. Agnes had never really been a big drinker but on the odd occasion she let her hair down and got wrecked. She was a nasty drunk. Oh yes, she was evil with her mouth once she'd necked a few glasses of vino. She could go one way or the other to be honest.

Rachel sucked in a large mouthful of air as she crossed the road. She knew it was now or never. At least if she tried to make amends and failed, she could go to bed each night knowing she'd tried to fix it. The summer night air was gentle and it tickled her hair as she crossed the road into the cul-de-sac. Her heart was beating rapidly and her legs started to wobble slightly. The lights of her mother's house were on in the front room and as she neared she could hear music being played. Celine Dion had always been her mother's favourite singer and she'd often belted out a few tunes when she was drunk. She was a good singer, she could hold a tune. Rachel edged closer to the living room window and peered inside. A warmth filtered her body and she gave an endearing smile. This was what she was missing, home was where the heart was. All the years that had passed she'd been so mixed up in all her traumas that she'd never realised how comforting a family could be in times of need. But they'd sold her out, banished her from the family without so much as a kiss my arse or anything. Okay, she'd fucked up a few times but surely they could understand her point of view. She was in a bad place at that time and her head was all over the place. Watching through the windowpane, she touched the glass with her fingertips. She wanted her family back and hoped they could see eye to eye now she'd realised her mistakes.

Suddenly Rachel jumped back from the window. Cath's husband appeared and draped his arms around her sister's neck. What a smarmy bastard he was! And there was her sister, none the bloody wiser, blinded by his lies and manly charms. Her mind was racing now. This guy would just put a spanner in the works and do his best to make sure she wasn't in their lives anymore. He knew Rachel knew the truth about him and there was no way he would put his neck on the line for her. Edging closer to the front door, Rachel stood fidgeting. Her hand slowly came out of her pocket and lifted up the letterbox. There was no going back now, she'd made her move. Looking around the garden, she realised they hadn't heard her. She tried again, she rapped harder. A light was switched on in the hallway, a shadow approached. The front door opened wide and Cath was still singing her head off. She clocked Rachel stood there and her jaw hung low. What the hell was she doing here? She tried to look happy but her disappointment was there for everyone to see. "Erm, is it me you want to talk to or have you come to see my mam?"

Rachel was searching for words but she was struggling, dry throat, clammy palms, small beads of sweat forming on her forehead. She swallowed hard. "I've come to have a word with you all really. Well, that's if you'll listen to me?"

Cath stood with the front door wide open and Agnes was shouting from the front room. "Cath, who is it, tell them to piss off, we don't want to buy anything." Cath raised her eyes and smirked. This area was well known for door-to-door salesmen and every night around this time, they were always knocking on the door trying to pitch a sale. Rachel walked inside and Cath closed the door behind her. The smell of her mother's home sent a sense of wellbeing through her. There was always a candle burning somewhere in the house and the vanilla fragrance from it was so inviting. The aroma gave her inner peace and started to make her relax. Cath opened the living room door and Rachel stood behind her playing with her hands. "Mam, it's our Rachel," Cath announced. Rachel edged into the front room. Dave nearly choked on his drink as he plonked down on the chair near him. She'd taken the wind right out of his sails and he was shocked to say the least.

Agnes tried to focus, her eyes were not what they used to be. It looked like her daughter but she had to reach for her glasses to get a better look. Her spectacles hung on the end of her nose as she tried to focus. Agnes swallowed hard and you could see so much pain in her expression. You could have cut the atmosphere with a knife. "Sit down, I'll get you a glass of wine," Cath whispered.

Agnes sat forward in her chair and looked her daughter up and down. She was half-cut and it could go either way. "So, to what do we owe the pleasure? Don't you dare come in my house trying to cause trouble! I'm not in the mood for it! Just spit out what you have to say, then you can be on your way." These were harsh words but she had her own reasons behind them. Every time Rachel had been here in the past she'd always caused murders in the house. Dave couldn't make eye contact, there was no way he was adding anything to the conversation, he was keeping well out of it.

Rachel took a deep breath and began. "I've come to say I'm sorry. I know I've said it in the past but this time I mean it. I've had a lot of thinking time and you all mean the world to me." Cath was blubbering, she always had a big heart and no matter what, she was always ready to give someone a second chance. She was a soft cow really, a bit over the top. Dave cringed as he listened further. "I've had so much trouble in my life and I don't know if I can take it anymore on my own. I've even thought of ending it all. I am nothing without you lot. Our Mikey's banged up and I don't know where my head's at from one minute to the next." Agnes picked her glass up and sipped at her drink, she was listening and never said a word. Cath came to her sister's side and tried to comfort her as she began to break down crying. "Mam, can you let me back in your life. I promise from this day forward I'll never let you down again. I just need to be part of something, part of this family again." Dave sat playing with his fingers, his eyes were all over the place waiting on his mother-in-law's decision. Rachel's eyes clouded over and a single fat bulky tear sailed down her cheek. This was a first and something that only ever happened when Rachel was at her wit's end.

Agnes crossed her legs and folded her arms tightly in front of her. Was her daughter after money? Was this just another ploy to have her over again? The amount of times this woman had lied and cheated to get what she wanted was endless and there was no way she was being fooled ever again. She'd cried rivers over Rachel in the past and said endless prayers just to make sure she was alright but at this moment, her own flesh and blood was knocking her sick. Her stomach was churning, half of her wanted to knock ten bags of shit out of her and the other half wanted to hold her in her arms and never let her go. Cath looked at her mother and urged her to say something. She was a right stubborn cow sometimes and she was the world's worst when it came to forgiving somebody. "So, Mikey's in prison again. Why does that not surprise me with a mother like you?" She reached over to the small table at the side of her and sparked a cigarette up. Here it was, the lecture. The 'I told you so' speech. "Didn't I warn you about where he was heading? I remember it like it was yesterday. I said to you he needs keeping in line. The way he's going he'll end up like his dad, a lowlife waste of space. And I knew I was right. I always am."

Rachel sighed and shook her head slowly. This was an impossible mission, she knew it was going to be hard but could she just sit there and keep her mouth shut and listen to her waffling about days gone by? Mikey was her life and there was no way she was letting anybody badmouth him like this. She'd tried her best to hold it together. "Mam, our Mikey has had a rough time. I blame myself for the way he's turned out. You don't need to kick me while I'm down. I've made mistakes, yes, but hasn't everybody?" She flicked a sly glance over at Dave. Cath was watching her from the corner of her eye and noted the way Dave reacted. "I just want to put the past behind us and start again if we can. I've missed a lot of years with you all and if you will forgive and forget we can all move on."

Agnes sucked hard on her cigarette and for a few seconds she digested what had been said. Cath was eager to put this situation to bed and it was in her nature to be the peacemaker. "Well, I'm all up for giving you a second chance. If what you've said here today is from the bottom of your heart, then I can forgive you. At least you've admitted your mistakes, so that's a start."

Agnes wasn't as sure as her daughter though. She hated putting her neck on the line just in case she was wrong. There was no way she was buying her daughter's sob story. If that was the case, where was she at Christmas? Mother's Day? Her birthday? She continued with caution. "How do

I know you mean it this time? You know what you're like when you're feeling sorry for yourself. You might just wake up in the morning and go back to your old ways. How can I take a chance on you when all you've ever done is lie to me and broken my heart? And it's not just once may I add!" There was silence, not a word spoken.

Dave coughed and cleared his throat, he was in Agnes's corner. The guy was a prick and somewhere in his thoughts he was only thinking about himself and watching his own back. Rachel was a loose cannon and he knew that sooner or later the affair he had with her would be in the limelight again. "I'm with your mother on this one, Cath. Rachel has caused nothing but misery in this family, every day she has a drama and who's to say she's not on drugs anymore. I mean, would you feel safe leaving money about where she is because," he screwed his face up and held his head to the side, "I'll tell you something for nothing, I wouldn't trust her. She's stolen from us in the past, remember your gold necklace that just went missing, the odd tenner here, the odd tenner there? I'm not sure she's all that she's making herself out to be. I wouldn't trust her as far as I could throw her."

Rachel had seen her arse, she hated that dickhead for bad-mouthing her. He'd made mistakes in the past too and was she sitting there blurting out his track record? No. She'd let bygones be bygones and never mentioned a single word about what went on. Cath's cage was rattled and she was the only one who was giving Rachel a break. She walked over to the table and picked up the bottle of wine. Tipping some into a glass, she filled it to the top and passed it over to her younger sister. "I say we make a toast to new beginnings, let's move on and see if we can all get on." She raised her glass high in the air and made a speech. Cath was pissed and she was wobbling slightly. "Let's raise our glasses, to new beginnings." She clinked her glass with her sisters and smiled at Dave and Agnes. It was hard to tell how Rachel's mother was feeling. She was keeping her cards close to her chest and giving nothing away. The music was turned back up now and Cath was singing her head off. Her sister seemed to be back in the family for now.

A little later, Rachel stood at the kitchen sink washing some pots. Agnes came into the room and stood looking at her. Here it was, the true Agnes. "You can leave them dishes. I'll do them in the morning."

"It's alright, I'll have them done in no time."

Agnes stood behind her and reached over and touched her hair. She lifted it up and closed her eyes as she inhaled the fragrance from it. Her daughter was clean for a change and her heart ached deep inside knowing what kind of a life she'd led in the past. The wine was talking now and Agnes was slurring her words. "You shattered my heart, every day that passed I wanted to speak to you. Do you know how that feels for a mother to watch her own child melting away right in front of their eyes? Not knowing if I'm going to get the knock on the door telling me you've been found dead?"

Rachel choked back the tears. Her mother did care for her after all. She turned around slowly and all she wanted to do at the moment was to hold her mother in her arms. She'd starved herself of affection for years but at this moment, all she wanted was to be in a safe place and be told everything would be alright. The words spoken now were on another level, hearts were opening and long-suppressed feelings were being expressed. "Mam, I should have listened to you but I just got it all so wrong in my head. I thought I knew best. I hated you for not looking after Mikey when I got sent down and I just couldn't get my head around it."

Agnes held a flat palm over her heart. "I couldn't breathe love when you got sent to prison. I couldn't look after myself, never mind my grandson. Our Cath was going to take him on but Dave was the one who said she couldn't. Don't you think it hurt me to know I'd let you both down? I've blamed myself time and time again for the path you took. Could I have done more? Did I listen enough? My mind was racing every night and I was making myself ill."

Rachel hugged her mother and the familiar smell she could remember from being a child was there again. Rachel's heart melted and her shoulders shuddered as years of emotions finally came to the surface. She'd not cried like this for years. Rachel was a blubbering wreck. "I just got lost, mam. I was a rebel and I couldn't stand to be told what to do. Our Cath was everything I should have been and I know I let you down."

Agnes gripped her tightly in her arms and looked her straight in the eyes. "We both could have done things differently. I know that now. I've never told you this but I did go to the care home to get Mikey back. I sat outside that place for hours in the pouring rain fighting with my emotions. In the end, I just walked away. I couldn't do it. I made mistakes with you and who's to say I wouldn't have ruined Mikey's life as well. I couldn't take the chance!"

Rachel was struggling to breathe, she was having a panic attack. Why had nobody ever told her this before? It could have made such a big difference. It could have ended all the years of pain she'd suffered. Agnes kissed the top of her daughter's head and smiled as she looked deeply into her eyes. "Let's turn the page and start again. We can both have a clean sheet now. Let's start a new chapter." Rachel nodded and for the first time in years she felt loved.

Dave walked into the kitchen and he was swaying about. He stumbled up to the both of them and patted his flat palm across Rachel's bum cheeks. "Yep, let's all try to get along now. Too much time has passed for us to all be at loggerheads."

Rachel pulled away from her mother. This guy gave her the creeps and as soon as Agnes left the kitchen she growled over at him. "Don't you ever think you can lay a finger on me again! You make me feel sick to my stomach and I'll never ever let you get under my skin again. Our Cath is your wife, just remember that. I took the blame for last time but if you come within an inch of me I'll cut your bleeding balls off."

Dave stood with his back against the wall. He smirked. He licked his lips slowly and made sure he kept his voice low. "You loved every minute of it, just like I did. I've never forgotten you know." There was a noise just outside the room and Rachel was spooked. Dave dipped his head behind the door and once he knew nobody was there he carried on talking. "You'll always be a slut in my eyes, love. You can't polish a turd. The two of them in there might buy your bullshit but I won't. You love cock and you always will. Anyway, if you ever fancy a quick knee-trembler you know where I am. We'd just have to be more careful this time wouldn't we? We don't want to upset your sister do we?"

Rachel was livid and she walked straight up to him and spat in his eye. "You dirty no-good bastard. I was young when you got a grip of me, I should have known better. I'll tell you now, if you ever come near me again, I'll tell Cath. I swear to you, I'll tell her everything."

Dave chuckled and ran his hand over his crotch, he was obviously turned on by the whole episode. "What, you think she'll ever believe a lying dirty skank over her own husband? Good luck with that," he chuckled. Rachel couldn't wait to get away from him, he made her skin crawl and given the chance she would have shoved a blade deep in his chest, stabbed the fucker up. He was dangerous and she knew in the future she would have to tread carefully where he was concerned. Rachel walked to the kitchen door and froze as Cath walked into the kitchen, she had taken her by surprise and she was sure she'd been listening to the conversation. Cath walked over to the kitchen sink and placed her glass carefully there. As she looked over her shoulder she gave Dave a look that could kill. She raised her eyes and snarled over at him. "I suggest you finish your drink. We're going home now." Dave didn't know which way to look, had she heard what he'd said or what? He obeyed his wife and never said a single word. Cath was in a world of her own and started to sing in a low voice.

Rachel picked up her coat from the side of the sofa and dusted it softly. Her original intention when she came here was to ask for some help with the money for her son but after what had been said here tonight, she knew she could never ask them for a handout again. She had to prove she was on the straight and narrow now. Agnes's eyes were closing as she sat back in her chair. It was late. She looked older than Rachel remembered her. The years of torment she'd caused her were visible in every deep wrinkle on her skin. The sleepless nights, the twenty-four-seven anxiety that Rachel had caused her. Yes, she'd aged her.

Rachel crept to her side and tapped her gently on the top of her shoulder. "Mam, I'm going to set off home now," she whispered.

Agnes was alert and tried to stretch her eyes open wide. She wriggled about in her chair. "You can stay here love. It's too late for you to be walking the streets at this time of night."

Rachel started to put her coat on. She was touched and those words meant everything to her. It was there for everyone to see. Agnes really did care about her daughter. This was the first time in ages that anyone had ever really showed that she mattered in their life.

Dave grabbed his car keys from the table and rattled them in his hands. "I'll run you home. I've had a few scoops but I'm alright to drive."

Cath growled at him and spoke in a stern voice. "You're going nowhere. You've had more than enough to drink. I'll pay for a taxi if you want Rachel?"

"No, no, I'm going to call in the late shop and get some fags and a loaf. It's not that late and I like the exercise. The fresh air will do me good."

Dave was out to cause trouble and he just couldn't keep his trap shut. "Yeah, let her walk. It's not like she will be in any danger is it. I mean, who'd want to touch that."

Agnes jumped from her chair and there was no way she was listening to his filthy mouth. He could be a right arse sometimes and he never thought about anything before he put his mouth into gear. "Oi, less of the snide remarks. I think you should go and make a black coffee for yourself, it's obvious you're pissed."

Cath dug deep in her purse and pulled out a ten pound

note. "Here you go cock, get a taxi. You take no notice of Dave. He just thinks he's a bit of a joker that's all. You know what he's like."

Rachel turned down the money, even though she could have done with it. "No, honest. I'll walk. Mam, if it's alright with you, I'll come and see you again tomorrow or something."

"You don't need to ask, just come here whenever you want, love. It's a fresh start remember." Rachel pecked Agnes on the cheek and squeezed her tightly in her arms. Bridges had been built here today and the family was reformed again. This was the happiest day of her life and as she left the house, she felt like the worries of the world had been lifted from her shoulders.

Rachel walked along the main road. For some strange reason she kept looking over her shoulder. Something was wrong, she was edgy as her pace quickened. The roads were quiet tonight and hardly any traffic was flying by. Nipping across a field, Rachel knew it would take at least ten minutes off her journey. The field was dark and as soon as she started to cross over it she realised she'd dropped a bollock. The thick brown mud gripped her feet and every step she took she felt like her legs were going to fall off. Branches crunched behind her, before struggled breathing could suddenly be heard. Rachel turned her head quickly but she couldn't see anything. She stood frozen, eyes wide open. "Hello?" she murmured. There was no reply. Mikey's mother picked up speed and carried on her journey home. Was her mind playing tricks on her? Was she imagining it? Every few steps she took she kept twisting her head behind her. Somebody was definitely there, hidden away in the shadows of the night. The silver moon shone brightly in the sky and made her way across the field safely. She would never come this way again. She'd put herself at risk, she could have been attacked. Rachel staggered over the last part of the muddy marshland. Just as she got out of the gates she turned around and looked behind her. There was a silhouette of somebody in the distance, she knew she hadn't imagined it. Who the hell was it?

Rachel sprinted down her garden path and shoved the gold key into the lock with shaking hands. She was so glad to be in her own home. Once she got inside she ran to the front window. All the lights in the front room were kept off as she peeled the curtains back. Her eyes tried to focus as she squeezed them together. There was nobody there, not a soul. But she could feel something inside her, a gut feeling that something was wrong. Turning the TV on, Rachel plonked down on the sofa and drew her legs up to her chest. She hated being alone at times like this and even though Sarah was a pain in the arse, she wished she would have asked her to stay with her tonight. Looking at the clock on the wall, the midnight hour was drawing close. There was no point sitting in the front room on her own. The gas had been cut off and she was freezing her tits off, teeth chattering. She was going to bed, at least she would be warm there. Standing at her bedroom window, Rachel gazed out. In the distance she could see a shadow of somebody stood on the opposite side of the road. Her head pressed hard against the pane of glass trying to get a closer look. This time she knew she was right, she could see perfectly. The man just stood looking over at her house, he never moved a muscle. She quickly moved away from the window. Had he seen her? "No, no, who the hell are you?" she whispered under her breath. If her theory was right, the person she thought was following her now knew where she lived. Her heart raced inside her chest and she had every right to be scared. She'd gained so many enemies over the years and knew this day would come sooner rather than later. The loan man had told her he would make her pay one way or another for the cash she owed him. Was this his way of making her cough up the cash? She didn't know. She had to protect herself and always be on her guard from this day forward. The clock was ticking and sooner or later the stalker would reveal themselves.

Rachel dragged the clothes from her body and shoved an old T-shirt of Gary's on. Pulling the duvet back from the bed, she jumped inside and shivered as the cold night air gripped her bones. Checking her mobile phone, she realised there was a text message she'd not yet seen. It was from Mikey. With shaking hands she opened the text and read the message. "Mam, I'm struggling in here, shit's going down. Please get up to see me as soon as. Tell Sarah I love her. If anything happens to me, I love you too."

Rachel read the text message over and over again. It wasn't like her boy to be weak. He never let anyone know if he was having a hard time. And what did he mean "if anything happens to me"? Perhaps the years of torment in his life had finally got a grip of him and like his mother, he'd had enough. Her heart was low and she didn't know if she could take much more. Rachel replied to the text. "Son, just be strong. I know I've let you down in your life but not anymore. I'll fix it all, don't worry about a thing. I'll be up to see you soon."

The message was sent and Rachel lay in bed staring into

space. Tomorrow was another day and somehow, someway, she was going to make sure every penny of Mikey's money was returned. Gary wouldn't be hard to find and she knew if she put her mind to it, she would uncover his hideout. Once he saw her, he would shit a brick and hand the cash back over. The moonlight shone through the window. Her eyes started to close slowly as she dragged the duvet tightly around her body. The house was creaking and with every noise she heard, her heart was in her mouth. She needed to pull herself together, this was no time to be falling apart, her son needed her.

CHAPTER TWELVE

Mikey stood inside Mark's office and he was edgy, his eyes flicked one way then another. Where the fuck was he? The screw said he would meet him here ten minutes ago. The two of them had a thing going now and despite all that Mark had previously believed in, he was now bringing contraband into the jail for prisoners. He had no other option. He needed the extra money. He didn't know what he was getting involved with. How on earth had he got wrapped up in such a dangerous game? If he got caught smuggling phones and drugs he would lose everything; his job, his home, his wife. He needed his head feeling if he thought he could get away with this. Someone would surely talk, they always did, the place was full of grassing fuckers who would love to see him fall flat on his face. But Mark was only dealing with the one inmate so far. Nobody knew he was bent and he was clever at disguising his crimes.

Mikey sat looking around the room. He shouldn't have been able to get inside this place but the door had been left unlocked. If Mark was caught breaching jail security, they would throw him out of the place quicker than he could have said he was sorry. This was a prison and every door had to be locked, no matter what. There were dangerous criminals inside this place, men who would gouge your eyes out without giving it a second thought. There was no time for mistakes. Mikey had always had a nosey nature and as boredom set in he couldn't help himself. His hand reached over to the desk in front of him and he started to read a few letters lying there. His eyes scanned the words but there was nothing of any real interest to him, just boring shite that he couldn't really understand, there were too many big words. There was a pile of files nearby and his fingers touched the top of them, twisting them around so he could see the names on them properly. There were some familiar convicts named here, guys that he knew from the wing and without a second's hesitation, he started to read about the criminals he was serving his sentence with. The first file he opened was Potter's. Mikey flicked the pages over and sniggered as he clocked the profile picture of his pad mate. The lad looked scared to death on this photograph, he looked like he was going to break down in tears on it, eyes wide open, cheeks creased. What a soft twat he was! Turning the white pages, he smirked as he read the notes on his convictions. It was all what he really knew really, nothing major, just fraud like Potter had told him. Mikey closed the file and noticed a bunch of red files on the other side of the table. This was juicier; some of these guys were fucked in the head. Mikey opened a few files and held a sour expression as he read some of the notes. Dirty scumbags, twisted bastards. His fist tightened and you could see whatever he was reading made his stomach churn.

Mikey studied another file for a lot longer than he should have, he never touched it, just sat gazing at it. Slowly, he dragged the notes closer to his body. His jaw dropped low as he read the name 'Dennis Milne' on the front of it. His cheeks sank and his fingers just ran over the name several times. Was this really his father? The man he'd missed in his life for so long now? He was taking forever to pick them up. At last, he slid the notes closer to his body, heart pumping, alert. His limbs seemed lifeless as he paused, head twisting around, unsure of his next move. Someone was here, the door handle rattled. Mikey pushed the paperwork away and tried to regain his composure. He would have got bollocked if he'd been caught rooting through stuff.

Mark was in a panic as he entered the office. He was fully aware that no convict should have been sat in his room alone, his cheeks were bright red. "For fuck's sake, who said you can come in here on your Jack? If anyone would have seen you, I'd be fucked. Don't ever do it again, do you hear me, ever!"

Mikey backed away from the table and for a few seconds he was in some kind of deep trance. Nothing was registering, his head was all over the place. Was his old man really in the same big house or was this just an old file? He wasn't sure. Mark plonked down at his desk and ragged his fingers through his hair. He was stressed and his head wasn't with it. His voice was low. "I'll meet the woman tonight at the usual place. I want no fucking about. There'd better be all the money there too. A grand, like we agreed."

Mikey snapped back to reality and replied in a sarcastic tone. This guy was a worrier and he was so on top. Mikey tilted his head to the side. "Isn't the cash always there? Just relax will you."

Mark wiped the invisible dust from his sleeve as he started to calm down. "This is the last lot too. I told you I would help you out but after this parcel it's back to square one. It's stressing me out too much. And, like I said, nobody must know about this."

Mikey's head was mashed and he sat forward tickling the end of his chin. He swallowed hard. "Boss, I've just clocked my old man's file on the table. Is he in this joint too?"

Mark quickly grabbed the inmates' files with shaking hands, he was fuming. This was a breach of confidentiality and he was going ape. "Don't tell me you've been looking inside them. For fuck's sake, you're going to get me the sack! What the fuck are you looking through all this shit for, keep your nose out of it in future you daft prick!"

Mikey maintained a serious expression and his tone was low. He was no big boy now, he was after something that mattered to him. He changed his tune. "I'm just asking that's all. You know I've not seen him for donkey's years don't you? Just answer yes or no, that's all. I don't need to know the ins and outs of a cat's arse I just need to know if he's inside this jail."

Mark loosened his black tie. He was sweating and wet patches were visible under his arms on his white shirt. Taking a few seconds, he checked nobody was listening. "Yeah, he's in here, but don't ask me anything else. He's on the other side of the jail. He's nothing to do with me. I just make sure his files are in order and all that."

Mikey smirked and his eyes lit up. "Well, fuck a duck. Me and my pa serving a sentence in the same nick. Can you get a message to him? Just tell him I've landed here and we could have a catch-up if he wants. Be nice to see what he's been up to all these years, the old fucker."

Mark's eyes were bulging out from their sockets, he couldn't look the inmate in the eye. "I can't do anything like that. Listen, from what you told me about your childhood, you don't need him in your life, he's bad news. He walked away from you, remember, sometimes things are better left unsaid. I'd keep my distance if I were you."

Mikey was on one. Who was this geezer to tell him when he could speak to his own father? There was no way he was keeping quiet, he was telling him straight. Fuck it, what did he have to lose anyway. "What's the big problem here?" he ranted. "I'm only asking you to pass him a message, where's the harm in that? I thought you was an alright screw and we could talk. Don't be going snide on me now."

Mark was backed into a corner and he knew this convict would end up giving him trouble if he didn't get the answers he was looking for. Why the fuck had he ever let him talk him into this? He was in it now and for the first time in weeks, he couldn't see a way out. It was always one more drop, one more parcel. Mikey stood and shoved his hands into his trouser pockets. He went nose to nose with Mark and looked him straight in the eyes. "The money will be there tonight. Just make sure you've got all I need. You're no different than me, remember that. Just because you wear a uniform it doesn't make you untouchable."

Mark wasn't sure what he was hearing, was this a threat? His ears pinned back and his chest was rising frantically. There was no way he was being blackmailed. He'd sort this inmate out if he was playing that card with him. No fucking way was he the underdog. No one was holding him to ransom, especially a fucking know-it-all prisoner. His voice was firm and he meant every word spoken. "This is the last time, the last parcel. Once it's done that's me out. Don't ever think you can use this against me because let me tell you something for nothing lad. I've shit bigger than you and I'll make sure you never speak again if you push my buttons."

Mikey didn't flinch. He was cocky, he knew he was the

one in control here, not this bent bastard. Mark was up to his eyeballs in it and if he thought he was bailing or ever getting out of this situation he had another think coming. Mikey edged closer to the door and gripped the handle tightly. As he turned back he kept a serious expression. "Listen, you bellend. I'm only asking for you to contact him, not to climb a fucking mountain. Take your head from out of your arse and sort it out will you?"

Mark rushed towards him and pushed his hand into the small of his back urging him out of the door. "I'll see what I can do. Fuck off now before someone gets onto you." Mikey bounced out from the office and never looked back. Mark slammed the door shut and stood behind it for a few seconds. This wasn't good, it wasn't good at all. Things needed sorting and fast.

Brendan Mellor was on the landing playing cards with a few other inmates. As Mikey strolled by he lifted his head slowly. His teeth ground together and his grip on the playing cards tightened. Mikey smirked over at him on his way past. "Alright there Brendan, are you doing a session down the gym later?"

Brendan looked at the other inmates who were sat with him and chuckled. "Have you heard this clown, lads? He's sold me out for a daft specky prick and he thinks he can still chill with me. Do one, you dick. I'm nobody's mug."

Mikey spun around on the spot. Brendan was dicing with death and the mood he was in, he would have floored him with one blow. There was whispering among the others who sat there. The prisoners sat back in their seats and waited for his response. Mikey's eyes closed and he licked his lips slowly, his fists starting to curl into two tight balls at the side of him and he was game to knock this cunt out.

Smithy came onto the wing just in time and he was shouting names out for the visits. "Come on lads, get your shit together, your loved ones are waiting for you. Get that sack and crack scrubbed, you never know you might get a feel of some pussy if you're lucky." Smithy was happy today and enjoying the banter on the landing. Mikey was still eyeballing Brendan and for a split second he didn't know if he was going to bang him out or not. Smithy came to Mikey's side and patted the top of his shoulder. "Come on Milne, you're on a visit today. Go and have a quick swill and line up to go over to the main block." Brendan was already up out of his seat and heading back to his pad to get ready. Mikey watched him from the corner of his eye and took a few steps forward. There was no way he was letting him get away with that, not a fucking chance on this earth. Who did the ginger tosser think he was trying to put him down like that in front of people? If he didn't sort this out now his status would be in jeopardy, no, this had to get nipped in the bud. Mikey quickened his step towards his pad, he was vigilant and made sure there were no screws about. Potter greeted him with a smile as he walked inside his pad. "I'm on a visit too Mikey. My sister and mother are coming to see me today, they said they have some good news in the letter." Mikey was quiet, he dragged a sock from his washing pile and walked over to the side of the table. Two tins of tuna were rammed deep into the grey sock and a knot was tied over the top of them. Shoving the weapon inside his jacket, he casually walked out from his cell, completely ignoring Potter.

Brendan was washing his face in the steel basin. He needed a shave really but time wasn't on his side and the bum fluff had to wait. Lifting his head up slowly, he saw a shadow meet the mirror. Soap had gone into his eyes so he couldn't see clearly, his eyes were starting to sting. Turning his head to the side with both his eyes watering, he was blinded as he searched for a towel at the side of him. A hand gripped the grey towel and rammed it hard into his chest, taking his breath away. Brendan was struggling to see and his legs were unsteady, he stumbled and fell onto the bed. Mikey just stood over him snarling. Brendan could see him now. "What the fuck are you doing here, go on, do one back up your own arse buddy." It was too much, he'd overstepped the mark. If he would have kept his mouth shut Mikey might have given him a talking to, but he'd done it now, he was fucked. Mikey dragged his weapon out from his jacket and flung the sock over his shoulder. It had power behind it now, this was going to hurt. Mikey's nostrils flared and without thinking, he steamed into Brendan. The sock crashed against bones, blood splurging onto the walls, this was way over the top. This was a savage attack. This kid had only given him a bit of back chat, there was no need for this. He was taking liberties, he was killing him. Brendan's head was pushed deep into his pillow and any calls for help went unheard. When he had finished, Mikey stood over his victim, his eyes dancing with madness. He was in the zone now and anything could have happened. His temper was boiling and there was no coming back once he'd started. He whacked the tins over Brendan's body and his own face was covered in small speckles of bright red claret. There was talking outside, Mikey froze, he stood back and wiped the back of his hand swiftly across his forehead. His heart was racing and small balls of sweat ran down the side of his cheek. "You're a rat. I don't give a fuck how long we've known each other, don't ever think you can mug me off in front of people." He spat onto his victim's face and stormed out of the pad. Brendan was in a bad way and his eyes were swelling with every second that passed, bright purple bruises. This lad was choking, he was turning blue as he tried to sit up, spluttering blood.

Back in his pad, Mikey plonked down on his bed and threw the sock over at Potter. "Sort that out for me, get rid of it."

Potter was flustered, he shot a look at Mikey's hand and could see there was damage, dried blood, small gashes on his knuckles. Standing up from the bed, he took hold of the sock and made sure there would be no evidence in the room that would associate his pad mate with any assault. Mikey lay on his bed staring into space, his chest was rising frantically and he was finding it hard to calm down. He touched every finger with his thumb slowly, he was counting. This action was what he'd learned in an anger management class when he was much younger. It was working now, he was starting to calm down, his breathing returned to normal. Potter stood over Mikey, he was eager to speak. Something had gone down and he was scared to ask what. What if they were rushed though, taken by surprise, he needed to be ready, tooled up. "What's up, has something happened?" Potter eyes creased and he was hoping he'd not rattled his cage while he was still angry. He could get a crack here if he wasn't careful.

Mikey growled over at him. "Just some dickhead chatting shit, it's nothing for you to worry about. There will be no comebacks, I've made sure of that. Stop flapping, you're doing my head in."

"Who was it, someone from the wing?" Potter asked anxiously.

"Brendan. He got what he deserved. I'm not arsed if he's a mate or not, he's a cock and I should have got rid of him years ago. The cheeky arrogant bastard."

Potter nodded and clinched his fist tighter. He was behind Mikey one hundred and ten percent and if his pad mate said this lad deserved it, then who was he to question him? But Brendan was a long-term friend, someone he'd chilled with on the outside. Potter swallowed hard and at that point he realised that friendship meant fuck all inside these four walls. It was a dog-eat-dog environment. Nobody was safe.

Mikey sat on the table waiting for his visitor to come through the doors. He was tapping his fingers out of boredom, eyes flicking from side to side. Sarah was coming today and he was more than happy to see her big smile when he first made eye contact with her. As the doors opened, a stampede of eager visitors flew into the room. Here she was, her eyes desperate to find him. This poor girl had lost weight, her face looked thinner and her body frame wasn't as full as he remembered it. He sprang up from his seat and opened his arms wide as she approached him. "I've missed you so much, come here and give me a kiss." Their bodies connected and you could see in his eyes that he needed this. Mikey felt the love rush through his body, the butterflies and shortness of breath. This was someone who genuinely cared for him, someone who could lift his spirits, calm the rage bubbling inside. Even the way her hair smelled sent calming waves through his body, she was his love, his girl.

"Do you want a drink or shall I wait until the queue dies down?" Sarah asked.

Mikey was still staring at her and his mind was on kissing her, nothing else. He stretched over the table and pulled her closer. This was what it was all about on a visit, the loving touches, the promises they would make to each other for when he was a free man. It was just jail talk though, nothing that could ever be taken seriously when a man was locked up behind bars. They said what they needed to, making sure they kept their loved ones happy. At the time they probably did mean to change but more often than not it was a load of crap. Words said in the heat of the moment. The blood rushed to Mikey's throbbing member, the desire to have sex. The kiss was passionate and if they would have been left any longer he would have mounted her. Stuck one right up her.

"Enough of that Milne," the screw shouted at the side of him. He walked over to the table and pulled Mikey away by his shoulder. The prisoner was blushing, cheeks beaming. His cock was hard and he was doing his best to control his urge to fuck her brains out. Sarah wasn't like the girls he'd met in the past. The others were just bangs really, no loving time during sex, just a shag but his girlfriend was special. There was no way in this world she would have let him get away with just a quick bang. Every time these two made love it was like the first time; lights low, soft music playing, gentle touches. Sarah always wanted to be treated like a lady and it had taken him ages to even get a crunch from her. She struggled with oral sex and couldn't see the point in it really. Mikey spoke to her about having a sixty-niner many a time but that also took ages for him to get her to agree. Even to this day she was still a bit prudish about having oral sex and never really let herself go when he was between her legs with his tongue. She was particular like that. Sometimes he hoped that she would feel at ease with him and let her inhibitions go but up to this day she was still shy.

Sarah blew a laboured breath and held his hand in hers. "My dad knows you are in here. The shit has hit the fan in our house, let me tell you. I told him straight. I said what kind of a man has his daughter's boyfriend beaten within an inch of his life? He's not spoken to me for days. It worries me when he's quiet though, he's up to something. Don't ask me why, I just have a gut feeling." Mikey was concentrating, he never flinched as she continued. "He's banned me from coming to see you. He said you're a crazy animal and I don't know you properly. I mean, how can he say that when he's not even spoken two words to you? He's judging you when he doesn't know shit."

Mikey could see her eyes clouding over and patted her hand to reassure her. This girl really did have his back, she would fight anyone who blackened his name. "Sarah, I don't have to prove to anyone what I'm about. All that counts is that you know me, nobody else. Fuck them, fuck them all."

She held her tears back and bit hard on her bottom lip. "But he's not even given you a chance. I've told him when you get out you want to find work and settle down but he's having none of it. It's so frustrating because he won't listen."

Mikey nodded and looked over at the queue on the other side of the room. "Will you get me a drink babes, a bar of chocolate too? I'm starving today I've hardly eaten a scrap." Mikey watched her leave and shot his eyes around the visiting room. Mark was on duty and he could feel his presence, the bastard was all over him, watching his every move. What was his problem? Mikey sat twisting his fingers, he took a deep breath and knew he would have to shake this mood off. His blood was boiling and he still couldn't rid himself of the anger he felt deep inside. It was hard to control, once it got a grip of him it would fuck with his head for days. Put him on a right downer. The anger issue he had started when he was in the care home. The workers there liked to refer to it as frustration, the hurt he felt about being away from his loved ones. What the fuck did they know about his life anyway? He was just a case number to them. Once their shift finished they didn't give a flying fuck about anyone or anything. They had their own happy lives to go home to; a family unit, a stable life. The anger just tortured him inside, it was like a volcano ready to erupt and lately it was getting a lot worse. It was waking him up in the middle of the night and playing with his head, torturing his mind.

Taking a few seconds and long shallow breaths, he held his head back and looked up at the ceiling. Sarah was back now and he wanted to make the most of their time together. "How's my mam? I spoke to her last night and she seemed okay. Happy even."

"That's all my doing that is. I told her how important family was and suggested she made friends with your nana." Mikey held his head to the side. Surely he'd heard this wrong. He asked her again and this time he made sure he was listening properly. "Yeah, she's been around a few times now. It's like she's never been away. Your Auntie Cath was there too with her husband. A lovely family get-together."

Mikey thought deeply before he spoke. This was a turn up for the books and he was struggling getting his head around it. "I'm happy for her you know. Even though she'd deny it, she's missed them all. Shit happens and I'm glad it's all been finally put to bed once and for all.

Perhaps now she will look at things more clearly." Sarah was giddy and she started to tell him about Rachel and her new outlook on life.

Mikey was sniggering and covered his mouth with his hand. He was cute when he smiled, his cheeks creased and the laughter came from the bottom of his stomach. He carried on talking. It was time to get to the nitty-gritty now. "Has she sorted my money out yet?"

Sarah sat back and folded her arms tightly in front of her. Why did he have to go and ruin things when they were getting on just fine? It was like a dark cloud had appeared right over their table. "She's been looking for Gary but up to now he's nowhere to be seen. Anyway, money isn't everything is it? And I've been thinking that when you get out you can start to find work. I'll help you, someone will see all the good things you have to offer."

Mikey swallowed hard. In fairness, his girlfriend could see no wrong in her eyes but to ask so much of him was starting to scare him. Grafting was the only way he knew how to survive; crime, hooky deals and robberies. A proper job could never give him the life he wanted. Things cost money and he could never be one of those men working shit hours for shit money. But as he looked into her eyes, he knew he could never hurt her like that. It would break her heart. She didn't ask for much and the least he could do was to offer her some kind of answer. "I know babe, but that money was for us and our future. I'm not letting it go, fuck that, the guy owes me dough."

Sarah knew she was pissing in the wind. She wasn't getting into this now, what was the point?

He had years left to serve and she would cross that bridge when she came to it.

Mark paced the floor and he was on the ball today, nothing was going to get past him, not on his watch anyway. Ok, he was bent, but that was stopping soon and he wanted to remain vigilant on the visits. Smithy was off today and already he was missing his wingman. Usually they worked together and they could spot a parcel being passed a mile away. Mikey tried to ignore the screw and carried on talking to Sarah. "So my mam has finally sorted herself out then?"

"Yes, how cool is that? I just knew there was something more to her, she was just lost, misunderstood."

Mikey smirked and scraped the chocolate from his front tooth. "We're all lost, we just need saving babes, that's all."

Sarah's expression changed as she moved closer to him. "She's not been feeling herself though. She said she thinks someone's following her. I told her she's imagining it but she insists someone's got her card marked."

Mikey nearly choked laughing. "That will be the weed that, it always sends her a bit paranoid."

"No, she's carted the drugs. She's had nothing for weeks." Mikey sat looking puzzled. Perhaps leopards did change their spots after all.

CHAPTER THIRTEEN

As Rachel walked around the shopping centre in a world of her own, she seemed at peace with herself. She was fresh today and her skin was glowing, rosy red cheeks. It was market day and she could hear all the traders shouting loudly trying to sell their wares. "Come on ladies, a bunch of bananas only a pound. King Kong even eats them they're that good, grab yourself a bunch." Rachel smirked, she couldn't help but giggle. His comment really tickled her. Harpurhey was somewhere she loved to live and no matter how many times she'd heard on the news that it was a deadbeat area she always enjoyed the humour of the people. They all looked out for each other, if you fought one, you fought them all. She strolled down the market aisles knowing she had a few quid to spend. This was a first, usually every penny was spoken for. Every payday she would have to pay her dealer what she owed them, usually she'd ticked about forty quid's worth of weed, sometimes more if she was stressed. But now there were no more drugs in her life and it was only now she realised how much of her weekly benefit was taken up by her addiction. She'd been a fool, she realised that now. A bright pink top caught her eye, a colour she loved. She'd not dressed in anything remotely colourful in years. Her clothes were like her mood; dark and dreary.

"How much love?" she asked the trader as she ran her fingers over the silk fabric.

The man was smiling now. He was all over her like a

rash. It was time for his sales pitch. "Two for a tenner love or five ninety-nine each."

Rachel knew the script like the back of her hand. She loved a bit of bartering and in her role as shoplifter she knew full well she'd have to cough up some cash. Thinking for a few seconds, she pushed her hand deep into her coat pocket. "I'll have this pink one and a purple one love. I've not seen anything this nice for time."

"It will look lovely on you, that will. I'll tell you something for nothing, these tops are like rocking horse shit. I swear Selfridges in town have sold out of them. I got them cheap if you know what I mean." The man tapped the side of his nose and checked the area behind him. What a load of shite this was. It was the same story whenever she bought anything around here, everybody had the spiel to make you think you were getting a bargain. Rachel smirked and handed the cash over. For the first time in ages she was smiling. Life wasn't that bad after all. Her usually morbid world was now an array of bright colour and her outlook on life was changing day by day. She had positive thoughts, a reason to get up each morning. She turned on the spot and set off to browse the other stalls. Rachel stood still and clocked a shoe stall not far from where she stood. And, even though she was trying to turn over a new leaf, she just couldn't help herself. Shoplifting was in her blood and she couldn't resist but lift a pair of black boots on the way past. She was quick and nobody clocked her. They went straight in her carrier bag, no messing about. It was cold today and her feet were perished. So it wasn't really a crime in her eyes, it was an act of looking after herself. Aromas of food floated around her as she neared a burger van. The smell of the onions was making her hungry, she felt pains in the pit of her stomach. After a few seconds she decided to join the queue with her mouth watering. She needed to taste the big fat burgers she could see being made.

"Rach, oh my god I've not seen you for years," a voice suddenly shrieked from behind. Rachel turned her head quickly and there she was, the biggest gobshite she'd ever met in her life, Gemma Lucas. Rachel had known this woman for over twenty years, they went to the same school together years before. Gemma was a storyteller and if something was going on in the area, she would be the first to know all about it. A proper shit-stirrer she was, a right mixing bitch. She casually patted Rachel's arm. "How are you cock, I've not seen you in donkey's years. Are you still up to no good? I bet you are, you'll never change you!"

Rachel was blushing and she watched as a few other customers turned around to get a better look of her. "I'm sound, love just doing a bit of shopping. What you up to?"

Gemma held a single hand on the side of her waist and here it was, the gossip, the rumours, the news in the area. "Your Mikey's in deep shit isn't he? One of the lads told me about him having Davo's money off. Is he fucked in the head or what? That crank will kill him."

Rachel just stood listening, there was no way she was airing her dirty washing in public. She kept cool and answered, "It is what it is, Gemma. I don't think our Mikey's arsed anyway, he's in the nick isn't he. At least he's safe in there for now."

Gemma licked her dry cracked lips and moved in closer. Her voice was low and she knew exactly what she was doing. "Well, that's why I'm telling you. Davo's been lifted and landed in the same jail as your lad. His girlfriend told me last night. I mean, I didn't even know Mikey had gone to the Farms did I?"

Rachel's faced dropped, what a grim reaper this woman was. She loved it really, she enjoyed seeing other people go under, watching the pain she'd caused. "Is that where Davo is then?" Rachel enquired.

Gemma was louder than ever and she was drawing attention to herself. "I swear on our little Daniel's life, he landed there last week. His girlfriend said he's still on the induction wing for now so he's not hit the main landing yet. You'd better warn Mikey because he'll be scheming to stitch him up. You know what he's like, he's as sly as they come."

Rachel was in no mood to listen to her anymore. It was her turn to get served and she turned her back on Gemma. This was bad news, Davo was a bad arse and she knew without a doubt he would be making a beeline for her son once he found out he was in the same jail. Rachel got served and said a quick goodbye to Gemma. There was no more talking, no more gossip, she had to get a message to Mikey. He was in deep shit, big danger.

Rachel had been trying her son's phone all day but he wasn't answering. There were only certain times in the day when he could get on the blower. It was way too early for him to take the risk of bringing the mobile out of its hideout until after bang up. Rachel sent him endless text messages, desperate to warn him that he was a marked man. Checking the clock on the wall, she smiled over at her mother. "Mam, I'm gonna get going. My head's been all over today and I'm knackered. I don't know if I'm coming or going. You don't mind do you?"

Agnes was reading her weekly magazine and dropped it onto her lap. Her eyes held sadness and her voice was endearing. Of course she minded, she hated being alone. "I thought we could have shared a bite to eat love, nothing much, just some pie and chips. It would be nice to have a bit of company for a change to tell you the truth. Night after night I sit here on my own. Sometimes I just wish your dad was here. I miss him so much!" Agnes' husband Ged had died ten years ago and every day her heart craved him by her side again. Rachel knew exactly what she meant and her heart sank. She raised a smile and looked at her mum.

Rachel was hungry and the thought of going home having to make something to eat was something she was not looking forward to. She'd have probably have only made a piece of toast, nothing special. She didn't take much persuading to stay a little while longer. "Go on then mam, I'll have something to eat before I go. I mean, it's not as if anyone is sat waiting for me is it?"

Agnes stood and walked to her daughter's side and patted her on the shoulder. "You're in no rush to find a man either love. You should spend some time on your own and sort yourself out. You seem to attract the wrong type anyway, dead-legs they are. Men who don't have a day's work inside them, cadging fuckers."

Rachel held her tongue, this was one debate she didn't want to get involved in. They would argue for days over it if she even made one comment regarding her relationship. Rachel stood and walked over to the living room window as her mother left the room. With her arms stretched high above her head, she peered outside. She was watching a moth flying deliriously near the window, crashing into the glass, spinning in the air, mesmerised by the light from inside the room. Moving the curtains slightly, she stood back and froze, her jaw dropped low. There he was again, she was sure of it, hidden in the shadows. Sprinting to the living room door, she yanked it open and stormed out of the front door like a full force hurricane. Her feet pounded the pavement and there was no stopping her, she was on her toes, sprinting, full steam ahead. Soon she was weaving through the traffic to try to get to the spot where she'd clocked him. Cars honked their horns and wheels were screeching. A van just missed her, she was dicing with death. Rachel reached the side of the bus stop. Her eyes flicked one way, then the other. There wasn't a living soul there. Her head twisted around, still nothing. She stumbled around the other side of the bus stop, nothing. Was she having a nervous breakdown here or was it her mind playing tricks on her? She was sure it was Gary, she knew he would turn up sooner or later when he was on his arse. That was his game, he would never just come and admit he was wrong, he would just stalk her until he found the courage to say sorry. Plonking down on the floor inside the shelter, she held her head in her hands. The wind howled past her, echoing inside her eardrums, she was sure she'd seen him, she would have put money on it. The sound of the traffic flew by and she was just sat there in her own little world, scared of the thought that she could be losing the plot. She cradled her knees to her chest and sat shivering on the cold pavement. Hold on, what did she spot, her eyes were wide open, her breathing stopped for a split second. Rachel scrambled to her feet and bent her body over slightly. The thick grey smoke from the cigarette was still circling above it, blowing side to side in the wind.

So, she was right after all. Somebody was there, otherwise where had the burning cigarette come from? She let out a laboured breath and started to head back across the road with caution. She wasn't going daft after all or losing her marbles. There was someone watching her. And if it was Gary, she was going to give him a smack right in the face for scaring her like this. What a wanker he was!

Mark sat down with his wife for tea. The mortgage had been paid and everything was rosy in the garden. Tracy had never asked where the extra money came from, she knew better than to question him. As long as the bills were paid, she wasn't arsed. It was her husband who had blown the money, so it was up to him to put it back. Gone were the days when she'd run around to her family begging them all to help bail her out. Tracy stabbed her fork into a chip on her plate. She was a right greedy bitch and her stomach was never full. She blamed it on boredom. She actually said that if her life was more exciting, she would never munch so many calories. The silver fork scraped along her plate. "You're quiet tonight, what's up with you?"

Mark played with the food on his plate and rolled a few peas around on the end of his fork. "Nothing, I'm just tired that's all. I've had a crap day, too. I swear, once I get the chance of something better I'm moving on. This job is killing me."

Tracy had heard all this before. Every day he told her about some inmate who was doing his head in. He'd had many a sleepless night about them as well. The prisoners just pecked away at his head twenty-four hours a day. It was always an endless battle to get up each morning for work and lately he hated every minute he was working in the prison service. Rolling his sleeve up slightly, Mark checked his watch casually. "I've got to nip to Smithy's soon love. He wants to borrow my squash racket."

Tracy sniggered and held the bottom of her stomach. "Well, you may as well give it to him. I mean, when was the last time you did a bit of exercise? I wasn't going to mention it but you are piling the pounds on lately. Especially around the waistline."

Mark gulped his glass of water back and shot a look over at her. What a cheeky cow she was. He'd never said what he thought about her weight gain over the years and here she was slating him in his own home regarding a bit of extra blubber, his 'winter warmer' as he liked to call it. Mark blushed and patted his stomach with a flat palm and tried to make a joke out of it. He was raging inside but kept his cards close to his chest. He raised his eyebrows and casually flicked a comment over to her. This would teach her to belittle him and make him feel worthless. "Yep, it happens to the best of us love. I think we both need to go on a diet. Your cheeks look like they're storing nuts for winter."

This was below the belt and he loved watching her face drop. Her expression changed and she clenched her teeth together tightly. "What do you mean both of us, you cheeky get? I've lost over two pounds this week, I'll have you know. You don't see me munching biscuit after biscuit do you? At least I bleeding try."

Mark smirked. He was clever like that, he could bring her down a peg or two whenever she got above her station. Tracy had a face like a smacked arse and you could have cut the atmosphere with a knife. She didn't say a word, she just sat snarling over at him. He'd done it now, he was in her bad books. Pushing her plate away from her, Tracy folded her arms tightly and her nostrils flared. She was fuming. How dare this bastard insult her like this? She'd seen her arse. "I'm going to bed early tonight and don't be waking me up when you get back in either. You can sleep on the sofa for all I care."

There it was, she just couldn't help herself. This was the usual sort of stuff that always followed any argument - the sex ban. The 'you can kiss my arse' moment. Mark whistled about the room and he knew he'd rattled her cage. "If you can't take it, don't give it," he mumbled under his breath so she couldn't hear him. "No worries love, I'll be as quiet as a mouse. I might even pop in the boozer if you're planning an early night and have a few scoops with the lads." Mark was on a roll, what a result he had - a free pass to go and chill with the local lads down at the pub. She said herself she was tired, so there was no way she could come back at him with any moaning about spending quality time with her. Bending down slightly, he pecked his warm lips on the side of her cheek. She was like an ice maiden, she never flinched. "Night love, sleep tight," he shouted over his shoulder as he left.

The front door banged shut and shook the house. Tracy was alone. "Fuck off, you smarmy bastard," she cursed as she booted the chair from under the table. Tracy pulled her top up and stared at her muffin top, examining every inch of it, grabbing the lard. Her husband was such an arsehole and he'd put her on a complete downer now for the rest of the night. How dare he bring up her weight gain! What a bastard he was, he knew exactly what he'd done. She picked her fork up and carried on eating the food left on the side of her plate, comfort eating.

Mark stood in the darkness waiting for the last parcel to be delivered. He would never do this again. The last bit of money from the drop was going in the bank. He would never get

himself in this state again. It was all stopping. The stress was killing him. A silver car pulled up at the side of him and turned its lights off, the engine just ticking over slightly. This was a quiet street and very few cars ever drove up it. There were a few lovers every now and then but they were always parked up away from prying eyes, out of sight not wanting to be disturbed. Mark had had a couple of nights here too; a drunken fling with the barmaid from the Fat Ox. Fuck buddies they were, always there for each other when times were hard, no questions asked, just pure filthy sex. Mark scoured the area before he stepped out from his hideout. His breathing was noisier than usual. He rushed toward the waiting vehicle and once he was at the side of it he opened the car door with shaking hands. This looked shady as fuck. Anyone who was watching this scene would have put two and two together and worked out what was going on. It wasn't rocket science. The man in the driver's seat was wearing a dark cap and the peak was pulled right over the top of his eyes. His body dipped into his seat. Mark sat on the passenger side as he handed over the goods. It wasn't that big really, but it was bound tightly together with clingfilm. Drugs, miniature phones, steroids, it was all there inside the bundle.

"You got the cash?" Mark asked, he never looked the guy directly in the eye. There was rustling, coughing and the sound of cash being counted.

The male's voice was chilling and he put the fear of

God in Mark. "There you go, you bent bastard. Make sure it lands too. But, remember," he paused and went nose to nose with him, "if it doesn't, I'll find you. And you don't want that to happen do you?"

Mark's heart was racing and he knew he was a sitting duck. He had to get out of there before things got out of hand. He counted the money quickly. It was all there, a done deal. The car door flung open and he jumped out, aware he could be stuck from behind. He never said goodbye, he just walked away at speed with his head dipped. That was a close call and he was made aware of how deep he was into all this now. The guy was right though, he was a bent bastard, bought for thirty pieces of silver, a dirty lying Judas. Mark's nightmare was nearly over in his eyes after this parcel landed. There would be no more sucking up to that little prick Mikey Milne. Yes, this was over and he planned to get his life back on track as soon as this parcel was out of his hands.

Marching down the street, he zipped his coat and turned his collar up to protect his neck from the bitter wind. He was gagging for a pint and maybe even a game of cards to help him chill out. His head was mashed. Sheila the barmaid was on her shift tonight, so if she was feeling a bit frisky later on, he could sling one up her before the night was over, a quick knee-trembler. Mark marched into the public house and ruffled his fingers through his hair. The wind had messed it up and he looked like he'd been dragged through a hedge backwards. There was lots of noise, laughter and banter between the punters. This was a man's pub and few women were sat about, except for the usual bikes that everyone had ridden at one time or another. The card table here was well known in the area and you had to be a fool or pissed out of your head if you ever sat around it. Men had lost everything in seconds here at the drop of a hat; cars, gold and life savings. Each and every one thought they had the hand to make a difference to their lives; the aces, the kings, the queens; but they never did. Sheila called it the devil's table. There were so many fights caused by the card games and we're not talking little scuffles here either. Punters had been stabbed, knocked out and even shot. Where there was money, there was always trouble and the Fat Ox was well known for it. The residents in the area had tried to have the pub closed down more than once. It was an eyesore and just caused youths to hang about near it. You could get whatever you wanted in this boozer. Knocked-off clobber, food, gold, drugs... There was always someone selling something right from the back of a wagon.

Mark stood at the bar and smiled over at the brassy barmaid. She was a right dirty hussy and had no morals. She had big tits and bright red lipstick plastered all over her lips. Once she clocked Mark she pulled her top down lower and made sure he got an eyeful of her perky breasts. This guy was on a promise tonight and without even saying a word to her, he knew she was game. A right dirty cow she was; anytime, anywhere, she was there gagging for it. Mark waited for his pint then turned his body and leaned against the bar. There was some serious money going into the pot on the card table tonight and he could see by the players' eyes this shit just got real. His eyes were wide open, eager to see who came out on top. The game was drawing him in, his eyes fixated on every card dealt. Patting the cash inside his jacket pocket he felt an adrenaline rush throughout his body. His palms were hot and sweaty and his heart was racing. What the hell was he doing, had he not learned from his mistakes? Mark swallowed hard and slurped a mouthful of his cold beer. Once a gambler, always a gambler he supposed. It was too late, there was no going back. His addiction took over. "Deal us in lads on the next round," he chuckled. Mark rubbed his two flat palms together and pulled up a chair. It was going to be a long night. A very long night indeed.

Rachel kissed her mother goodbye and headed home. Agnes stood at the front door and watched her until she got to the end of the street before she went back inside. She always did this. No matter who came to her house she always walked them down the garden path. Rachel was aware that her stalker could be watching her. She would take no shortcuts tonight, she was staying where people could see her. With every step she took, her heart started pounding a little bit more inside her ribcage. If any fucker tried grabbing her, she had her front door key lodged in between her knuckles ready to gouge their eyes out. She was alert and aware of her surroundings. Rachel finally reached her garden path and it was fair to say she was relieved. A woman wasn't safe at the best of times in this area so especially not at night. She knew how easily she could have been attacked from behind. There were always stories in the news about women being attacked, there were some sick twisted bastards out there who would think nothing of killing another human being, slitting their victim's throats, raping and abusing them before they ended their lives.

Sliding the key into the front door she turned her head quickly, eyes wide open. There was heavy breathing, rustling. "What the fuck do you want!" she screamed as she nearly jumped out of her skin.

"I've come back. I just needed to get away while all that shit was going on. I know I sold you out but my arse was flapping. You're alright, Davo would have left you alone and given me a right good hiding."

Rachel punched her clenched fist into Gary's chest, not just once, she pummelled it like her life depended on it. She was knocking ten bags of shit out of him. "Rachel, for fuck's sake. I'm back now," he protested, "come on, give me a break will you!"

What kind of fool did he think she was? Did he really think he could have her over and she would just let it go? Not a fucking chance! This woman was livid and she was looking around the front garden now for a missile to launch at his big, daft, ugly head. "Get my son's money back, you lowlife thieving twat. I knew you were low Gary but never in a million years did I think you would nick from me. How low can you go? You disgust me, you make my skin crawl you worthless wanker."

Gary was backed into a corner and his eyes were wide open. He stuttered as he held his hands over his head trying to protect himself. "What fucking money, I haven't touched any."

Rachel growled and booted him right in his leg. "You lying, dirty cunt. I know it's you who's had it away. Don't even try to deny it."

Gary made sure he got her in a death grip and held her hands tightly behind her back. "Just shut the fuck up for a minute and listen up, yeah." Rachel spat in his eye and she was nearly free. "I've not touched a penny of any money. Are you right in the head? Come on Rach. I love you and to think you would have me down as something like this knocks me sick."

Gary let go of her hands, she was still snapping. "Well, if you didn't take it where the fuck did it go? Did the fucking money fairies nick it?"

Gary held a blank expression and shrugged his shoulders. "Just let me come in and we can sort this out. Fuck me, I'm a lot of things but don't ever put my name down for robbing from you."

Rachel pushed him away with her hands deep into his chest. She booted him again in his shin. "Go fuck yourself, over my dead body are you getting into this house. Go and get the money back and then we can talk, otherwise piss off and crawl back under the rock you just came from."

Gary hung his head as he marched from the garden. He was watching his back too, there was no way he trusted this lunatic. She was like that Rachel, she was a sniper. The minute his back was turned she would lamp him one, swing a killer blow. "I'll let everybody know about you as well, Gary. Mark my words, your name will be shit around here. Nobody likes a shady cunt, a lowlife robbing bastard. Go on, piss off and don't come back." Rachel was stood at her garden gate, her hands gripping it tightly. Her shrieking tones could be heard by all the neighbours. You could see them peering out of the windows. Everybody loved to watch a bit of drama on the street and Rachel was giving them value for money. Gary was gone now and she hung over the garden gate gagging for breath. He was such a lying hard-faced fucker, did he really think she'd come over on the banana boat or what? He'd had the money alright. There were no two ways about it. What now though? She was fucked. How on earth was she ever going to get her son's money back? She was up shit creek without a paddle. Something had to give, she had to get a break somewhere, surely? She turned slowly. This woman had been dragged through the mill, her heart was low and she couldn't take anymore. Every time she took a step forward something always dragged her back down. Sad really, because she was trying to change, to right all the wrongs she'd done over the years. It was such a hard thing to do though. Everything was going tits up. Rachel opened the front door and once she got inside she stood looking around the hallway with dismay. This was it, her life in a nutshell. No man to love her anymore and her boy locked away in prison. As if from nowhere her eyes flooded with tears and she fell to the floor sobbing her heart out. "When's it going to stop, ay, when is all this shit going to end! I can't take it anymore. I just want it to stop!"

CHAPTER FOURTEEN

The doors were finally opened on the landing and the inmates were eager to get out and go for their showers. Shouting and banter was exchanged, this was prison life. Mikey emerged from his pad with a white towel under his arm and some shampoo and soap in his hand. Potter was close behind him as always. Everyone knew the script for getting a wash in the morning and inmates had a pecking order to follow. The prisoners headed down to the shower cubicles and spirits seemed high. Mikey headlocked Potter and was dragging him about the landing playfully. "Come on, you can wash my sack for me," Mikey joked.

The other criminals were laughing and joined in the friendly banter. "Potter can be the landing wood washer. He can do a sack and crack washing service." The youth at the side of them chuckled. Mikey howled laughing and let go of Potter who was struggling to find his feet. Once he was steady he pointed his finger over at the men. "You can piss off you lot can. I'm no dirt-box merchant. Any of you come near me and God help me because I'll stick a blade right in you."

Whoa, where's all this coming from? Who had died and made him captain of the ship? Potter was bouncing now as he continued to walk along. He was taking his role as Mikey's wingman seriously. I suppose he was learning the ropes as he went along but hats off to the guy, he was starting to look the part. Potter had some good news to share. His family were moving back to where they used to live in Cheshire. The family business had taken off and their money worries were over. There was even a job waiting for him when he got home. He'd already decided to go straight, or at least try. Mikey hung his towel around his neck as he walked into the showers. There were cocks and balls all over the show. Nobody was arsed about showing their wedding tackle off. It was funny how each inmate clocked each other's nobs too, they would never look at it directly. No, it was always a sneaky peek. Mikey stripped off and this inmate was packing, his dick was huge.

Potter swallowed hard as he got an eyeful of it. "Fuck off away from me Mikey. You make my pecker look like a slug."

There it was now, everyone's eyes were on his privates. Honest to God, the prisoners walked over to where he was stood and got a good butcher's at it, no hiding, no shame. It was official. Mikey had some meat on him, he was hung like a donkey. The showers were cold and you could hear the perishing moans from the men as they washed their bodies inside the cubicles. Singing, whistling, this was a happy place this morning.

Mark watched the lads coming back from the showers. He caught Mikey's eye and he was trying to grab his attention. His neck stretched and he coughed to clear his throat. "Oi, Milne, can I have a quick word with you?"

Mikey shot his eyes across the wing and changed direction towards him. Once he got there he stood tall with his hands held behind his back. "What's up boss?" This lad was so fucking cocky and it was no wonder he got people's backs up. Just the look in his eye was enough for somebody to want to punch his lights out.

Mark checked around him and made sure he took the inmate to a secure place where no CCTV could see them. "Here, get a grip of this. Like I said, it's the last one."

Mikey took the parcel, looked the screw straight in the eye and smirked. "You'll do as I fucking say. You're in it now."

Mark clenched his fists into two tiny balls at the side of his legs, his knuckles turning white. He had to come back with something, there was no way he could have this runt calling the shots. His voice was firm and he meant every word he said. His ears pinned back and his nostrils flared. "You daft cunt, do you really think you can win against me? You're forgetting where you are lad. I run the wing not fucking you."

Mikey clicked his tongue inside his mouth and rubbed the end of his nose with a flat palm. "You don't scare me. You're a bent screw. All it takes is one word from me and your number's up."

Mark ran at him and slammed him up against the wall with his hand around his neck. His warm breath in his face, spit flying all over. "Go on, you just test me. You'll see what I'm all about, go on I dare you." Mark went nose to nose with him and whispered. "You've heard about prisoners stringing themselves up haven't you? Lads who nobody could believe had taken their own lives; the question you need to ask yourself is – did they take their own life or was it me who ended it for them?"

Mikey wasn't flinching, he just stared right back at the screw and smirked. What was up with him, why didn't he just walk away and let sleeping dogs lie? He had to reply, show no fear. "You see that scar on your cheek, pal. Word has it that it was an inmate who did that to you. It just goes to show that you never know where a blade will come from. We both have shit we can pull out of the bag don't we? Think about it, let me see," he rolled his eyes and licked the corner of his mouth. "Yeah, a junkie will slice you up for a few bags of brown. No questions asked, job done."

Mark was pissing in the wind here and he knew something had to give. There was no way he could continue like this, he was making himself ill. But he needed money again. The card game he played had taken all the cash to pay his bills and he was back to square one. Mikey stuck his chest out and pushed Mark out of the way. "Any chance you can get that message to my old man?"

Mark snarled. "Fuck off Milne, just get out of my sight before I do you some damage."

Mikey may have won the fight today but the war was far from over. He'd got the screw's back up and he knew he wasn't safe anymore. This cunt could stitch him up, plant stuff in his pad, get him shipped out. He had to tread carefully now, watch every move he made.

Brendan Mellor sat in his new pad rolling a cigarette. Blowing a thick cloud of grey smoke from his mouth, he sat in deep thought. His face was still badly bruised and you could see he'd taken a right beating. The prison had moved him to a new wing and were about to ship him out to a new jail, he was just waiting to be moved. His street cred in the jail had gone now and if he went back to the wing they would all be waiting for him to fight back, put up a challenge. Keys jangled outside his door, he was alert, eager to see what they wanted. The door opened and Smithy stood smiling at him. "Here you go, a bit of company for you." Brendan lifted his eyes and his jaw dropped. He knew Davo from the out and he was speechless. This man looked hard as fuck, muscles pumped, thick set neck, he wasn't someone to be messed with.

"Alright," he said to Brendan.

"Yeah, cool bro." Davo gave a sour look over at him and Brendan could have punched himself. Where the fuck had the word 'bro' come from? It was just a habit and how he spoke on the street. What a complete tosser he felt now. His cheeks were bright red and he dipped his head low, ashamed of the choice of word he'd used. Smithy stood at the door and watched Davo throw his bags to the side of the room. He jumped onto his bed and looped his arms behind his head. "Sorted this boss, cheers for getting me away from that wing, it was a fucking nightmare full of raging bagheads and riff-raff."

Smithy chuckled. He knew the wing where this inmate had come from and he was right, it was a shithole with the dregs of society serving time on it; the down-and-outs, the men who had lost all respect for themselves, offenders who wouldn't last two minutes on the outside. For some of the prisoners this place was their second home. Smithy left the room and locked the door behind him. This was going to be good, how was Brendan going to handle this? The prisoner sat on the edge of his bed biting his fingernails hard.

Davo turned his head over towards him and gave him the once-over. "Who's done you in then? Fuck me, you've took a good arse-kicking haven't you?"

Brendan was relieved that this man had even given

him the time of the day. He sucked in a large mouthful of air and answered him. "Just some twat who'll get what's coming to him. He got me when I was unaware, stole a few blows on me."

Davo rolled over on his side and wanted to hear more. "What and you've not come back at him with anything, stab the fucker up, don't just take it on the chin. I swear, I would fuck the cunt right up."

Brendan was thinking aloud and he was getting above his station again. He was chatting shit trying to make himself look like the big man. "Don't you worry, Milne is getting it. As soon as I see my chance I'll twist the shady fucker up. We were mates you know." Brendan's eyes were wide open and he was twisting his fingers rapidly. "He sold me out. Honest, we were a team until we landed in this shithole. And then he went all snidey. Mikey's changed, he thinks he's untouchable."

Davo digested what his new mate had just told him and licked his lips slowly. "What's the geezer's name again?"

Brendan sighed and shook his head, still trying to get his head around why his brother-in-arms had fucked him over, "Mikey Milne" he said.

Davo sprang from his bed, his eyes were dancing with madness, the vein pumping rapidly at the side of his neck. "Oh, so this is where the cheeky cunt landed. What wing is he on?"

Brendan was puzzled and answered him with caution. "He's on B-Wing. He thinks he's the fucking daddy over there because he took the main man down."

Davo smirked and kicked his trainers from his feet. "I need you to sort a few things out with me pal. Let's see Milne fall flat on his arse. He'll shit a brick when he sees me."

Brendan was such a gawp and he was none the wiser as to what was going down here. All he knew at this moment was that he was going to get his mate done in. Who was this guy and why did he want Mikey? Brendan filled his pad mate in about how things were running on the opposite wing and by the end of their chat, Davo knew the ins and outs of a cat's arsehole. Brendan was a right blabbermouth, a grass. He sold Mikey down the river and he was more than ready to make sure he got what was coming to him.

When he had finished Brendan tickled the end of his chin and held his hand out towards Davo. "Don't you worry. Anything you want to know about that rat I will find out. What's he done to you anyway, are you going to fill me in?"

Davo looked over at the window at the skyline and spoke slowly. "He knows what he owes me and unless he sorts it, he will be leaving here in a body bag. He can run but he can't hide."

Brendan punched his clenched fist into the air. He was loving this, it was payback time. "Kick his fucking head in for me mate. He's fuck all to me anymore, kill the cunt, knock his teeth out."

Davo lay back down on his bed and nodded his head slowly. The clock was ticking now and Mikey Milne's days were numbered. He'd show this clown how he rolled. Nobody fucked with Davo, nobody.

★

Mark stood on a corridor not far from B-Wing. It was quiet here, not like the rest of the prison. It was eerie, haunting. An old man walked past Mark and smiled at him sheepishly. The guy must have been at least sixty; bald head, silver-rimmed glasses hanging on the end of his fat and stumpy nose. "Morning sir," the old geezer said as he strolled past him. Mark nodded and screwed his face up slightly. He had no time for this offender, you could tell. Walking up the landing, he stopped at a cell door and seemed to take forever before he stepped inside. Slowly, with a flat palm, he edged the door open wide. "Alright Dennis, I just wanted to pass you a message from your lad. He's on my wing and he's heard you're in the same jail."

Dennis nearly collapsed. He was frozen, eyes wide open, lips trembling. He ran to the window and stuck his head through the bars having a panic attack. Dennis was suffocating and finding it hard to breathe. Mark hesitated, after a few seconds he walked closer to him and checked he was alright. "He just wants to know if he can see you. Yes or no?"

Dennis ran his fingers through his thick grey hair. This guy looked a lot older than he was. His yellow tobacco-stained teeth stood out from his mouth as he gripped the bars with force. "Why does he want to see me? Has he said. Fuck, fuck, fuck!"

Mark was fed up already and hated being on this wing. "Listen, I'm just passing a message from your son. Personally, I wouldn't give you the time of day but ay, that's just me. Do you want to see him or what? I've not got all day."

Dennis closed his eyes and his cheeks creased. He was thinking out loud. "It's been years, what would I say to him? I'm an old fool who's been locked up for years. He was a kid when I left him. I don't know him anymore. I'm a mess, a fuck up. A dirty rotten hanging twat."

"You said that, not me," the screw sneered. Mark started to edge his way out of the door. He had no time to listen to all this shit. It was a yes or no, a simple answer like he'd already told him.

Dennis turned on the spot. He had to make a decision one way or the other. He ragged his fingers through his hair and squeezed his eyes together tightly. "I'll see him. I want to see him."

Mark stood with his hand resting on the doorway. He could have done without this and didn't need the ball-ache of setting up a meeting. He sighed and shook his head. "I thought you didn't want to see him. I mean, it's not like you're a role model to him is it. In fact, if I was him, I would put you six foot under."

Dennis gritted his teeth tightly together. He was no shit-bag and prison life had taught him a thing or two about defending himself. This man had been hurt inside these walls, there were deep gashes all over his body, he'd had boiling water flung all over him. His time inside the jails over the years had nearly killed him off. Fifteen years Dennis had been inside the system and he never thought he would see the outside world again. His sentence was coming to an end in the next few months and he'd already told his mental health worker that he didn't think he was ready to face society again. This was his world, this was where he felt safe. Prison was all he'd known for most of his life. Mark studied Dennis for a lot longer than he should have. A cunning smirk appeared on his face and he tapped his fingers on the side of the door. "I'll sort it out for tomorrow. It might be a bit hard to get him over to this side but I'll try my best."

Dennis was frantic and he stormed over to Mark in a

panic. "Don't bring him over here," his eyes were bulging from their sockets. "I want to meet him in at one of the offices. Somewhere quiet, a place nobody can see us talking."

Mark paced back from the door. "I'll see what I can do."

Dennis watched the screw walking back down the landing. He scanned the area and stood glued on the same spot for a few seconds. This was all too much for him to take. He stormed back inside his pad and smashed the door shut. It was always a shame to see a grown man cry and this convict was blubbering, heartbroken. He scrambled over to his bed on his hands and knees and shoved his hand under his pillow. A small photograph appeared as his fingers unfolded. It was a snap of Mikey when he was younger. A wave of emotion choked Dennis Milne and his legs buckled from underneath him. He was a quivering wreck now, sobbing his heart out, gasping his breath. He never thought this day would come in his life. What would he say to him, how could he explain his life and the choices he made? This man was a mess. Dennis pressed his mouth firmly against the photograph of his son. He was speechless and not a single word left his mouth. This was going to be so hard, so fucking hard.

★

Davo stood talking to Smithy, he was his new allocated officer. The pair of them were having a bit of banter and they were discussing gym routines and the best exercises to do; v-sits, weight bench and squats. In fairness, Davo was tanning the steroids on the out and only really pumped iron when he was going out with a new girl to impress her.

Davo stood there in his white fitted vest, chest expanded, hands held behind his back. Mark came to join the join the group. He was in no mood for anybody today and the stress was showing more than normal. He slammed his flat palm on the wall and pressed at it with force. "I fucking hate Mikey Milne with a vengeance. On my life, he just presses my buttons."

Davo's ears pinned back, he was listening now. This lad's name was all over the jail. "I thought you were making progress with the kid, you said yourself he was just misunderstood, what happened to all that?" Smithy replied.

Mark stood with his hands in his pockets and let out a laboured breath. "Yeah, that was then. I've had a rethink, he's a prick. A cocky know-it-all. He winds me up."

Davo stepped closer to them and squeezed the top of Mark's shoulder. This was the time to get them on board. The screws in the jail turned a blind eye when shit was going down, everybody knew that. It was the law of the land. Davo sneered. "You just give me five minutes with the cock and I'll make sure he never gives you any shit again. That's all I need, five minutes. You know, nudge, nudge, wink, wink, say no more lads."

Mark was shocked and although he shouldn't have, he nodded his head. He was ready to wipe the smile right from Mikey's face. "Yep, don't you worry about that. I'll let you kick ten tons of shit out of him. He just gets right under my skin. I would like to see him fall flat on his arse I'm telling you straight."

Davo winked at Mark and without a word being said, you could tell these two would be having words again in the very near future. Smithy backed off, there was no way he was getting involved in shit like this. Yeah, he knew what went on behind closed doors but this was something he wanted to keep his neck out of. Davo watched Smithy head back into his office and stood looking down the landing. He cracked his knuckles and knew anytime soon Mikey Milne would be lying underneath him taking a good hiding. Mark stood with him and took him over to a quiet part of the corridor. When nobody was looking, he stepped inside his office and pulled a red file out on the table. "Just come in here a second Davo," he shouted. Mark had a cunning look in his eye and with a single finger he pushed the notes forward. Davo was unsure at first and stood looking puzzled. Then it clicked. He read the name and slowly, with caution, dragged out Dennis Milne's personal file. His eyes flicked one way then the other. The pages turned with speed as Mark stood at the office window making sure nobody came in. The deed was done, whatever Mark wanted now was understood by both parties. Davo nodded and backed out of the room. Mark stood at the glass window and watched him walk back to his pad. He smirked to himself and sucked hard on his gums. If Mikey Milne wanted trouble, then bring it on. He was ready.

Mikey lay on his bed. His expression seemed different; he was cool and calm. Potter finished writing his letter and plonked down on his bed to chill. "Why don't you ever write Sarah a letter? Tell her how much you love her and all that?"

Mikey raised his eyes, "I'm shit at feelings and that. And, come on, imagine me writing all that 'I love you' shit."

Potter chuckled and pulled two pieces of white lined

paper from his pad. "I can help you if you want. I know you struggle with reading and writing. I'm pretty good when it comes to expressing the human heart. I've never really sent a letter as such but I've written a few nice

letters to my friends."

Mikey ran his fingers through his hair. "What, you write girls letters and don't send them. What's the point in that?"

"No point really, it just helps me clear my head from time to time. I've loved a girl for years but never ever told her. Pretty gutted about it now but time has passed and it's too late. Every night my head was mashed with her and I just needed some way of channelling my energy. She drove me wild, I swear, every minute of every day she was in my thoughts."

Mikey had never really had time to talk about love before and this inmate seemed to know what he was talking about. Perhaps he could pick up some tips, learn the art of romance. "I feel a right dickhead even saying 'I love you' though. Sarah always tells me I should say it more often but I really struggle."

Potter's eyes were wide open. This conversation was right up his street. "It's the way a person can make you feel inside, the ache in your heart when you're not with them. The need to touch and kiss them."

Mikey sat up on his bed. Did he really feel all these things for Sarah or was he just plodding along with her. He held his head to the side and thought. "Yes, I guess I do miss her sometimes. But not when I'm out grafting and she's ringing me every two minutes."

"How does it feel when you kiss her, does she give you butterflies?"

Mikey let his guard down. "My Sarah is sweet, I think she's slowly but surely teaching me how to love somebody. Come on Potter, growing up I never had love, nobody ever said they loved me as far as I can remember."

"What, so your own mother never told you?" Potter replied, shocked.

Mikey dragged his knees up to his chest and rested his head there. "It wasn't like that growing up. When my dad left she lost herself and went down the wrong path, she was off her head half the time. She couldn't even love herself, never mind me." Potter could see the pain in Mikey's eyes and was in two minds about whether he should give him a cuddle. Mikey continued. "I gave up on love a long time ago. It only ends in tears. But Sarah, she's different, she makes me believe that two people can be happy and have fun. Her home life has been so different to mine and sometimes I get quite jealous that she has so many people who care about her. I'd be happy with just one family member giving a shit if I'm being honest with you."

Potter pondered his own upbringing, "I was lucky, I suppose. My parents did everything by the book. No sex before marriage, bought a house and then had children. I think sometimes they both wish they had seen more of life, done more things. It's like they are just waiting to die now. Of course they have the business but without that, I think they would have said goodbye years ago. They don't even like the same kind of things, my dad is a bookworm and my mother sits knitting any chance she gets. I never want to end up like that, shoot me now if I do! I want to find a girl who wants to go on an adventure with me, explore life, see the sights."

Mikey burst out laughing. "No chance of that for me

and Sarah. Her dad hates my guts and if I'm being honest with you, I don't think I'm good enough for her. Let's face facts here. It's only a matter of time before some smarmy cunt comes along and sweeps her off her feet. How can I compete with a guy who's working and has a good education? She'll get sick of me in the end, they always do." Mikey's eyes started to cloud over and he swallowed hard. "It's just life though isn't it? You take the good with the bad and see where you end up."

Potter could see he was struggling and tried to shed some light on the matter. "But look what's happening now. You're going to see your dad after all these years. It might be a turning point. You two could even start a relationship again and have a father and son bond."

Mikey liked the sound of that and moved his head slowly. "Yeah, I suppose it would be nice to have him in my life again. When we're both out of this shithole we can even go to the match together like we did when I was younger. He likes his footy does my dad. He's a proper United fan too. He used to sit with me watching it on the TV and you should have seen him when they scored, he went fucking ballistic." Potter could only watch as his pad mate flicked through his memory bank. Mikey was so happy talking about this happy time in his life and he was glad that he had found his dad again. The meeting was set for first thing the next morning and Mikey was buzzing.

The lights went out on the wing and Mikey pulled out a small mobile phone from his arsehole. He'd had it plugged there all day. Slowly he started to unwrap it. Potter was still amazed that anyone could shove anything up their ring piece. He was intrigued that it actually stayed up there but as of yet he'd not had a go at concealing anything. He had no plans to plug anything in the future either. It wasn't right in his eyes. Once the power button was turned on, text alerts could be heard, there were loads of them. Mikey flicked the button and made sure the phone was on silent. Before he starting reading them Potter sprang up from his bed and seemed to have something on his mind. "Can you sort me a woman out? I know I'm not like you but there must be someone out there that you can get to write to me, they don't even have to come and see me, just a few letters here and there."

Mikey blanked the unread messages and he was in the zone. Now they had social media on the blower the world was their oyster. Mikey was a dab hand with the ladies and he was going to put Potter on the map. Yes, it was as easy as that. Mikey opened Facebook and urged Potter to come and join him on his bed. "Here you go lad, the land of pussy. It's been a while since I've been on here but you never forget how to pull the hotties. Honest I met pure girls on here, gagging for it they were, dirty slags." The two of them spent hours sending friend requests to girls now. Potter was eager to get even one message back and it didn't take long. The phone was on fire now, there was pussy galore. At last, Potter was learning the tricks of the trade, he was excited and never before had he talked to so many girls. This Fuck-book was the best thing ever.

Why had he never been on it before?

Dennis Milne watched the silver moon shining through his window and stared at it as if it held all the answers to his problems. There was no way he was sleeping tonight, not a chance on this earth. A single fat bulky tear rolled down his cheek and he wiped it with the side of his hand. His chest was rising frantically and every now and then he seemed to lose his breath. Tomorrow was D-day. There could be no more running... He owed his son an explanation as to why he'd never been in touch with him. Was he strong enough? Could he look him in the eye and tell him the truth?

CHAPTER FIFTEEN

Rachel was smoking like a chimney. Her head was in bits and nothing was making sense anymore. Gary was a lying twat and her blood was still boiling. He had more front than Blackpool, he even believed his own lies. Sarah came into the front room holding two cups.

"Have you heard anything from Mikey? He never rang me last night which is unusual?"

Rachel shook her head and it was time to fill Sarah in. "Davo's in the same jail. I've tried getting in touch with Mikey but I've heard nothing, zilch up to now. I hope his pad hasn't been spun. I bet he's down the block or something. I mean, he always replies to me, why not last night?"

Sarah's mouth was wide open. "You mean the guy who he's had trouble with?"

"Yep, the one who ragged me about. He's bad news and if he gets his hands on him he'll leave him for dead."

Sarah gasped and sat back in her seat. She seemed distracted today and her mind wasn't on the job. Her bottom lip trembled. "My dad is sending me away he said. There's a job down in London that his pal has sorted out and he's putting pressure on me to take it." Rachel was listening and never said a word as she continued. "I've told him I'm going nowhere but he said he'll make sure I go if it's the last thing he does. He's evil you know. He'll just take me down there kicking and screaming. He doesn't care about Mikey and the love we have."

Rachel voiced her opinion without thinking. "It might be for the best. Our Mikey's away for a long time and this job could change your life."

Sarah snarled and slapped her clenched fist down on her thighs. "Well, thanks a bunch Rachel. I thought you would have told him to take a running jump not bleeding side with him. I've told you how I feel about Mikey and you should help me to support him."

Rachel wasn't with it and she put her mouth into gear without thinking yet again. "Mikey could be the biggest mistake you've ever made. He's my own son but he's not cut out for the life you want him to have. People like us fuck up, let people down. He might think he can make you happy but, come on, he's got nothing going for him. You're used to a different style of life. I know Mikey and he'll feel like he'll never fit in."

Sarah snapped and this was not what she wanted to hear today. "I'd give it all up for Mikey any day. I don't need nice things and money means nothing to me. We can make it work, something will give. We can be so happy. Nobody makes me feel happy like he does."

Rachel looked at her and her heart sank. She had her own problems to deal with at the moment and her head was in bits trying to think of ways to come up with the missing money. Sarah was on one and sat staring into space. She'd come here for a bit of peace from her own parents and now she was getting stressed here too. Why was everyone against her? She loved Mikey with all her heart and nobody was going to stop her going to see him, not even her father. Rachel didn't know the half of it. Sarah's dad had knocked her about, slapped her right across her face. He was desperate to get her away from this deadbeat and would do anything in his power to keep his princess free from harm. Sarah rolled up her sleeves slightly and ran her slender finger over the bruised skin and the purple and yellow blemishes. This was true love, she could feel it in her heart, nobody would stop them being together, nobody. She would never give up on the love of her life.

Mikey stood on the landing, he was edgy. He couldn't keep still and his forehead was sweating. This was a big day for him and one he'd imagined in his head for as long as he could remember. Flicking invisible dust from the top of his shoulder, he turned his head as Mark marched up behind him. He was quiet today and seemed like he had the world on his shoulders. Mikey was giddy, his feet tapping on the floor at the side of him. He forgot all about the war he had going on with this screw and spoke to him like they were best friends. "Thanks for this. It means a lot. I know sometimes I can be a prick but just ignore me. It's the way I am sometimes."

Mark pulled a sour expression. This inmate could get to fuck if he thought he was getting a conversation out of him today. He wanted to smash his head in, snap his jaw, put him on his arse. Mikey walked through a small door to the left of the corridor. He'd never been to this part of the jail before. It was quiet and deserted. He scanned around and tilted his head; there wasn't a sound, what a strange wing this was. Where were all the inmates? The floors here were highly polished and it looked like nobody had walked on them in months. Mark stood at the steel door and held it open with his hand. "Go in there and wait. I'll go and get him." Mikey went into the office but remained on his feet. His heart was in his mouth and his stomach was turning. Here it was, time to meet his old man.

★

As Dennis walked along the corridor his legs buckled. Every now and then he had to stop to regain his breath. Mark had no patience whatsoever for this inmate and carried on walking. He could have died for all he cared, dropped down dead, he didn't give a flying fuck. Dennis lifted his head slowly as another inmate appeared on the landing. He looked over at Dennis but never spoke a word. What the hell was this place? Nobody seemed normal, there was no conversation, no banter. Mark was losing his rag and shrieked behind him. "Are you coming or what? I've not got all fucking day." Dennis used all his inner strength and moved away from the wall. He didn't expect any sympathy from this screw. They were all the same in his eyes and usually he never gave them the time of day. He had to pull himself together, do what was needed. With his head held back he sucked in a large mouthful of air and his lungs expanded.

He was ready now, ready to face his fears. Mark stood at the door and kept his hand there until the inmate was at his side. He whispered into his ear. "You get ten minutes you sad old cunt. Make it quick and may I suggest this is the last time you see your son. Who would want to know a waste of space like you anyway, you're the scum of the earth."

Dennis looked him straight in the eye and his hot stale breath was in his face. He was scared of nobody in authority and this rat was getting told. "Listen, you jumped-up prick.

I'll do what I want. This is my time in this shit-hole, not yours. Are you forgetting how dangerous I can be, I'm sick in the head - the doctors said so, so take that onboard before you start giving me your shit. You understand me now, yes?"

Mark was fidgeting, his eyes were all over the place. "You don't scare me, Milne. Men like you should be hanged. Just get in the room before I change my mind you sick bastard." Dennis chuckled to himself. Any fear he had now left his body. His adrenalin was pumping and he would stick one on this screw if he needed to.

Mikey's heart was in his mouth and he swallowed hard as the door swung open. Here he was, after all these years. Mikey was finding it difficult to breathe, he was having a panic attack, his cheeks were bright red. His legs folded from beneath him and he became like a small child again. Dennis hurried to where he'd fallen and scooped his boy into his arms. He rested his head on his son's shoulder and you could see his knuckles turning white as he pressed his fingers deep into Mikey's skin. He whispered into his ears. "It's been so long, son. Too many years have passed. I'm so sorry."

Mark watched the commotion from behind the door and squirmed. Everybody had a weak point and no matter how hard Mikey appeared to be, this was his heart, his lifeline. "Dad, I've missed you so much. I tried to find you but nobody knew where you'd gone. I had nobody. I needed you. Why didn't you come back for me?"

This was heart-wrenching to watch, there was so much pain in his eyes, desperation. Mikey was relieved that he'd finally found the missing pieces. Dennis was a quivering wreck, he didn't know which way to turn. It was all too much for him. He choked up. "I had to go, son. Things were bad between me and your mam and I would have ended up killing her if I'd stayed a moment longer. She lies, she knows nothing about me really, she just makes it up as she goes along," Dennis's voice was high-pitched as he continued. "But son, I never left you. I tried to speak to you, to gain contact but she fucked me off every bastard time. I should have tried harder, I should have done more."

Mikey was an emotional wreck. His fingers dug deep into his father's shoulders and he hung onto him for dear life. He never wanted to let him go. "It means nothing now. What's done is done. I'm just so glad I've found you again." Mikey wiped his nose on his shirt cuff and tried to regain his composure. What the hell had happened to him, where was the big man everyone was used to seeing waltzing about the landing with not a care in the world? This was a completely different side to him, one nobody had ever seen before. Mikey and Dennis sat at the table opposite each other and Mikey was chuckling. "Wow, I can't believe you're even in here. What are the chances of that ay, it's fate."

Dennis dipped his head slightly and tried to change the subject. "You look like me when I

was younger. Handsome fucker aren't you?"

"Yep, at least I got something good from you. My mam said all the bad things I've got in my life are part of you. You know what she's like, she still hates you."

Dennis closed his eyes slowly. His words stabbed deep into his heart. "I've thought about her, you know. I often wondered if we could ever have been happy. Perhaps, I suppose, but we were both just too young."

Mikey chirped in. "My mam's hard work. You don't have to tell me about her, I've lived with her. She's quietened down a lot over the years. Still a big gob though, that will never change."

Dennis raised a smile and he couldn't take his eyes off his son. "So, tell me about you. We've

got years to catch up on. I want to know everything, do you have a girlfriend, kids?"

These two were really getting on and before long it was like they were never apart. But pretty soon, Mark walked inside the room and stood with his hands on his hips. "Right, finish off. I've got to get you back to the wing before roll call."

Dennis turned his head to face him and tried his luck. "Can't you sort out an extra ten minutes, boss? Come on, we've not seen each other for years."

Mikey was alert and waiting on the screw's answer. "Nope, just move your arses. I've done what I said I would do and that's it." Mikey sat up straight in his seat and rocked back in his chair. He shot a look over at Mark and his eyes were wide open. "He said we just want ten minutes more. It's not a lot to ask is it, sort it out and stop being a cock."

Mark went beetroot and he couldn't take much more of this blackmailing shit. He gritted his teeth tightly together and walked a few paces closer to the table. He slammed his hand down and made sure these two got the message. "I said end the fucking visit."

Their eyes locked and for a split second it looked like the screw was ready to strike a blow. Dennis could feel the tension and stood to his feet. "No worries. Mikey, we can sort something out. I'll have a word with the guvnor. Let's do it properly and go through the right channels." Mikey was raging in the pit of his stomach and even now he still wanted to one-bomb Mark.

"Dad, ask if you can get moved over to my landing. It's sorted over there and I'll look after you."

Mark burst out laughing and covered his mouth with his hand. Dennis's jaw dropped and he wanted the floor to open up and swallow him. "No, I'm alright where I am. I'm on the older block, it would do my head in with all you gobshites every night. I like my own space." Mark sucked on his gums and he held a cunning look in his eye. Dennis was uneasy and he was starting to sweat. "I'll be in touch son. Keep your head down and keep out of trouble." Mark walked behind the older prisoner and led him back to his cell.

When he was left alone again, Mikey held his head in his hands. His eyes clouded over and for some strange reason he had no control over his emotions anymore. The years of frustration, the days gone by when he needed someone to love him all came to the surface. He had to pull himself together, nobody could see him like this. Stretching his eyes, he quickly wiped his nose on his sleeve. This day was one of the happiest of his life. One he would remember until his dying day. Fancy meeting his old man in the slammer after all these years, it was uncanny. The sides of his mouth started to raise slightly, at last Mikey Milne had a father in his life. Even now in his head he was planning a future with his old man. Football matches, a few beers down the local; a few games of darts or pool…

★

Rachel walked along the main road. Sarah had gone home

hours ago. She was in a mood and never really spoken after she'd told her she'd be better off without her son. But could she blame her? Anyone would have been upset. Sarah was very touchy and took things to heart. It was like Mikey's mother had sold her out. The chippy stood facing Rachel and ever since she'd been off the drugs all she was doing was eating like a horse. Every single minute of the day she was craving some kind of food. Chocolate was her new addiction, thick creamy pieces of it.

She ate bars of it at a time. She was no longer stick thin, her waistline was now invisible and none of her clothes fit her anymore. Rachel jibbed across the road dodging the traffic. The smell of the chips was more than she could bear. Walking into the chippy she inhaled the aroma of the food. Her senses had a mind of their own now and she could smell and taste everything she ate. "I'll have pudding, chips, peas and gravy please. And, a buttered muffin." Rachel hung her head over the counter and watched every movement the assistant made. Once the chips were on the white tray she reached over and nicked one. The chip was piping hot and the daft bleeder nearly burnt her mouth off. "Can I have loads of salt on them darling and just a bit of vinegar?" Rachel rubbed her palms together and couldn't wait to scran the lot. Once it was all wrapped up neatly she headed home. All that was on her mind was to eat her food. Her plan was to fill her stomach and maybe watch a late night movie on the TV. That's all she did now most days, she was a different woman. Of course she went to visit her mother but most of the time she liked her own company, her own space.

Rachel walked down the path at the side of her house and clocked a man stood there. He looked at her and started to approach her. Rachel quickened her pace and was about to get on her toes. "Rachel, can I have a word," the voice shouted behind her. She stopped dead in her tracks, it must have been someone she knew. The man was pacing towards her and she swallowed hard. She owed no drug debts anymore so whoever it was wasn't looking for beef. "Any chance me and you can have a quiet word. I'm Sarah's dad."

Rachel looked the geezer up and down and she could see he came from money; black shiny shoes, crisp white shirt and not a hair out of place. Even the way he smelled was like nothing she'd ever smelled before. Where was the harm in talking to him? She was no longer scared and invited him into her house. Rachel showed Sarah's dad into the front room. "Sit yourself down in there. I'm just putting my food on a plate and I'll be with you. Do you want a chip butty or anything?" The man was too busy looking around the house and didn't reply. Rachel unwrapped her grub and stood picking at it, she was a right gannet and couldn't get it into her mouth quick enough. "I won't be a minute," she yelled into the front room as she shovelled the food inside her mouth.

Rachel was still devouring her food as she sat down. Sarah's father watched her from the corner of his eyes and pulled a sour expression. Quickly checking his watch, he began to speak.

"I'm Gerry. I'm here to see if you can help me with my daughter. Let's call it a business venture."

Rachel shot him a look and already she wasn't liking the sound of things. "What do you mean business?"

Gerry sat forward in his seat and cut to the chase. He

was a busy man and he was used to people doing as he said. You could tell by the way he was looking at Rachel that he thought he was the one controlling the situation. "I'll be straight with you. You might not like what I'm about to say but I'm going to say it anyway. My daughter means the world to me and since she got in with your son nothing else seems to matter to her anymore. She's too good for him. You know it and so do I."

Who the fuck did this smart bastard think he was calling her boy like this? If he wanted trouble she'd give him trouble. His sort didn't scare her and she looked him straight in the eye. "I beg your pardon, don't you dare come into my house disrespecting Mikey. Sarah loves him so there is nothing you can do about it. Leave her to it and let her make her own mistakes."

Gerry snarled over at her and things were about to get messy. "I'm not asking you. I'm telling you, love. We can do this the easy way or the hard way. Sarah is moving to London and that's the end of it."

"So, why are you here telling me, tell your daughter instead?"

Gerry pulled a cheque book out from his jacket pocket and plonked it down on the table. "Like I said, it's a business meeting this and I'm sure you can help me out." Gerry searched his jacket pocket and pulled out a silver pen. "Name your price. Go on, you just tell me what you think your help is worth and we can discuss it."

Rachel held her head back and sniggered. "Do yourself a favour and fuck off out of my house. Do you think there is a price on my son's happiness?"

Gerry was used to business deals and this was second nature to him. He always got what he wanted in the end and you could see he wasn't leaving today without the result he desired. "Five grand, there you go. I'm sure that will make a big difference to your life. Take yourself on holiday, get some new clothes. By the looks of you, you could do with a few new garments. It's up to you."

Rachel gulped, did she hear him right, five grand. Taking her time to answer him, she played it cool. "Are you right in the head you or what? Get it into your thick head that I'm not doing fuck all to stop Mikey and Sarah being together. You should want her to be happy, what's up, is she embarrassing you or something? Our Mikey is a good lad, he has his hang-ups but don't we all."

Gerry was pissed off, this was a lot harder than he first thought. He changed his tone and spoke in a calm manner. "Sarah has so much going for her. This job in London is the chance of a lifetime. If she misses it she'll regret it for the rest of her life. I'm sorry what I've said about your son and perhaps he is a good lad but see things from my point of view, I just want the best for my girl."

Rachel was listening now, she'd thought the same thing herself and even though she hated admitting it, she knew in her heart that somewhere along the line her son would let Sarah down. "I agree with you but how do you expect me to help? Mikey is her world and she would go ballistic if she thought I was conspiring with you to split them up."

"Just tell her he's ended it. I know Sarah, she won't question it, she's like that, she'll just walk away. She won't beg any man to love her, no way."

This was sounding better by the minute. In the long run Mikey would get over her, it wasn't like he was short of female attention. Rachel sat thinking and pulled her legs under her bum cheeks. Like Gerry, she was all about making a few quid. She was pushing her luck here but she had to give it a go. "Ten grand and I'll sort it. Don't try and argue the price because that's what I need."

Gerry rolled his eyes and shook his head. This woman was hard work, he thought she would have bitten his hand off for five grand, he'd underestimated her. They both sat staring at one another with poker faces, neither was blinking. Rachel's heart was pumping and she knew this could be the turning point in her life, there would be no more worrying about the money Gary had nicked, she could put it to bed and know her son still had a nest egg to come home to. "How do I know you can make her leave?" Gerry asked.

Rachel stared over at him and popped a fag in the corner of her mouth. "She will listen to me. I'll tell her Mikey has met somebody else."

Gerry digested what she'd just told him and it seemed to make sense in his head but he was a business man, he had to negotiate the fee. "I'll give you five grand up front and then once she's left I will settle the debt. You know it makes sense."

Rachel lit her cigarette and blew a thick cloud of grey smoke over at him. "She'd never have fit in here anyway. Our Mikey would have let her down. I've told her that myself, time and time again I've said it. She's a lovely girl, it's such a shame."

Gerry wasn't listening anymore. This woman was just justifying the reason why she'd sold her own flesh and blood out. She was a disgrace and she should have shown him the door once she realised why he was here. Gerry picked the pen up and wrote the cheque out for half the amount. He stretched over to pass it to her but kept his fingers pressed tightly on it. "Just for the record – if she doesn't leave this money here will be coming back to me. Don't try and have me over because I'll have you sorted out at the drop of a hat."

"I'm a woman of my word. If I say I'm going to do something, then I will. And as for you having me sorted out love, there will be no need. This money will help our Mikey start his new life when he's a free man. It's what he deserves."

The money changed hands and the deal was done. Gerry stood up and edged closer to the door. "Just make sure she's ready to leave next week. I don't care what you have to do or say, just make sure she never comes back here again."

Rachel listened as the front door slammed shut. A chill passed over her body and she rubbed at her arms slowly as goosebumps appeared on her skin. Holding the cheque in her hand, she sat staring at it. Was it blood money or was it the right thing to do? Of course she liked Sarah but Gerry was right, she was ruining her life. Flicking the lights off in the front room, she headed upstairs to bed with a heavy heart. Sarah was going to be heartbroken, she had to make sure she never tried to contact her son again. This was going to be tricky, she had to think it through. Everything had to be right for her to believe it, every detail had to be thought out. Rachel plonked down on her bed and stared at the ceiling. Why was life never straightforward? There was always someone getting hurt. Reaching over to the bedside cabinet, she pulled out a writing pad. Biting the end of the pen she began to write a letter to her son from Sarah. What a snidey bitch she was. How could she break his heart like this? He would never forgive her.

CHAPTER SIXTEEN

Brendan Mellor was on the landing scouting about, seeing what was going on. He could see Mikey Milne from where he was stood, he froze, his heart beating ten to the dozen. This cunt was getting it, as soon as he got the chance he would make this fucker pay for every bruise he gave him, stick a blade right in his back, stop the cunt from breathing.

Mark stood back from the corridor, he was also watching Mikey. He had to stop him, he couldn't take it anymore. This kid was running him ragged, calling the shots, pushing him to the limit. Mark spotted Davo from the corner of his eye. He moved quickly and tried to get his attention. "Oi, here a minute, I need a word." Davo marched over to the screw and leaned on the wall at the side of him. Mark's voice was low and he made sure nobody could hear their conversation. "I want you to pay Mikey's dad a visit. Let's start with his old man first, then we can move onto him."

Davo cracked his knuckles and held a look of disgust in his eyes. "It would be my pleasure, just put me in a room with him for two minutes and I'll destroy him. Get me a blade and I'll cut his bollocks off."

Mark was winding him up now, adding fuel to the fire. Making sure the job was going to be done successfully. "You read his reports right?"

Davo's nostrils flared and his chest expanded. "Fucking dead right I did. Get Mikey in the same room as well and I'll make him watch me do him in."

Mark was white and the colour drained from his

cheeks, he was trembling. "I want Mikey out of the picture for good."

Davo wasn't sure if he'd heard him right so he asked him to repeat himself. "You mean end it for him right?"

Mark was struggling to answer him, but what choice had the prisoner left him. Every day he was asking for more and more and he didn't trust him, he was a liability. "Just do the dad in first and we can sort Mikey out after that. I want that runt to suffer and feel pain just like he's caused me."

Davo was game as fuck and his ears pinned back. "I'm ready now. Just take me where I need to go. I'll be quick and nobody will see a thing."

Mark knew that Dennis's wing was quiet at this time and it was all systems go. He jangled his keys at the side of his leg. "Come on then, remember, I want him wasted, near death."

★

Dennis lay on his bed with his arms looped behind his head. On the floor was a letter he'd written for his son. He wasn't good at talking and in his own mind there were a few things he needed to get off his chest; personal things, heartfelt feelings. Things that had kept him awake at night, regrets over the choices he'd made. The notes were stacked high. He must have written at least ten pages. The cell door creaked open and Dennis was startled. This was an ambush, a raid. He knew it for sure. He cowered into the corner of his bed and all he could do was protect himself as the attack got underway, hands over his face. It was terrible, blood squirting all over the room accompanied by sickening smashing and cracking noises. Davo went to town on Dennis and he was stood over him, white saliva foaming from his mouth. "I'll kill you, cunt. Just like you killed that poor young boy. How would you like me raping you, ay?" Davo grabbed Dennis's cheeks together, lifted his lifeless head up and spat in his eyes. "You're a queer cunt, a fucking kiddy-fiddler. You don't deserve to live on the same planet as us!" His fist swung back and here was the killer blow. As the punch connected with Dennis's head, dark red claret sprayed from his mouth. His body folded onto the floor and his legs shook a few times before he stopped moving. How could this have been allowed to happen? This prisoner should have been on a high-risk wing, nobody should have been able to get to him.

Mark stuck his head inside the cell and gripped hold of Davo by his arm. He looked down at Dennis and knew his orders had been carried out to the letter. "Come on, get the fuck out of here, before somebody clocks you."

Davo roared like a lion and punched his clenched fist onto his chest. He was full of rage and his eyes were bulging. He ran over to Dennis for the last time. He swung his leg back and booted his victim right in his face, crushing his skull. The inmate's body lifted up from the floor and dropped back down with an almighty thud. It was a massacre. His attacker ran from the cell. His job was done here and Dennis was a goner.

Mark locked the pad up with shaking hands and pushed Davo away. "Go on, fuck off, get back to the wing," he stressed. This man was a lunatic and he was still in the zone, he looked like a man of steel, fearless.

Davo was dangerous and God help anyone who crossed him, he was like a caged animal. "There you go. If that cunt's still alive in the morning, I'll show my arse. I want his son now, I'll rip his fucking head off too."

Mark told him again to leave, his arse had gone. The sound of their feet scurrying along the corridor, keys rattling, struggled breathing. They needed to be quick before anybody spotted them. Mark was in a panic and he knew there would be a big investigation the moment Dennis was found. Paedophiles were always being targeted in jail and most of the time the screws turned a blind eye to assaults on them. Sometimes, though, they let other inmates give them a sly dig, a few belts. Dennis had always declared his innocence in the crime he'd been found guilty of but the facts were there for everyone to see. Yes, he was there when the young boy got killed but he always declared he wasn't the one who'd done it. He'd never revealed anything to the police and covered up for the real murderer. The story had been all over the papers at the time and the victim's parents were still fighting to make sure Dennis never got out of jail. It was such a horrendous case and the details would make your toes curl. Richard Parker was only twelve years old when he lost his life to these sadistic bastards. Dennis claimed he'd only popped around to the house where he was staying and it was fair to say he was off his head on drugs. He didn't know Len, his mate, had taken a kid off the street and brought him into the house. Everyone who heard what happened to this poor lad before he met his death would never look at the world the same again. Even the jury found it incredibly difficult to listen to the evidence regarding the case against Mikey's dad. Dennis was off his head and couldn't recall what went on but his semen was all over the lad's clothes, how could he not remember a single thing? Most thought that this man deserved the beating he'd just received. If he had really committed such a horrific act, then Davo wasn't alone in wanting to finish him off and end his life.

Yet there were so many flaws in Dennis's case that no one knew for absolute certain and he had always maintained his innocence. Had Mikey's dad been framed or was he really a dirtbag, the lowest of the low? It didn't matter now either way – Dennis was dead and the truth would probably never come out.

Davo stood in the shower room washing his hands and face. Bright red speckles of blood sprayed all over his skin. Mark stood behind him urging him to hurry up. Davo looked into the mirror and rubbed a single finger down the side of his nose, eyes wide open. "Just Mikey left now and the job's a good 'un." Cold water hit his face and he blew a laboured breath. "Does he know about his dad being a wrong-un?"

Mark shook his head and raised his eyebrows high. "He hasn't got a clue. It's a shame really. I would have had great enjoyment in breaking the news to him."

Davo rubbed his wet hands on his jeans and chuckled. "I think it's time for you to put me on B-Wing. Let's get this party started. I want to play about with him first, where is the fun if I just snap his jaw. I want him to suffer, humiliate him in front of everyone."

Mark was smiling. This was music to his ears. He'd show the cocky bastard once and for all. His tone was chilling as he answered him. "Yes, that's a great idea. I'll get you moved over tonight so when he wakes up in the morning he'll get the shock of his life. Promise me you will break him down, bit by bit, day by day, break the cunt in half."

Davo started to walk towards the door. "Move me and Brendan over and I'll show you what I'm about. First thing in the morning all the lads are going to know just what

Mikey's dad is in here for. Let's see who's laughing then, ay?"

The pair of them shook hands and Mark felt that his torment was coming to an end. Once Mikey Milne was out of the picture for good he could get back to his life and live without fear. Mark watched Davo go back to his pad and smirked. Revenge was sweet, very sweet indeed.

Sarah sat waiting for Rachel in the café on the precinct. She should have been here over twenty minutes ago, where the hell was she? Sarah sipped the last bit of her drink and peered out of the window. It was raining again and fat raindrops hammered the pavements outside. Sarah pulled a book from her bag and buried her head into it. She was studying hard now as her exams were just around the corner. Night after night she had her head stuck in some kind of revision book, it was boring and laborious. The door opened with a bang and Rachel stood there soaking wet through. She shook her hair and dragged her coat off. "Fuck me, where did that rain come from. I look like a drowned rat. It just came from nowhere. It was sunny before."

Sarah folded the page back slightly on the book she was reading and closed it. "I know, it was a good job I had my umbrella in my bag otherwise I would have been like you."

Rachel went to the counter and ordered herself a cup of coffee. She was gabbing with a woman at the side of her and cracking a few jokes. She was common as muck, foul-mouthed and didn't mince words. She did cheer people up though. Rachel had a knack of making people laugh when she was on form, potty mouth she was. Once she was at Sarah's side, Rachel sat down and swiped her hair back. It looked like rats' tails. "I've not got long, love. I'm going to my mam's tonight for my tea, so I'll just have a quick brew with you and get on my way. She moans if I'm late, you know. I swear, she proper spits her dummy out if I'm not there on time. I think it's because she's lonely. Our Cath's coming tonight with Danny. I can't say I'm looking forward to that I can tell you," she wasn't shutting up – she was waffling, she didn't even stop for air. "Cath's lovely you know but that prick she married makes my blood boil. I'll just try and bite my tongue while he's there. He knows he'll get no change out of me anyway. I'll put him on his arse if he lays one finger on me." This woman was going for gold, she was having her say no matter what. Sarah was sniggering to herself. When Rachel was on one she was so funny, the expressions she pulled were something else.

Sarah sat listening to her and waited until she could get a word in edgeways. "I've got to study for my exams. It's doing my head in, honest it's stressing me out. Night and day I'm at it, nothing seems to be registering. My mind is a blank."

Rachel slurped at her drink and she could have done with a blast of nicotine before she delivered the bad news. She took a deep breath and here it was, the betrayal. "Sarah, our Mikey has been on the blower. He was on for hours last night. He's asked me to talk to you."

Sarah sighed. "Didn't you give him my new number yet, he's not rung me. I should be first on his list, not you."

"Yeah, course I did but he thinks it's better if he doesn't speak to you."

Sarah froze, she looked confused. "What do you mean

by that? Rachel, don't start all this again because if you are trying to make us split up it's not going to happen."

Rachel touched the top of her hand and stroked it slowly. She dipped her eyes. "Sweetheart, this is so hard for me to say to you and I know it's going to break your heart but it is what Mikey wants."

Sarah held her breath and a red rash started to appear on her neck, itchy, irritating. "What's happening Rachel, you're scaring me now, just say what you have to. Don't beat about the bush."

Rachel looked out of the window and closed her eyes for a split second. The words were on the tip of her tongue. She just had to pick her moment. Act like she cared. "It's over. Mikey wants you to find somebody else. He thought he loved you but he's been talking to a girl while he's been in the nick and he thinks he's fallen in love with her."

Sarah's eyes were wide open. Was she hearing her right? No, this was just a wind-up for sure. "Shut up lying Rachel. You're so funny sometimes. As if Mikey would ever do that to me. We're in love."

This was so hard and Mikey's mother was struggling. There was no other way to say it, she had to tell her straight. The details would let her know how serious it really was. "He met her on Facebook and she's been up to the nick to see him quite a lot. I know you don't want to hear it but that's why he's not been having you up all the time to see him. I knew something wasn't right with him you know, but I just couldn't put my finger on it."

Sarah slammed her hand down on the table, she wasn't taking this lightly. "Are you for real? Is he really seeing somebody else? What about our plans for the future? The promises we made..." Rachel tried to comfort her but

Sarah pushed her away. "I know love, I know. I told you a long time ago that things change when you're locked away and he said he's realised that you two will never work out. You're from different walks of life, you see. Mikey will always be a criminal, he realises that he can't change who he is for you. It's all too much."

Sarah was holding back the tears. Her mind was spinning and nothing was registering. "What, and some other girl can make him happy? Give me his number. I'll ring him myself. This doesn't sound like him one little bit."

Rachel had to dig deep and it was killing her inside seeing Sarah hurting like this but she had a job to do, she had to dig deeper. "The girl he's seeing was one he met when he was out of prison. It kills me to tell you this but she's pregnant." What a horrible bitch Mikey's mother was! There was no need for this, she was destroying her. Sarah welled up and tears rolled down her cheeks. She sat watching the rain outside the window and never said a word. Rachel tried to put a hand on her shoulder for comfort but she moved her away as if she was diseased.

Sarah sobbed, her shoulders were shuddering. "He's broken my heart. I loved him so much and this is the way he's treated me. I would have waited forever for him, done anything to make him happy. You know that don't you?"

Rachel agreed and tried to console her. "I know you would have love but now you can move on and find somebody new. Someone who deserves you," she rolled her eyes and sighed, "because, let's face it, our Mikey would have wronged you sooner or later, it was just a matter of time. Men are like that Sarah. I've been there, got the video and bought the t-shirt. Nothing lasts forever and if you believe happy endings are real, then you need to give your head a shake. Cinderella has a lot to answer for. There are no Prince Charmings in this world. They're all cunts the fucking lot of them. Always cheating with other women and keeping secrets. Never trust a man love, ever."

Sarah snapped. She still believed in true love, it still existed in her eyes. It was something beautiful and magical. "They might be the kind of men you meet, but not me. I believe in love and Mikey was all I needed. Why has he done this to me? Go on! Tell me why! When I gave him my heart. I gave him everything!"

Rachel was stuck for words. How could she answer this? But, she had to do the job, make sure she left Manchester for good. She had to make sure she put Mikey behind her. She flipped and upped her game. "You're talking out of your arse, woman. I wasn't going to mention this but you need to know so you can move on. Mikey brought girls back to our house loads of times and, if we're laying all the cards on the table here, I've heard them having sex too." There was no need for this, it was such a brutal blow and totally uncalled for. She was destroying her. How could she say something like that? Sarah was devastated and Rachel was kicking her while she was down. Sarah wafted her hand in front of her face, she was having some sort of panic attack. Rachel was concerned for her wellbeing and took her outside to get some fresh air. "Come on love, take deep breaths. It's just the shock that's all. You'll be fine soon. Breathe, come on, take deep breaths."

Sarah gripped hold of Rachel's coat and ragged her about, she was hysterical and not in control of her actions. "I bet you had something to do with it. You've never liked me from day one. Well, you've got what you wanted. Fuck you and fuck your son." Rachel's mouth was wide open.

She'd never heard her talking like this before, this was another side of her that she'd hidden away. "Mikey will regret losing me one day. I hope him and his little family will be happy together. I've got hopes, I've got dreams and he can kiss my arse if he thinks I'll ever have him back after he's shoved it up someone else." Sarah was gasping for breath but she still had more to say. "And you're not much better either, you two-faced cow! How dare you sit in the same room as me when you knew he was unfaithful all along? You have no morals woman. You should be ashamed of yourself."

Rachel had heard enough and she wasn't letting anybody speak to her like this. She owed her nothing. "Whoa, keep it shut before I shut it for you. Don't shoot the messenger. I'm only telling you what I was told to. I know you're upset but don't start to take it out on me. Life goes on, just deal with it." Rachel was showing no compassion whatsoever but what did Sarah expect? Rachel was never one for holding back. She shot straight from the hip and didn't mince words. "Anyway, I've told you now, so there is nothing more to say. It's not like we're friends is it? If we're being honest here, we only put up with each other for Mikey's sake. You're not my cup of tea and you never will be."

Sarah was holding her own and she was livid. "Don't you think I didn't know about you? Do you think for one single second I enjoyed your company? You knock me sick and no wonder your son hates you. Yes, he told me that. What kind of worthless piece of shit leaves her son to fend for himself when he's only a child."

That was it, Rachel had heard enough. She twisted her hands inside Sarah's hair and dragged her around the back of the café. There was rustling, groaning and the sound of feet scraping the floor. "Don't push me Sarah," Rachel screamed. "I'll scratch your fucking eyeballs out if you carry on. Go on, fuck off out of my life and leave my son alone. I'm glad it's happened. I'm buzzing he's finally fucked you off. You thought you were too good for him anyway. It was only a matter of time before he carted you."

Sarah was wriggling to break free and she was stronger than Rachel first thought. She was giving as good as she got. Mikey's mother had bitten off more than she could chew for sure. Sarah grabbed her hair and swung her around like a rag doll. Rachel lost her footing and the tide turned very quickly. It was Sarah's shout now and she was straddled over Rachel ramming her finger deep into her cheek. "Don't you worry, I'm gone. I'm glad I don't have to look at your pathetic face any longer. You deserve everything that's coming your way. You're an evil woman, do you hear me, sick in the head!" Sarah spat at her and started to walk away.

Rachel sprang to her feet and took a few seconds to find her bearings. "Go on, run back to mummy and daddy you posh bitch. You need to learn to stand on your own two feet you do, learn the hard way like I fucking did."

Her words fell on deaf ears, Sarah was gone. Rachel straightened her hair and dusted the thick brown mud from her jeans. She was genuinely upset and had to take a few seconds to regain her thoughts. "Fuck, fuck," she mumbled as she stamped her feet on the floor. She never intended for things to get this bad but she had to do it, she had to make sure Mikey had his money on his release date. Everything in life had a price and she would do anything to make sure her son had a chance of a better future. Rachel's head was in bits and she was in no mood to go to her mother's house anymore. She was filthy and needed a wash. A quick text to her mother soon sorted that out. So what, she'd moan but she could handle her. Rachel was going home to clean herself up. All that was left now was to tell Mikey the same thing. It would hurt him, she was sure of that, but he was made of stronger stuff and in a few weeks he would back to normal.

Mikey flicked through Facebook on his iPhone. Potter was at his side and he was loving every minute of the social network. "Add her, send her a message. Ask her to come and visit me," Potter shrieked.

Mikey sniggered and scrolled through everyone's posts.. "Just chill, I've already got a few birds on the go for you. You can't rush in and seem too eager. The ladies love a bad boy so cool down and stop stressing." Mikey held the phone from his face as it started to ring. "It's my mam, fuck me what's she doing up at this time it's nearly two in the morning." Without wasting a second more he answered the call. Rachel sounded distressed and Potter could hear every word she said. Mikey's expression changed and he ragged at his t-shirt. "How long has he been here for? Is this for sure, it might just be gossip?" Potter was hanging on every word and he could tell by his pad mate's body language that something was not right. He moved back over to his own bed and dragged his duvet around his shoulders. Mikey finished the call after a few minutes, with all the colour drained from his cheeks. He punched a clenched fist into the wall and banged his head against it repeatedly.

Potter had to say something, he couldn't just sit there

like a prize prick. "Mikey, is everything alright? You look like you've seen a ghost."

Mikey didn't reply straight away, he just sat staring into space. As he spoke his bottom lip trembled. "Sarah's binned me. She's found somebody new. What the fuck is going on? She said she loved me?"

Potter was lost for words. What could he possibly say that would take the pain away? Heartbreak was a painful emotion on its own, but locked away behind bars the love he'd lost was going to be a hundred times worse than it would have been on the outside. Mikey pulled Sarah's photograph from the wall and dragged the cover over his head. Nobody could ever see him like this. He was strong and fearless. He had a name to protect. Potter could hear sobbing sounds from where he lay and he knew better than anyone that this lad could switch at any second. He was keeping well away, he never muttered a word.

Mark marched two inmates along the landing with their belongings. Smithy watched from his office and he could smell a rat. He stretched his neck out hoping to get a better view. No inmate got moved during the night shift. This was something that happened during the morning shift. The prison was already on lockdown and the guvnor was already going ballistic as to how a prisoner could be beaten to near death and nobody had seen a thing. Dennis Milne was barely breathing when a screw found him, he was hanging on for dear life. The briefing earlier that week had made Smithy even more suspicious about his work colleague and the way he was acting. He knew he was hiding something. He barely spoke to him anymore, he was always jumpy and looking over his shoulder. Smithy watched from the shadows and kept a low profile. He flicked the light off in his office and stood taking everything in.

Mark opened the door to the new pad for the lads. "Right, get your heads down and let's see a few faces drop on here tomorrow morning when you raise your ugly heads out onto the landing. Mikey Milne will shit a brick for sure. Like I said, I want you to make him suffer. I'll give the nod when it's right to take him down. Promise me you won't fuck things up!"

Davo threw his belongings on the bed as Brendan stuck his head through the window. "My word is my bond. But don't make me wait too long. I want to do it sooner rather than later." Mark stood frozen for a few seconds. He knew what he wanted and everything had to happen slowly. The other officers had to see Mikey slipping down the ranks, they needed to see he was no longer the daddy on the landing.

Mikey checked Potter was asleep at the side of him. The night was a lonely place when someone was upset. He looked over at the night sky and tears ran down the side of his cheek. Perhaps he could call for a listener. The prison service always had someone on hand to talk to when inmates were feeling low. Would it help him though? It still wouldn't bring his girl back, it was pointless. Sarah had fucked his head up big time, he genuinely loved her. Okay, he acted like she was the one who was doing all the running when in fact he loved her with all his heart. But how had he allowed himself to fall in love, let his guard down? As a rule, he never gave his all in a relationship. He'd seen so much heartache over the years and always promised himself he would never put himself in that position. Only fools fall in love. Mikey paced the cell with a cigarette hanging from the corner of his mouth. He needed to speak to her. The rejection was killing him inside. He knew it was a big ask for her to wait for him but it was her that said she would wait forever. What a lying slut she was! She was no different to the other girls he'd met. She'd probably met one of her own kind. Yes, a guy with money and a fancy car. He'd blow it up if he had the chance, torch the bastard.

Potter stirred in his bed, he must have heard him moving about and opened his eyes slowly. His voice was low as he rubbed his knuckles into the corners of his eye. "Do you want me to make us both a drink? I know you're upset, you're bound to be. Talking sometimes helps you know." Mikey screwed his face up. If he had a pound for every time some know-it-all had told him it was good to talk about his problems, he would have been a rich man. They were all nosey fuckers trying to get inside his head, mess it up and stop him thinking for himself. "I don't need to do fuck all. Just get your head back down and get some shut-eye. I'll be over it soon. It's just been a bit of a shock that's all. My main concern is the big bastard who's landed in the nick. I told you about Davo didn't I and the beef I had with him on the outside?"

Potter nodded his head. "Yeah, he seems like a right head the ball. I'm glad I've never met him."

Mikey gave a sarcastic laugh and sat back down on his bed. "Well. Hold that thought, he's been shipped here to this jail. He's a bad arse and I know he'll have something up his sleeve for me."

"Just front him, just ask him what the crack is and if he

Bang Up

wants a one-on-one, a straightener to sort it out?" Potter suggested.

Mikey swallowed hard and lifted his eyes over to his pad mate. "Get a grip lad, the guy is a maniac. You don't know about him, he would eat me up for breakfast and shit me out of his arsehole."

Potter was wide awake now and he was unable to get back to sleep. He walked over to the small table with the kettle on it. "I'll do us a drink. If what you're saying is right then we have to be prepared for whatever he throws at us. You know I've got your back don't you?" Mikey sat chewing on the side of his thumb. He knew he could fight, swing a punch, so why was he crapping his pants? If this man wanted a fight then he may stand a chance. But Davo didn't work like that, he was a crafty bastard, he liked his victims to suffer. There were so many tales about this guy and some of the things he'd done to other gang members were off the scale. He liked to humiliate them, piss on them, shove his dick up their arse. Potter stirred the sugar around in the cup and drained the teabag. "I don't know what to suggest for the best. It might be a case of you get to him before he gets to you. I've seen you scrap Mikey you're hard as fuck. I'll tell you something for nothing, I wouldn't like a belt off you."

"You might be right, I'll take the cunt down, stick a blade in him. I'll let him know I'm game too."

Potter passed Mikey his drink and sat down facing him, he rubbed at his arms as a cold chill rippled over his skin. "Trouble just follows you doesn't it? It's like you're cursed or something. I mean, some of the shit you've disclosed to me is horrendous. I don't know how you've survived for as long as you have. Anyway, on a positive note, your dad is

297

back in your life now and you can both start to move on. How does it feel after seeing him again after all this time? I know I've not mentioned anything about it before but it would be good to hear how you feel." Potter was staring at him waiting on a reply. Usually, Mikey would have kept this information to himself but he was vulnerable and needed to open up, release all the anxiety he had rushing through his veins. He took a mouthful of the hot, sweet tea. Four sugars he had in each brew. Mikey had always had a sweet tooth and even though he knew it was no good for him he still craved the sugary drink.

"It was weird Potter. Do you know when you look at someone and even though you know someone, you don't really. His face has aged so much and I couldn't stop looking at him. My mam always told me I looked like him and I couldn't see it until I was face to face with him."

"How did you feel inside, was there still a father and son bond, did you feel it?"

Mikey thought about the question and took his time to answer it. "It felt strange, I suppose I just wanted him to hug me and tell me everything was going to be alright. As a kid growing up he always cuddled me and put the effort in to be a good father. It was the beer and the drugs that ruined him though. I remember him being in some right states, fucked in the head he was when he'd been on a bender."

Potter sighed and picked at his nose. "My family is pretty boring compared with yours. Nothing really happens at our house at all. My parents are straight members, they get up go to work and come home and go to bed. I don't know how they live like that really. Meeting you has already given me a different outlook on life. I need excitement, to challenge myself, not to be a boring prick anymore. No wonder I can't get a leg-over. I'm boring as fuck; a geek, a proper dickhead."

Mikey chuckled and nodded his head. "Yeah, you are a bit wet behind the ears. It is like you lived in a bubble and not experienced anything in life. I still can't believe you're still a virgin. Pussy is mint."

Potter licked at his lips and just the mention of girls made his temperature rise. "How do you know where to put it?"

Mikey opened his eyes wide and he smirked. "What, your cock?"

"Yeah, how do you know where it goes?"

"For fucks's sake, you just bang it in. You'll know when you're there, just give her a good fingering first, explore and you'll find it."

Potter looked worried and you could see the idea of sex with a woman scared the life out of him. "My dad told tell me about the birds and the bees a while back but he never explained it like you just have. He went around the houses and told me when two people love each other that's what they do to show each other they care."

Mikey's mood was lifting and he couldn't help but giggle. He just took it for granted that all men had the natural instinct to know what to do in the bedroom. His own father had never told him shit, he just picked it up as he went along. Mikey lay down on his bed and let out a laboured breath. "Oh well, fuck it. If I'm single then I'm single. A couple of hours on Fuck-book and I'll be back in the game again. You can't keep a good man down can you? It looks like I'm back in the mix then."

Potter smirked as he went back to bed. "Nope, I knew

you would bounce back. It's just that Davo who needs sorting out now. I'm right behind you, don't forget that." The room was silent and all you could hear was Mikey's breathing. His nose was blocked and he sounded like a sleeping pig. "Night Mikey,"Potter whispered.

"Get to fucking sleep you wuss," Mikey sniggered back.

CHAPTER SEVENTEEN

Rachel sat at the kitchen table munching on some hot toast, butter dripping from the sides of it. The radio was on and she was singing along to it. The money from Gerry was safe now and she'd completed her task of splitting her son and Sarah up. Today she was going to the jail to see her son and she was already planning in her head what she was going to tell him. As far as she knew Sarah was in London now ready to start her new job, there was no coming back. Her quest had been completed. Mikey had shattered her heart into a million pieces and she would never forgive him for his infidelity. Gerry had been worried about her at one point and he was sure she was going to run away but as time went on, he could see she was ready to move on. Rachel ran her fingers through her hair and sat staring into space, the lack of sleep lately was showing on her tired skin and every day she woke up tired. The letterbox rapped and Rachel headed to the front door. As she held her toast in her hand she lifted the catch. Rachel's body was twisted up in minutes, screaming, shouting, blood spraying about the hallway. What the hell was going on, somebody must have heard her screams? Why was nobody coming to help her? This woman was getting beaten within an inch of her life.

★

Mikey made his way onto the landing. There was a group of prisoners gathered nearby chatting and playing cards.

He looked fresh this morning and the session at the gym had really cleared his head. The rage inside him was curbed for now and he seemed to have his temper under control. Mikey sat down and picked up a newspaper to scan the local news. "Fancy seeing you here," a voice from the side of him chirped. Mikey lifted his head and his jaw dropped low. Brendan Mellor was at Davo's side and he was smirking too. "Me and you need a chat don't we?" Mikey's nostrils flared and his breathing became rapid. Should he steam into him now?

What the hell was he waiting for? Kick his fucking head in before he makes the first move. He scanned the room for a weapon to whack over Davo over the head with but there was nothing in sight. Everybody's eyes were on him now, waiting on a comeback.

Mikey sat forward in his seat and kept his eyes on the newspaper. He couldn't show fear, he had to see it through. "Ready when you are Davo, just say where and when and I'll be there."

Davo was a snapper and he was trying his best to keep his cool. "Listen, you cocky prick, don't even think you can chat shit to me. I'll break your fucking nose in front of everyone if you carry on."

Mikey raised his eyes and growled over at him. Brendan was licking arse and he caught his eye. "See you've got yourself a new bitch then Davo? You better watch him though he's a shady fucker, he'll sell you out at the drop of a hat."

Brendan was cocky and now he had the back-up he was more than willing to voice his opinion. "I hope Davo fucks you up. It's about time someone knocked you down a peg or two. I for one will be laughing my cock off when he does too."

Mark was watching everything from the corridor. He was biting his fingernails, intrigued by Mikey's courage, he'd underestimated him. Davo made sure Mikey was listening and spoke in a loud voice to the rest of the inmates. "Did you all know about Dennis Milne getting kicked to fuck. He's in a bad way. I wonder who done him in?" Mikey was white and his fists curled into tight balls at the side of his legs as Davo continued. "You all know Mikey's dad is a nonce right?"

There was whispering among the prisoners, they were nudging each other, their eyes wide open.

Mikey sucked hard on his gums and stood to his feet. There was no way he was letting this go... "My dad's no nonce. So, don't start rumours you prick."

Davo marched over to Mikey and, leaning into his ear, whispered, "Your old man got what he deserved and I loved watching his face squirm when I kicked his fucking head in. You know he raped a young lad don't you, stuck his cock right up his arse." Mikey closed his eyes for a split second and without thinking he twatted Davo. Smithy was on his way down the corridor, he could see the fight starting. He sprinted towards them and raised the alarm. It was too late, these two prisoners were at loggerheads, fighting like gladiators.

Brendan was ranting and you could see the evil in his eyes. "Do him in Davo, put him in a body bag, kick the shit out of him."

Mikey was fast and he got a few digs in before Smithy and the rest of the officers got between them. Davo was trying to break free and he was shrieking at the top of his voice. "His dad's a fucking paedo, get Milne off the wing.

He's probably a kiddy-fiddler just like his old man."

The other inmates shot a look over at Mikey and you could tell now that his card was marked. No matter what he said after this, he wouldn't be able to sleep tight anymore. They would get him, it might not be now but he was marked for life. "Come on, you cunt. You want some do you? I'll show you what I'm all about," Mikey yelled.

Mark secured him and brought him to the ground with a loud thud. The handcuffs were on and he rammed his knee in the middle of his back. "Just calm down, keep fucking still." Mikey was dragged to his feet, his body bent in half as they rushed him from the wing.

Davo was twisted up too and he was up in arms. "This is far from over. I'll kill him, I'll end his life," he ranted.

★

Mark stood talking to Smithy. Mikey was down the block now and he was going nowhere. Smithy was agitated and he had something to get off his chest. "What do you know about Dennis Milne being twisted up? Come on Mark, you know more than you're saying. How did Davo know what he was in for? I'm not green, so don't insult my intelligence. You set it up didn't you?"

Mark stood with his back held firmly against the wall and his nostrils flared. "I had to do something Smithy. It's all just gone tits up. I was in bad debt and I just got involved, I had no other choice." Smithy took a few seconds to digest what he'd just told him and dragged him by the arm to a quieter place. Mark was in bits and sank to his knees. "He was going to grass me up. He knows too much. I'll lose it all; my wife, the house, the fucking lot."

Smithy let out a laboured breath and ragged his fingers

through his hair. "What the fuck have you got yourself into? Please tell me you've not been bringing any shit in for this lot?"

Mark choked up and lifted his eyes to the ceiling. "I was on my arse, I needed to do something. I know it's a mess but what else could I have done?"

"For fuck's sake, are you right in the head? You could have spoken to me! I would have helped," Smithy blurted out.

Mark held his head in his hands and his body shuddered. "You've done enough for me. I even fucked that up and gambled the money you gave me. I always fuck everything up, everything I touch, I ruin."

Smithy watched his pal crying and tried his best to comfort him. "We can sort this. We can get Mikey moved from the jail. No one will believe him anyway, he's a criminal, you're an officer, are you forgetting that?"

Mark wiped his snotty nose on his black jumper. "I'm in too deep Smithy. He will make sure he stitches me up. He said so himself."

"So let's set him up, plant something in his cell, get him starred up. He'll soon see when he keeps getting spun. We hold all the cards here not him."

Mark realised how serious this was, he could have landed in the slammer too for his actions. There was a banging noise in the distance. Mikey was booting at his door and screaming at the top of his voice. "I want to see my dad, take me to see him now. I'll kill some fucker if you don't. Please tell me where he is, please. I just need to make sure he's alright."

Mark cringed and squeezed at his fingers. "Look at what I've done. It's all my fault. I should never have let it get this far. Look what I've done to Mikey. His head was fucked enough without me adding to it all. Please, don't bubble me. If I lose my job then I don't know what I would do."

Smithy was in a predicament now. Yes, he'd help stitch Mikey up with a few illegal objects in his pad but he was asking much more of him, something that he didn't want any part of. Mikey sank behind his door and his shoulders shuddered, there was so much emotion, he was falling apart. Everything was falling into place now. All the snidey comments his mother had made over the years, all the times she'd told him his father was a bad man, it all made sense now. So why did he need to see him, why did he want to hold his old man in his arms and tell him everything would be alright? To tell him how much he loved him. His head was all over the place, head spinning, mind racing. He roared like a caged lion and banged the back of his head on the cell door. This was the real Mikey, the child inside him crying out for somebody to help him. He'd lost everything that ever meant anything to him. His girlfriend was gone, the father he craved and all the memories he held inside his head meant nothing anymore. It was all shit, a crock of shit and lies. Mikey dragged at his skin as if it was diseased, pinching, biting at it. Small wounds started to appear on his skin, bright red blood oozing out. Mikey placed a single finger inside it and scrawled the word "help" on the door in his own blood.

Rachel was coming round, her eyes were swollen and she could barely see. There was a dark figure sat facing her, a big, round, tall figure. "Wakey, wakey," the voice sneered.

Rachel's head wobbled from side to side, blood trickling from her top lip. She was injured and her body was weak. "Who are you, what do you want from me?" The man's voice was chilling, his identity still hidden away under his baseball camp. "I told you I would be back one day didn't I?"

Rachel took a deep breath and tried to focus on the features she could see. "I don't understand, Gary is that you?" Her attacker moved a few paces forward and knelt down near her. She could see him now. The baseball cap fell from his head and he pulled his hoody down. Rachel strained her eyes, she was confused. "I always pay my debts Rachel. No one ever gets one over on me. You wronged me remember that."

This was all too much for her to take, she started to cower into the corner. "I don't know who you are, please, just leave me alone."

His voice was louder now, powerful, as he watched her shaking like a leaf. "I cried for you for months, years even. I cried my eyes out and you just moved on. We could have been happy, you said you would wait for me."

Rachel moved her hands away from her face and studied her attacker further. Her back was flat against the wall and her eyes wide open. She knew this man, she knew his voice and she'd loved him once.

"John," she gulped.

This was bad, he always said he would come back for her but why had nobody told her he was out of jail? The authorities should have informed her, a phone call, anything. They knew the script with this man and knew he was a serious danger to her. But Rachel had moved about, changed addresses, she was hard to find at the best of times.

No wonder the police couldn't find her. She had to do something, calm him down. "John, it wasn't like that. You were away for years.

I got mixed up in all kinds of shit and no one was there to protect me. I needed you and you left me."

John Pollock snapped and his voice shook the room. "I was in a prison cell you daft slag, rotting away while you was shagging every Tom, Dick and Harry. You said we were forever, 'always' you said, you dirty slapper." His words were slow and meaningful.

If Rachel got out of here alive she would be a lucky woman. "John, I know you're hurt but please, don't do anything you'll regret. We can talk about this, put it behind us. We can even be friends again."

She'd taken him by shock now, he didn't know if he was coming or going. He punched a clenched fist into the side of his head. "No, no, you're not getting inside my head anymore. I have a job to do and I don't care if I spend the rest of my life in prison. I will make sure you pay for the way you dumped me."

Rachel could see a spot of hope in his eyes. She couldn't just give up, she had to try to save her life. "John, I never stopped thinking about you. I loved you with all my heart. I never stopped loving you if I'm being honest with myself. Let me make us a drink and we can talk. We had some good times me and you, happy memories, remember?" He was listening now and she seemed to be calming him down. "Our Mikey treated you like his dad too, he respected you. It broke his heart when you went to prison. None of us ever forgot you." John broke into a gentle smile and she knew she was starting to get through to him. She carried